WITHIN THE WOODS

TONY URBAN

PACKANACK
publishing

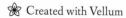

For Shane. I miss you, my friend.

I am going far away to the land of robbers and ghosts.

— HUTTER, NOSFERATU

CHAPTER ONE

May 26, 1989

"I've had enough of that bastard." Harrison Roberts' hand caressed the raised, red welt on his cheek without even realizing what he was doing. "I'm never going home."

It had been less than an hour since his father had hit him. Not hit, whipped. The old man had laid into him with his leather razor strap and even though he was pushing fifty, the fucker was still quick, especially when it came to unleashing his anger on his sons.

The first blow caught Harrison on his hip, the end of the strap circling around to catch his ball sack with a whip-cracking, stinging blow that sent him to his knees. As Harrison was going down, the old man was already bringing on round two and their combined motions resulted in the strap colliding with the boy's right cheek.

An inch higher and he might have lost an eye and the shock was almost as intense as the pain. Harrison instinctively tucked and covered his face with his forearms as he waited for the attack to recommence.

Instead, the old man dropped the strap and bent at the waist, trying to examine the damage he'd wrought. "Shit, Harrison. Look what you made me do. Little asshole."

Larry Roberts tried to pull Harrison's shield of arms free to get a better look, but the boy held firm. That was a mistake.

"Well fuck you then!" His father said, then used a calloused hand to shove Harrison sideways where he toppled into the kitchen table. A rib connected with the stove and the boy felt pain arc up his side like an electric shock.

It had been a bad night to ask his father whether he could spend the summer in Ohio. To spend the summer with his mother. That's what set the old bastard off. Harrison had suspected it might go this way, but he'd been missing his mom bad and she promised him she'd done her dozen steps and was going to meetings and was sober as a lawyer.

That didn't sound right. Sober as a... What? It didn't matter. What mattered was that she could now talk to him without slurring her words. Without her half of their telephone conversations descending into jibber jabber.

She told him she missed him. And loved him. And he could tell she meant it. And why shouldn't he be allowed to see his own mom? It's not like his gas jockey father was in the running for the parent of the year award.

As he sulked through the humid, black night Harrison realized he wouldn't miss anything in his shitty-assed hometown. Certainly not his father. Not the lame friends who he knew called him trailer trash behind his back. And especially not his little brother, Garrett who was such a pussy that, in the battle royals that often broke out in their homestead, usually took their dad's side. Little traitor prick.

He was so caught up in his hate that he didn't hear the vehicle approaching him from the rear. Didn't notice it at all until the headlights illuminated the narrow road that had been a dusty haze of cobalt fog a few seconds earlier. Only then did Harrison turn to see what was coming. He half-expected to see the front end of his old man's '74 pick up, but this engine wasn't wheezing and the brakes weren't whining. Besides, after the beating, he was certain he'd escaped through his bedroom window unnoticed.

Pretty sure.

Harrison realized he was holding his breath and let it out in a big whoosh that finished up about the same time he could identify the approaching vehicle as a Saab or maybe an Audi. One of those foreign boxes that looked and felt out of place in rural PA which was ruled by Chevys and Fords and Dodges with the occasional Toyota thrown in for flavor by some yuppie wannabe.

As the car rolled to a slow stop, the lights were bright enough that Harrison had to shield his eyes with his hand. He couldn't make out the driver through a windshield that was little more than a black hole in comparison.

"Which of the three are you?" A voice called out. It was ageless and smooth and masculine.

"Huh?" Was all Harrison could think of as a response.

"I asked 'which of the three are you?'"

Harrison heard the car door open, but the engine remained on. A steady, reliable purr that was so quiet it didn't even drown out the buzzing and whistling insectile noises that had filled the night before the car's, and this man's, arrival.

"Huh?" Harrison repeated, then realized he was sounding like a dumb hick who didn't know a word longer than three letters. "Three of what? Do I know you?" He tried to count in his head, satisfied when he realized at least one of those words had been five letters long.

The lights blinked from low beams to fogs and Harrison's young eyes quickly adjusted. He could see the man now. He looked about halfway between the old man's 47 and Harrison's 16. He had blond hair that was little more than a buzz cut and his tanned skin showed through, making his skull look like a peach with a smattering of fuzz. And he was smiling. That helped Harrison relax and some of the night's anger and pain seeped away when presented with this jovial, friendly face.

"The way I figure it, there's only three types of people out on the road at two a.m. Someone that's car broke down. Someone that's out and about and up to no good. And someone that's running away from it all."

The man's grin - Harrison thought it made him look younger than he really was - didn't leave his face. "Now I haven't passed any disabled cars, so I bet I can aim to eliminate that first one. That just leaves two and should make your answering a bit easier."

"Maybe you missed one."

"I doubt it, but you go ahead and fill me in."

"Well, maybe I'm out getting some exercise and I have to do it at night because I ain't got no sweat glands and can't do it in the heat of the day."

The man laughed, a sweet sound to Harrison who came from a house where such noise was as rare an occurrence as Haley's Comet. "I'll give you that, Son. That never occurred to me. How long have you been suffering from such a terrible malady?"

He'd moved to the front of the car and Harrison realized he was smaller than he sounded, then thought that didn't make much sense. How did he think he could deduce a person's stature by their voice? Sometimes he felt as dumb as the old man said he was.

"Aw, I just made that up."

"So, you're up to no good after all?"

"You pegged me. I'm a criminal mastermind out wreaking havoc."

The man nodded and pursed his lips in a gesture Harrison took as sarcastic admiration. "I suspected as much. Why, I bet you're out raiding some old granny's strawberry patch. Or maybe you're upending trash cans and blaming it on nefarious raccoons."

Harrison shook his head. "Wrong again, Mister. You see, I've been out here for hours, just biding my time, waiting for some stranger to come along in a fancy European car which I could steal and drive to Mexico, robbing banks and shooting up bars all the way from Pennsylvania to Tijuana."

"If that's the case, then I shall hand over my keys and let you get on with it. After all, who am I to throw a cog into such grand plans?"

It was Harrison's turn to laugh. And that felt so damn good he began to think his life wasn't so bad after all.

"Seriously though, kid. Is everything okay?"

Harrison realized the man was looking too hard at his face and his new smile and cheer dimmed while he felt the bruise grow hotter and, he imagined, redder. He considered covering it, on purpose this time, but that would make even more of a spectacle of it. "Yeah, I'm fine."

"You sure? I can give you a ride if you need one. And I won't ask any questions you don't want to answer."

Harrison looked past the man, to the idling car. It didn't look like a serial killer's car and, even though that made about as much sense as predetermining someone's size based on their voice, he decided to go with it. "All right then."

CHAPTER TWO

THE MAN KEPT HIS WORD ABOUT NOT ASKING ANY PRYING
questions, but Harrison found himself volunteering his story, or
at least parts of it. The unburdening of it made him feel twenty
pounds lighter.

The man's name was Vince Dupres and he didn't live in Sallow
Creek, but about twenty miles and one county over. Harrison
wasn't great with directions, but even he knew they were traveling away from Ohio. That was okay. He didn't consider himself
in any great rush and he was enjoying the company.

He was anyway, until Vince put his hand on his thigh. At the
man's touch, Harrison felt his sack shrivel up to the approximate
size of a prune and he imagined it looked about the same. My
shitty luck, he thought.

At first, he tried to ignore it. Told himself that Vince was simply
giving his hand a break from the steering wheel and missed the
armrest. That if he pretended it wasn't happening, and Vince
realized that kind of affection wasn't being reciprocated, that the

man would see the error in his ways and they could write the whole thing off as a monumentally awkward misunderstanding.

Awkward disappeared like the road behind them when Vince's hand travelled four inches north and landed on Harrison's crotch. His long, almost delicate, fingers gave it an encouraging caress.

Without giving it a second of thought, Harrison lashed out with his left arm and back-handed Vince in the face. There was a little crunch, like stepping on a peanut shell, and then two rivers of blood raged from the man's nostrils.

"Get your hand off my dick, you queer!"

The car - it was an Audi, Harrison had realized earlier after seeing the interlocking circles on the dash - swerved violently, bouncing over the berm and heading toward the ditch before Vince regained control. He whipped it back onto the road where it fishtailed, then lurched to a stop so abrupt that Harrison narrowly avoided smacking his own face into the windshield. He had a moment to think how ironic that would be, both of them with broken noses, before Vince's shouts filled the car.

"Ungrateful shit!" His voice wasn't smooth any more. It was thick and pinched and pained. "You broke my nose."

That came out like '*no-th*,' and Harrison almost laughed, but a look at the man's frantic, gory face put a quick end to that.

"I oughta call the cops on your ass." *A-th*.

"You're the perv! Feeling me up like I'm some kinda hooker."

"Out of my car! Now!"

Harrison fumbled for the door handle, his hand missing it the first time.

"Are you fucking deaf? Get out!"

Harrison found it on the second attempt and plunged out so fast that he stumbled and almost fell. As he steadied himself by planting his hands in the grit and shale at the edge of the road, he heard the tires shriek as the car disappeared into the darkness ahead.

"Fuck you, fag!" Harrison knew the man was already too far away to hear his taunts, but it felt good to yell. To scream. "Asshole!" Yeah, that felt real good. "Cocksucker!"

He wondered if cocksucker was an insult to queers. Probably not.

"Ass pirate!"

Ah, that was a nice one. He was trying to think up other creative profanities to shout when he realized how quiet it had become. He glanced around and saw nothing but black spires rising on either side of the road. The lifeless husks of pine trees stretched fifty, maybe sixty, hell, maybe a hundred, feet in the air. They looked almost high enough to touch the stars. Only there weren't any stars. The sky was as barren as the needle-less branches of the dead evergreens.

He stared skyward, at the black abyss, realizing he was on White-horse Mountain and only ten or so miles from home if you could make the trek in a straight line, but it was at least triple that on the twisty, winding roads. He was in the middle of fucking nowhere. The odds of another car coming along before dawn had to be smaller than he imagined Vince's faggy pecker to be and he sighed.

He thought about turning around and retreating, defeated, his dreams of running away from home, from his father, as broken as Vince's nose. No, he thought. I'm not going back. Because, if I go back, I'll never get out. I'll end up as miserable and ordinary as the old man. And Harrison knew he was better than that. He had a future and it was so damn bright he was gonna need shades.

Through the dead trees, light pierced the darkness. A pinprick at first and he thought it might be a flashlight beam. "Christ, Harrison, who the fuck would be out here this time of night? You're losing your shit." But what was it then? A firefly on steroids?

The light moved closer. Slow and steady and he again thought it was a person walking toward him. Maybe there was someone out here. Maybe a conservation officer was on patrol and had heard him screaming like a lunatic and was coming to investigate.

"Hey?" Harrison didn't mean for it to sound like a question, but his voice lilted up at the end anyway. "Sorry if I bothered you. Some creep was trying to come on to me."

Too much information, dumbass.

No one answered but the light's forward approach continued. It had been a hundred yards away, but it was closing in steady and picking up pace.

Seventy yards.

It was coming on too fast to be someone walking with a flashlight, Harrison realized. No one could move through the woods that fast without tripping over a fallen branch or shrub or smacking headfirst into a tree.

Forty yards.

It's someone on a motor bike or three-wheeler. The speed made more sense once that thought took hold. But it was soundless. Those things didn't sneak up on you. They were loud.

Twenty yards away.

The brightness illuminated the trees that filled the void between them and threw ebony shadows at Harrison like daggers slicing through the night. He tried to see what was behind the light. What was creating it, but it was too intense.

And quiet. Shit, even the bugs had zipped their lips. Did bugs have lips, he wondered. They had mouths so they must, right? He shook his head to clear the nonsense and, maybe, open his ears. But it was like he was stuck inside a vacuum. The only sounds were his breaths, which came spilling in and out rapid fire.

The light has ceased being a light. It was a pure white fire that obliterated everything around him and he could see nothing but the white. Hear nothing. Not even his own breaths now.

Judge, he thought. His mother promised she was sober as a judge.

That was Harrison Roberts' final thought because not even a second later the light enveloped him, and all the boy could think or feel or comprehend was pain.

CHAPTER THREE

GARRETT ROBERTS WAS TIRED WHEN HE AWOKE AND peddling his bike up Pleasant Hill wasn't helping. The night before he'd tossed and turned to the point that he thought his bed springs might break. Every time he came close to sleep, it wriggled away like some wild animal and he found himself wide awake all over again.

Part of the insomnia was caused by the drama that had gone down a few days earlier. His father and Harrison's argument. The ensuing fight. The hitting. Even from the unseeing confines of his bedroom, Garrett understood it had been a bad one. Maybe the worst ever. And afterward, he heard muffled sniffles from Harrison's room and knew his older brother was crying.

For a fleeting moment (very fleeting), Garrett had considered crossing the hallway to Harrison's room to try consoling him, comforting him, or even just giving an ear to bend. But Garrett knew better. If he dared crack open Harrison's bedroom door, he'd be the one on a receiving end of a beating. Because anger was like a boulder that rolled downhill and squashed everything in its path.

Besides, Harrison had brought it on himself. He should have known better than to ask to spend the summer with their mother. Geez, Garrett knew it and he was only twelve. After walking out on the family six years earlier, Bonnie Roberts had been little more than a ghost haunting the periphery of their lives, doing nothing but causing trouble.

She said she was sober now. A lie she'd told a dozen times before. Harrison might fall for her BS, possibly because he'd known her before the addiction to cheap booze had swallowed her up. Known her when there was still something about her worth loving. When she was a real mother capable of care and nurture. But, Garrett knew better. His mother was a lost cause.

He also knew it wasn't right that his father used the razor strap for punishment when a wooden spoon or an actual paddle would suffice, but usually you could avoid the beatings if you used your head before opening your mouth. But Harrison never seemed to comprehend that. How his brother could be four years older, yet so much dumber, was one of the greater mysteries in life.

The other reason, the main reason, Garrett couldn't fall asleep was because there were only two days of school remaining before summer vacation. Two days and the hell that had been sixth grade would be over, done with, gone. He had little hope that seventh would be any meaningful improvement, but at least there would be a three-month reprieve.

Almost a hundred days. Over two thousand hours of freedom. It was summer vacation he thought about while he sucked wind trying to make it to the top of the hill without dying. It looked impossibly far away, especially for a boy his schoolmates usually referred to as Blob-erts or Blubber Guts or Piggy. Beads of sweat on his forehead turned into salty rivulets that trickled down his gentle, but broad face. As he wiped it away, he saw a katydid had landed on his handlebars and that made him smile.

The duo trudged along until Garrett heard a car approaching from his rear and steered the bike off the road and onto the shale berm. That also gave him an excuse to stop. After all, safety first. His chest heaved and he made pained whooping sounds as he swallowed up big mouthfuls of air.

The vehicle was closer. He half-turned toward it, his kind, optimistic nature causing him to raise his hand in a genial wave and to smile, even while he felt like his lungs were on the verge of imploding. Before he even got a glimpse at the driver, he heard—

Reeeeee! Reeeeee! Reeeeee!

The pig squeal taunts had haunted him throughout the latest school year. Before that, the teasing was mostly limited to nicknames and putdowns that he'd tolerated. Sometimes one was so creative and unique that even he got a chuckle out of it. The sound effects though? Those, he could always do without.

He watched as a primer-colored Chevy Nova slowed beside him. Two older boys who Garrett knew by their faces, not their names, were in the front.

The driver leaned across the seat. "I'd give you a ride, Fatass but you'd probably blow out my shocks!"

The passenger laughed maniacally and then the car sped away with an extra punch to the gas pedal. The tires spun, kicking up a cloud of dust. Garrett waited for the storm to clear, then walked his bike the rest of the way up the hill.

As often as he was teased, mocked, humiliated, he'd never grown used to it. Every attack was a fresh wound that sliced all the way to his soul. At least, that's how he imagined it when he was feeling sorry for himself and being overly dramatic. He knew boys weren't supposed to let things like this bother them. His own father told him that often enough, sometimes with a hard slap in the belly and an aside like, 'If it bothers ya so much, do something about it.'

After cresting the hill, he straddled his bike and let it fly. The next two miles were all downhill or flatlands and at times he built up so much speed he wondered if a sonic boom might follow in his wake. All the while he thought about his friends and how they'd spend their summer.

Garrett coasted into the parking lot, adding his bike to dozens of others. As he pushed the front wheel between the bars of the rack, he noticed the katydid was still aboard. "Wow, buddy, you're a long way from home." He reached down and timidly touched the insect's vibrant, green thorax. It cocked its head at a neck-breaking angle but didn't depart.

He hesitated, still looking at the bug and wondering if it would be able to find its way back to whatever field or forest it had been living in. That seemed impossible. Surely it would get lost along the way, or splattered against a truck's windshield, or smashed under some careless oaf's foot before it made it a thousand yards.

Garrett thought that, to something so small, traveling a few miles would be like a man rocketing to a distant galaxy. It was in town now, far from the wheat fields and ryegrass, from the mites or ticks or whatever it usually ate. And he felt bad for it because it was all alone in this new, foreign world.

The first bell rang and Garrett knew he'd have to run to make it to homeroom. He hated to leave the katydid there, all by itself, but understood he was helpless against nature taking its inevitable course.

He lumbered toward the two-story, industrial-looking school and pushed through the front doors, making a right into the main hall and heading toward his room. Even before he arrived there, he forgot about the insect because a twelve-year-old boy's mind isn't all that different than flipping through TV channels every few seconds. Soon enough, some new, interesting thing comes along and whatever had been playing before fades away to nothing but a memory.

CHAPTER FOUR

LUNCH WAS THE HIGHPOINT OF GARRETT'S SCHOOL DAY. Not because the food was good. It was not. But because that was when Garrett got to see his friends. After sharing the same homeroom with them from kindergarten through the sixth grade at the smaller elementary school, his quintet had been cleaved and dismembered at Sallow Creek Junior High, each part of the whole sent to a different mad scientist to be fiddled with and experimented upon.

The only class he shared with any of them was Reading, where he was separated from Jose Supranowicz by three rows. Despite his given name, Jose was as white as the rest of this friends. As white as the rest of the entire town except for Mr. Thompson who ran the junkyard. And now Jose's face was even whiter than normal.

Garrett followed his petrified gaze and, when he saw what was coming, understood all too well. A trio of boys marched toward the lunch line and any students in their way drifted to the sides, giving them unimpeded access.

At the front, leading the way with the preening, puffed out chest of an exotic bird, was Nolan Haddix, one of the main reasons Garrett so hated sixth grade, and hated school in general. Nolan Haddix was, to Garrett, one step up from Satan.

Behind him were RJ Petrillo and Matt Ross, two of Haddix's obedient lackeys. While neither had displayed the creative cruelty of Haddix, these two were just as mean and eager to dish out punishment of both the physical and psychological kinds.

Petrillo wasn't much taller than Garrett, but he was lean and covered in ropey muscle. A heavy, gold necklace dangled from his neck and a diamond stud earring glistened in his left ear. Matt Ross was the tallest of the three, probably because he'd failed the third grade twice. He was stocky, filling out his Metallica t-shirt to the point where it looked a size too small and wore a vacant, vaguely confused expression on his face most of the time.

Garrett tried to slip out of their way before being noticed, but it was too late. As if on cue, Haddix snatched the collar of Garrett's t-shirt and threw him sideways. He careened into the stainless-steel assembly line behind which bland food was doled out by black hairnet-wearing lunch ladies who acted more like factory workers than cooks. He dipped to one knee before steadying himself.

"Watch where you're going, Blob-ert," Haddix said. His cohorts snickered.

Garrett stared at the lunch ladies with the pleading eyes of a prey animal, but they either ignored him entirely or looked at him with *not my problem* expressions pasted on their ordinary, disinterested faces.

RJ Petrillo stepped in front of Garrett, his upper lip pulled into a sneer. "You look like a *Fraggle*. Anyone ever tell you that?"

Garrett looked away, silent.

"One of the real fat ones. With the big noses and greasy hair and dirty clothes."

Garrettpushed his mop of dusty, brown hair out of his eyes without even realizing he was doing it. He knew exactly which Muppet Petrillo was referring too and now he'd forever associate it with himself. Yep, he was never watching that show again.

"He's no *Fraggle*. A faggot, maybe." Haddix stood with his crotch in Garret's face. A sour, pungent aroma wafted from it. "That it, blob-ert? Are you all fat and gross because you eat your feelings? Don't want your grease-monkey daddy to know you like packing fudge?"

A small crowd of girls - pretty, popular, perfect girls - stood close enough to overhear the goings on. They huddled together like gossipy hens, tittering. When Garrett looked at them, their lilting laughs only grew louder.

Jose had backed away from the fracas but scowled in silent disapproval, an act of support that Garrett appreciated, especially when faced with a crowd of otherwise passive onlookers. Like any good bully, Haddix homed in on this wordless disobedience immediately.

"You got a problem with me, Pedro?" Haddix asked as he stomped toward him with footfalls so harsh Garrett thought he could feel the linoleum quiver beneath him.

Jose opened his mouth to respond, then came to his senses. Haddix was, after all, a good eight inches taller and looked like he was already on the downside of puberty. Despite his name-brand clothes and designer sneakers, his skin was a shade of pink that made Garrett think of Piglet from the *Pooh* cartoons and his face was littered with mounds of zits whose yellow heads looked like miniature volcanos ready to blow. If he wasn't so damn scary and mean, he'd have been the butt of jokes himself.

Jose stared up at Haddix, jaw sprung like a broken hinge. He'd picked up the habit of breathing through his mouth after getting his braces earlier that year and his lips were chapped so bad most of the time that Garrett thought they might spontaneously bleed. The younger boy gaped at the bully liked a cowed dog awaiting his punishment, but instead Haddix moved on.

"Suck my sack, you dirty spic," he said as he cut in front, snatching the maroon tray from the top of the stack. He lurched down the line, filling it with enough food for three normal students. Petrillo followed on his heels. Ross, bringing up the rear, leaned down, aligning his face with Jose's, and belched. When the smell hit, Jose wrinkled his nose.

"Sorry," Ross said. "Must have been the burrito I had for breakfast." He left them and rejoined the others.

"Do they even know I'm white?" Jose still scowled, now with more confidence as Haddix's attention was elsewhere.

After holding back until Haddix and the others proceeded to the end of the line, the boys both grabbed trays and examined the day's offerings. It was the second to last day of school, but the last day for lunch and the cafeteria workers had presented an odd assortment of leftover entrees. Broad noodles slathered in red sauce, French bread topped with mozzarella cheese and diced ham, hot dogs, and something brown that might have been Salisbury steak or meatloaf or maybe shoe leather from the home ec room.

Garrett passed on the entrees, instead grabbing a Styrofoam cup of lumpy chocolate pudding and two half-pints of chocolate milk. It cost and extra dime which he handed to a lunch lady whose name tag declared as 'Maud' but who they all referred to as Mighty Mole because of the perfectly round, quarter-sized growth that punctuated her forehead like the dot on an exclamation point. A trio of wiry, black hairs jutted from that mole, so long that they waved like streamers under the lazy ceiling fan.

As Mighty Mole dropped Garrett's payment into the cash box, she gave his body an unapproving survey. "Ever think about trying skim?"

Aside from announcing the monetary sum of his purchases, those were the first words Mighty Mole had ever spoken to him and Garrett was so damn shocked that he was dumbstruck.

He was wholly aware of his girth and if he dared forget, someone like Nolan Haddix was always around to call him something awful, but Mighty Mole, with her droopy jowls, was no beanpole herself. She had no business judging but, since he couldn't tell her that, he did his best to ignore her and bounced to their usual table, Jose close behind.

Ray Mayhugh was already seated. His tray was empty save for a container of apple juice and a brown napkin.

"Did you inhale your lunch or something? Eat the silverware too?" Garrett said as he took the seat across from him.

Ray had been staring at his mostly empty tray and glanced up, startled by their sudden arrival. "I don't feel too good, man."

Garrett regretted his choice of seats. He had no desire to start off the summer sick and turned his head to the side, hoping to avoid Ray's exhaled, and possibly germy, breaths.

"You got the flu or something?" Jose said, then took a bite of the hotdog he'd chosen for his main course.

Ray saw it and his skin seemed to switch from tan to green like he was part chameleon. "Oh man, it's the hotdogs. You know they're pretty much my favorite food, right?"

Garrett nodded. He'd once seen Ray down five foot-longs at a minor league baseball game they'd gone to a year or so earlier.

"Yeah, well we were playing Head's Up Seven Up in math class today and you know how I never get tapped?"

Garrett and Jose nodded. None of them were anywhere in the vicinity of what might be considered popular. That's why their bond was so tight. But even amongst the outcasts, Ray stood out as an easy target. About half of it was his body odor, which wavered between mild onions and a dead skunk depending on the day's heat and Ray's own activity level.

The other half was due to his clothes. They were the kind of worn out, outdated shirts and pants that would have been tossed in the dumpster at Goodwill. Poorly fitting attire that had obviously been used and abused by every older male cousin and uncle in the Mayhugh clan. In a school where your wardrobe was a heaping portion of the recipe for acceptance, Ray had drawn the shortest of short straws.

"So, I didn't expect to do anything but lay there with my head on the desk smelling my armpits all period. But then, out of the blue, I got tapped. Or hit, to be more specific. Someone gave me a good smack on the back of my head and smashed my face into the desk, but I didn't care because I finally got to play."

He took a breath and continued. "So I thought real hard about who was strong enough to hit me like that and when it came my turn to try to pick out who it was, I zeroed in on Todd Joyner because the other six of them were four girls plus Sam Whittaker and you know how skinny he is and then there was Reed Smith and I don't think he'd ever pick me, not even just to be an asshole. So, I called out Todd and it was him!"

"You know, Ray, lunch is over in twenty minutes. Think you can wrap this up before then or should I ask Miss Zimmer if I can skip Social Science?" Jose said as he chewed on his hotdog.

"Oh ha-ha. Real funny, Jose. You're about as funny as AIDS," Ray said, but he must have realized his tale was dragging and got on with it. "So, anyway, I was up at the front of the class with the others and Mrs. Moon had just said, 'heads down all around' and I was thinking about who I was going to tap. I thought I might go for Shannon Walker because it would give me a chance to touch her. You know, she has such pretty hair. I bet it's real soft too. But before I could even take two steps in her direction, Valerie Arden jumped up from her desk and bolted for the door. She didn't get halfway there when—"

Ray raised both of his hands to his mouth and threw them out in an explosive motion. "*Blargh!* She barfed all over the floor. Oh geez, guys, it was awful. And right there, in the middle of the huge pile of barf was a piece of hot dog that must have been three inches long."

"That's longer than your pecker," Jose said. He'd moved on to his potato wedges and drowned one in ketchup.

Ray ignored him. "It was laying there, sort of pointing at me. Like an accusing finger or something. It was awful. I'll never be able to eat hot dogs again." He sighed and looked at his empty plate as if that was the most terrible thing to happen in his entire life.

"It was just a little puke, Ray. No big deal," Garrett said, trying to take the edge off his friend's visible trauma.

"No!" Ray shook his head vigorously. "Barf's the worst thing in the world. It's like shit that comes out of your mouth."

Garrett grimaced, losing his own appetite halfway through his pudding. "I'm pretty sure that would be worse than barf."

Again, Ray shook his head. Garrett thought his noggin might pop off his neck if he didn't stop doing that. "Uh uh. With shit, it's at least all digested and unrecognizable."

"Except corn," Jose added. "And peanuts."

"With barf, it's still identifiable. Like, it was halfway inside you but then got pissed off at you for trying to eat it and fought its way back out. It's almost obscene."

"Obscene? Sounds like my type of conversation." The voice belonged to Shane Vinyan who had appeared with his lunch tray without any of the others noticing.

Shane was the fourth member of their cadre, and, Garrett had realized a few months ago, he was on the verge of being handsome. Sometimes he worried that it wouldn't be long before Shane realized he was out of place amongst the rest of them and would leave their group in the dust, trading them for cooler, better friends.

"Not the good kind of obscene," Jose said.

"Well that's tragic," Shane said as he sat down beside Ray. "What's shakin' bacon?"

"We're trying to decide what's worse. Barf or shit," Ray said.

"Jesus, is this the kind of high-level discourse you boys partake in when I'm not around?" He shook his head mocking disapproval. "Anyway, that's easy. Barf."

"What if the shit comes out of your mouth instead of your butt?" Ray asked.

Shane raised an eyebrow, comically high an act that reminded Garrett of a ventriloquist's dummy. The boy's constellation of freckles and pale, red hair added to the effect.

"Well, that complicates matters. Are we talking about firm, high fiber sort of logs of shit coming out of your mouth, one big piece at a time? Or liquified and pureed like the Halloween when Lynn ate all his candy as soon as he finished trick or treating and didn't make it to the bathroom?"

Garrett stared into his open chocolate milk container, the brown liquid swirling around, random bubbles popping. He wasn't thirsty now either. "Please, make it stop," he said.

"I heard my name. Which one of you sons of bitches said it and was it good or bad?"

They turned almost in unison to see Lynn Ohler approaching with his sack lunch. He flopped down beside Garrett.

"That was me," Shane said. "Lynn, settle a debate for us. When it comes to barf versus shit— "

Garrett stood. "I'm done. You idiots have ruined my final lunch of sixth grade." He swept his uneaten pudding and un-drunk milk into an oversized black trash can.

"Oh, Garrett, we didn't know you were so delicate," Shane said, his laugh had the hard edge of a crow's cackle. "How will we ever make it up to you?"

"I don't know, but you've got all summer to try."

Summer. That sweet word had them all smiling. Even Ray. They had no jobs, no trips, no plans. Just three months to screw off and do the kind of stupid crap that only bored twelve-year-old boys could dream up. Garrett had no clue what they'd come up with, but he was sure it would be unforgettable.

CHAPTER FIVE

GARRETT'S APPETITE RETURNED WITH A VENGEANCE around 6 p.m. that evening. The house was still empty which was no great shock. The entire weekend, Memorial Day, and the second to last day of school had gone by and Harrison still hadn't come home. In passing thought, Garrett wondered if Harrison had bothered going to school or if he skipped that too. Either way, his brother was at the top of his class when it came to idiocy.

Their dad wouldn't be home until after he closed the gas station at eight, so Garrett grabbed two slices of ham from the fridge and cooked them on the grill. He then nuked a can of creamed corn for a side dish. He didn't bother making a plate for Harrison, knowing his brother could fend for himself if he decided to make an appearance. Garrett did put together a meal for his dad, because he knew the man was putting in 14-hour days and rarely took the time to eat anything nutritious.

While his brother hated their dad, Garrett loved him, even if the words, 'I love you' were never exchanged in the household. He accepted the beatings as a part of growing up, as one of those life challenges everyone promised would make him into a man, even though he knew those were lies. His friends, at least the ones who had fathers, didn't get smacked or hit or whooped. But life could always be worse and he'd take an occasionally violent father over an absentee mother six days a week and twice on Sundays.

After eating, another hour passed before he heard the wheels of his dad's truck crunching through the gravel driveway. There came a backfire as the engine shut off, then the boom of the door closing. Garrett set the microwave for two minutes and waited.

Larry Roberts was tall and wide with an unkempt mane of gray hair that glistened under the canned lights as he stepped inside the trailer. A nub of a cigarette was pinched between his lips and he took one more drag before tossing the butt out the doorway and into the yard. Larry dropped his keys and wallet onto an end able as he kicked off his work boots.

The man groaned as he slipped free of his uniform shirt, which had his name embroidered above the breast pocket, and let it fall to the floor. His pale, exposed torso made the grime and grease that coated his hands, and which was smeared haphazard across his face, look even more filthy.

As Larry rubbed a shoulder that was swollen with arthritis, the microwave shut off with a trio of beeps. Garrett retrieved the food and carried the plate to their small kitchen table. The Formica top was chipped and gouged and marred by numerous black cigarette burns.

"What'd you make good?" Larry asked as he approached.

"Ham and corn."

"Kernel or cream?" Larry got his answer when Garrett set the meal before him with the flourish of a waiter in a fancy restaurant. "Good choice. That ham's dry."

Garrett grabbed two cans of generic grape soda from the fridge, setting one before his dad and claiming the other for himself. Larry popped the top of his can and took a long swig.

"Thanks, Gar."

Garrett smiled. His dad was the only one who called him that and it made him feel special because his dad would have never dared call Harrison 'Harry' even though most everyone else did. "Welcome."

He wished he'd have made something for dessert. Not for his father's sake as the man didn't have a single sweet tooth in his entire mouth, but for himself. Oh well, he'd have to wait and satiate himself later with a candy bar from the shoebox he kept under his bed. "Anything new at the garage?"

Larry dredged a piece of ham through the creamed corn and shook his head. "Slow as shit." He shoved the food into his mouth and didn't speak again until it was chewed and swallowed. Larry Roberts might not bother to wash his hands before eating, but he had the good sense to not talk with his mouth full. "Got a call from one of the secretaries at the high school earlier. Told me Harrison didn't bother attending today."

Garrett stared, unsure whether there was a question to be answered.

There was. "You know anything about that?"

Garrett shook his head slow, once to the left and once to the right, remembering Ray's earlier head bobbing and being careful not to overdo it. "I didn't see him this morning. Thought maybe he got a ride with one of his friends."

"You mean he has some?"

A smile tugged at the man's mouth, but he didn't fully give in to it. Garrett liked the man's humor on the rare occasions it made an appearance.

"A couple. Wade Lowell. Dean Sanford. And one of the Wagner twins but I can't tell them apart."

Larry's only response was a curt nod and another mouthful of food. Garrett thought about bringing up the fight and Harrison sneaking out but thought better of it. Instead he downed half his soda in three long swallows.

His father pulled a crumpled pack of Winston cigarettes from his pants pocket and lit one. He took only a short puff before resting it on the nearby ashtray, which Garrett had earlier emptied of butts. The silence dragged on until Larry was three fourths through his ham. So quiet for so long that Garrett twitched with surprise when he spoke again. "You and Harrison don't mesh well, do you?"

Garrett bit the inside of his bottom lip and shrugged his shoulders. "He says I'm a pain in his a—" he stopped, swallowed. "Pain in his butt. Calls me 'the embodiment of a human hemorrhoid.'"

"Surprised he knows the meaning of a word like embodiment."

There was another hint of a smile and Garrett couldn't stave off one of his own. "It was probably the Word of the Day in remedial English."

"Don't take everything he says to heart. Harrison's full of

hormones and anger. And it's got worse since your mother..." He didn't extrapolate on that. They both knew the details.

"Anyway..." Larry pushed his plate aside. He'd left a few bites uneaten, something that never happened. "Suppose I should call around to the parents of those boys you mentioned. See if your brother's shacking up with one of them and being a bother."

He returned the cigarette to his lips and stared in the general direction of the kitchen window. Garrett didn't like the look in his eyes, mostly because he couldn't decipher it. Sadness? Disappointment? Whatever it was, it was a foreign look on the man's grizzled face and Garrett wanted to make it go away.

He considered saying something. Maybe telling him that he was a good dad. Or that he knew he was trying. Garrett even opened his mouth but when he did, no words came out. Growing up in this household hadn't prepared him for being candid about things like feelings and emotions.

Larry took a long drag that created nearly an inch-long string of ash that threatened to fall onto his leftovers and Garrett couldn't understand why he didn't tap it away. The way it hung there, precarious, made him nervous.

"I taped *Jeopardy* for you."

That was something he always did and stating the fact out loud made little sense, but it seemed the spell had been broken. Larry blinked and when he turned his face back to him, Garrett was glad to see that mysterious, melancholy mask was fading.

"Well, thanks, Gar." He pulled the cigarette from his mouth and smashed it out in the tray. "But did you watch it and memorize the answers already?"

"I didn't."

"That's a good boy. But if you get the final answer right and it's not something in your wheelhouse like movies or US history, I'm gonna be skeptical 'bout that." The elder Roberts stood and moved to the trailer's cramped living area.

As Garrett gave the dishes a quick and rather careless wash, he heard the recliner squeak, the TV turn on, and the whine of the VCR tape rewinding. He hoped Harrison stayed away all evening, so the home would be free of the tension that pulsed like electricity off a live wire whenever he was around. Maybe they'd even stay up late enough to watch *L.A. Law*. Garrett knew his dad was making an effort. As the fattest kid in his school, he understood no one was perfect. And if you cared about someone, you needed to accept them as they were. Warts and all. Not how you wished them to be.

CHAPTER SIX

SHANE VINYAN CHECKED UP AND DOWN THE HALLWAY three times before unzipping his bulky backpack and revealing the contents to a crowd of five onlookers. Three of them, Frank Howell, Sam Jerczyk, and Todd Joyner were in his own class while Randy Kowalski and Steve Hillstrom were a grade up. All watched with the type of avid eyes usually reserved for wolves or similar predators. Impatient. Hungry. Needful.

"Come on, already, Vinyan. Homeroom starts in five minutes," Sam said, reaching for the bag. For the plastic sheathed contents inside it.

Shane pulled it back. "Patience, my friends." None of them were his friends though. Not really. They were customers. Marks, even. If Shane had been a carny, these rubes would have been the type he eyed up with an excited and enthusiastic grin as he suckered them in for a turn at Spill the Milk or Shoot 'em Up. "No lookie loos allowed. Not until I see some green."

The boy's expressions went sour, but they dug into their pockets and came out with fistfuls of cash and change. "Happy now?" Sam asked.

"As a clam." Shane had come prepared and pulled out three of the plastic sleeves. He fanned out the first two. The covering at the top was clear and revealed the upper quarter of magazines. *Playboy. Penthouse.* Accompanying the names were the tops of women's heads and oversized, permed hairdos, but the rest of the women - the good bits - were shrouded behind blackness. "*Playboy's* five dollars. *Penthouse* is eight." And if you're feeling particularly generous..."

Shane slipped free the third title as deftly as a card shark. *Hustler.* "I only have one of these beauties and it will set you back an Alexander Hamilton. Or two Honest Abe's. Or ten GW's. I'm not particular."

Randy and Todd gasped audibly. Frank Howell seemed confused by both their reaction and this new arrival. "What's *Hustler?*"

Todd Joyner shook his head. "You've never seen a *Hustler?*"

"What's so special about it?"

"*Hustler* shows it all," Shane said.

"So does *Playboy.*" Frank folded his arms, which looked almost girlishly thin.

"No. Not even close. *Playboy's* like the pretty girl next door. Her titties just grew in and she's feeling a little naughty, so she decides to show off a bit. All strictly look but don't touch. And brief glimpses at that. Meanwhile, *Penthouse* is like your slutty cousin. You know, the one that wears the mini-skirts that just barely cover her ass and the tops cut so low you can practically see her belly button."

Shane gave Randy a knowing glance, as the girl he was describing was a mirror match for Randy's cousin, Pamela. "And if you give her a couple bucks she'll let you stick your hand down her shirt or up her skirt. And she likes it."

Randy's cheeks blazed red and, inside, Shane congratulated himself for such a stinging zinger.

"Both of those girls are fun. But *Hustler*..." He let out a soft, low whistle. "*Hustler* is the whole shebang. *Hustler* is that chick you see standing at the bus stop when you go to Pittsburgh to see the Steelers play. The one who winks when she sees you and calls you over with her finger. And as long as you've got cash in your wallet, she'll let you do anything you want."

He looked from one boy to the next, slow, deliberate. "Anything at all. That, my friends, is *Hustler* and after you look at this baby," his fingers tapped the cover. "You'll know so much about the female anatomy that you could open up your own medical practice."

Young Frank stared at it, trying to see through the black, blocking plastic as if he'd suddenly developed X-ray vision. "Looks like just another skin rag to me."

"You're welcome to your opinion." Shane returned the magazines to his pack. "And if you boys aren't interested, I can present these to Nolan Haddix and his crew. I'm sure they'll appreciate them."

"Those assholes will just beat your face in and steal them from you," Todd Joyner said, his voice dripping with false bravado and Shane noticed that Todd glanced around to make sure none of Nolan or his crew had overheard the remark.

"Nah," Shane said. "They might be rough around the edges, but those young men understand that pornography of these standards is hard to come by in Sallow Creek"

"Screw you, Vinyan. My dad's got a stack of old *Cavaliers* in his sock drawer," Frank Howell said. "I'll save my money and snag one of them."

"Fine by me. But when you're looking at those broads in torpedo tit bras and panties up past their belly buttons, I want you to picture your pop holding that very same magazine while he piddles his pudd." Shane zipped the bag halfway closed. "And like Sam said, homeroom starts up soon so if you aren't in the buying mood, I'll be on my way."

He was prepared to walk but knew it wouldn't come to that. They always protested. He always threatened to sell the rags to someone else. And they always caved.

"Wait!" Sam grabbed him by the wrist.

Always.

Sam handed him a five. "I'll take the *Playboy*."

Shane slipped it between Sam's math and science books. "As my good friend Jose would say, many gracias."

The next minute and a half brought a flurry of transactions as Shane sold 14 more magazines and had a cool seventy-eight bucks in his pocket. Only Frank remained empty-handed and, about the time Shane was ready to move on, Frank pushed a wrinkled and weathered ten-dollar bill in his direction.

"The *Hustler*."

The other boys looked to him, resentful and a little in awe, the way nickel slots players stare at the whale when he bellies up to the poker table.

"Good choice, my friend. Very good choice."

They finished their dealing and Shane, whose stock was down to a mere nine magazines, closed his bag as he headed toward room 217 - Mr. Twerdy's homeroom.

He'd hoped to finish the day up a hundred bucks and now he was certain he'd top that by a good margin. It helped that it was the last day of school and most of the boys knew that he, their dealer, would be harder to find. They needed to stock up for the summer and Shane was all too happy to oblige.

Shane had been selling porn to the young men of Sallow Creek Middle School for most of the school year. He got the magazines from his parents' pharmacy where they were kept behind the counter. Hidden away from innocent, or judgmental, eyes and available only to those brave enough to walk up to the cashier - oftentimes Shane's own mother - and ask for them.

They only sold a handful a month at the store, which meant the leftovers had to be returned for credit. That was when Shane got the brilliant (in his mind) idea to sell them at school. He'd gotten away with it for three months before his father caught on.

Steve Vinyan, pharmacist, town councilman, and all-around upstanding member of the community, was prepared to be outraged, but when Shane explained his entrepreneurial adventures, the forty-eight-year-old man could do nothing but run his fingers through his salt and pepper hair in mild shock. "Sixty-two dollars, huh?" Steve asked his son.

Shane had nodded. "I keep getting more customers each month."

Steve smiled a little at that, then bit down on his lips and tried to appear fatherly. "If your mother knew this, she'd have a conniption."

Shane wasn't sure what a conniption was, but he knew his mother and found it easy enough to connect the dots. "Well, I wasn't planning to tell her."

Steve's right eye squinted down to a slit. "No. I didn't expect you were."

"And I'm careful, dad. I promise."

His father had remained silent for a long moment, working things out in his own way. "I've always believed a boy has to learn how to swim or sink on his own. So, you carry on with your little business, but you're reimbursing the store for the wholesale cost."

Shane nodded, eager and excited and handed over the money due.

"And if you ever get caught..." Steve held his hands up in a not guilty posture. "I knew nothing. And if you dare insinuate otherwise, you're disowned. Got it?"

He gave his dad a hard embrace, and the business lived on.

As Shane passed room 213, he saw Garrett on the opposite side of the hallway. He took quick, almost prissy, little steps and kept his head tucked, like a turtle half-retreated into its shell.

"Garrett!" Shane called out, loud enough to be heard over the clamor of other students racing to homeroom.

At the sound of the voice, Garrett emerged from his shell, then maneuvered his way through the crowd in a way that reminded Shane of the *Frogger* arcade game they used to play at the bowling alley before they got bored of it. He was waiting for the splat as Garrett got run down, but it never came.

Garrett was a little out of breath when he arrived. "Hey."

"Hey back." Shane tried to make eye contact, but Garrett's attention was elsewhere. His distracted gaze wandering around the hall. "You got a hot date or something?"

Garrett finally looked at him, eyes narrowed. "What?"

"Who are you looking for?"

"Oh. No one, really." But his eyes drifted back to the stampede of students. "Harrison wasn't home again this morning. I thought maybe I'd see him around."

Yesterday, Garrett had educated Shane about the goings on in the Robert's trailer. He'd been surprised to hear Garrett stick up for his dad after the man had beaten the shit out of Harrison with a belt or something just as bad. No matter how big a douche Harrison was, and Shane knew that he was a douche of the extra-large variety, that wasn't right. While he had a healthy respect for his own parents, they'd never laid a hand on him in anger and, so far as Shane was concerned, that was the way it should be.

"He hasn't been home since last Friday?"

Garrett shook his head. "It's okay though. He's probably just skipping."

"What kind of mental defect skips the last two days of school?"

Garrett threw a smile his way. "My brother."

"Ah, yes. That one. I see said the blind man as he pissed into the wind. It all comes back to me now." Still, it seemed weird. He almost said as much but the fire engine-red bell mounted on the nearby wall shrieked like an air raid siren over their heads. One-minute warning. "Meet up after dismissal?"

"Sure. Where?"

"Luigi's?"

Any joy that had clawed its way onto Garrett's face vanished. "I don't have any money."

Shane patted his bulging pocket. "Well, it just so happens that I'm flush with the green stuff."

And like a rainbow after the storm, Garrett's happiness returned. "Magazine day?"

"Magazine day."

"Okay then! See you there!" Garrett hurried toward his own homeroom 202, his double-wide hips sashaying girlishly.

An older boy whose name Shane did not know, nor care to, passed Garrett and unleashed a whiny oink. The boy chortled, as did several other students in the vicinity. Garrett's shoulders slouched, his head tucked, and his pace quickened.

Shane had heard many of the awful things the other kids said about Garrett, the names they called him both behind his back and to his face, and while he never joined in - he would have disemboweled himself before joining in - he never spoke up against them either. He didn't speak up now either. And he hated himself a little bit for that.

He tried to push the negative thoughts away as he fled in the opposite direction, eager to sell his remaining magazines and start summer rolling in more dough than Mrs. Pillsbury herself.

CHAPTER SEVEN

THE OVERWHELMING MAJORITY OF THE STUDENT BODY THAT was inclined to dine on pizza after the last classes of the school year had taken up residence at Clair's. That made the most sense as it was only a few blocks from the school. A straight shot down Columbia Avenue.

As a self-professed pizza connoisseur, Garrett had to admit, their pies were pretty damn good. The sauce had a sweetness that he thought paired especially well with spicy pepperoni. But Clair's was also the restaurant where the jocks and cheerleaders and rich kids hung out. After being forced to spend nine months in their presence, he had no interest in sharing the same quarters outside of school.

His other pals felt the same way and that was why Luigi's had become their place. It was an unkempt dive that set on the northeast corner of the diamond in the middle of town, squeezed between a thrift shop and a jewelry store. According to the rumor mill, Luigi's was a front for the owner's drug dealing business.

Garrett didn't care if they sold baggies of pot or even cocaine out of the backroom though. All he cared about was devouring the pizza which was drowned with so much cheap mozzarella that grease dripped from the slices when you picked them up and you needed multiple napkins just to get through one piece. Add in his best (only) friends, and it was the perfect kick off to summer.

As Rick Astley promised he was never gonna give you up via the crackling overhead speakers, Garrett chewed away and watched Lynn add five heavy shakes of hot pepper flakes to his own slice.

"I don't know how you can eat it like that," Garrett said.

The flakes absorbed the grease and clung to the pizza as Lynn lifted it to his mouth. "I like it hot. Like me."

Shane gave a hard chuckle at that, one so loud an elderly couple three tables over, who happened to be the only other customers in Luigi's at 1:30 in the afternoon, turned and stared with sour expressions.

"Manners." The old woman, her gray hair pulled up in a tight bun, shook her head.

"I left manners at home this morning, Ma'am. But I'll try to keep it down."

Shane turned his back to her, but Garrett saw the two senior citizens lips moving and knew it was all bad. He mouthed, 'Sorry' and gave what he hoped was a winning and remorseful smile, but the old birds only shook their heads again and stopped looking in their direction.

He didn't understand why old people had to be such assholes to kids. Had they forgotten all about how great it was to be young?

Or maybe they remembered and that was the problem. They were jealous.

A gagging, wet coughing fit from Lynn drew Garrett's attention back to his friends and he watched Lynn suck down two thirds of his Coke without pausing to take a breath.

"You dumbass." Ray's words came out garbled as he said them through a mouthful of half chewed pizza.

Lynn finished drinking and gave a salute that came off less Army and more Nazi than he probably intended. "That's Captain Dumbass to you, Private. Show some respect."

Ray raised his fist, slow and deliberate, then rolled out his middle finger. "How's that for respect, Sir."

"That'll do." Lynn used a spoon to scrape off some of the pepper flakes, then took another bite. That one went down without choking on it.

"Does your butthole burn after you eat hot stuff like that?" Jose had finished off his piece.

"No," Lynn said. "Does yours burn after your dad shoves his fat kielbasa up your poop chute every night before bed?"

Jose's face flared red. Along with being the smallest of all of them, he seemed the most innocent, or maybe naive. He never swore, never talked about sex. He wouldn't even take more than a passing glance at Shane's magazines unless the others cajoled him into it.

"He does not," Jose said and even Garrett (who was usually a half-step behind when it came to witty comebacks) had to admit that was a real stinker.

"Oh, that's right. He's too busy doing your pretty baby sister," Lynn said and blew Jose a kiss.

Garretthalf-expected Jose to have some kind of emotional outburst, but the boy surprised him by giggling. He threw a used-up napkin at Lynn, which ricocheted off the boy's thick glasses onto his shoulder, before landing on the grimy floor.

Garrett looked toward the old couple, apprehensive and expecting more harsh looks, but they hadn't noticed. Nonetheless, he scooped the napkin off the floor and added it to the growing pile of trash that littered their table.

One slice of uneaten pizza remained on the pan. Shane, Jose, and Lynn had each had one. Ray and Garrett had two. Garrett knew that the last slice was by all right's, Shane's since he'd paid for the pizza, and their sodas, but still, he stared at it, his belly rumbling.

When he looked up, he saw Shane watching him. "Have at it, Garrett."

"No. That's okay. I'm full." Garrett wondered if that sounded as much like a lie out loud as it did in his head.

"Well, I'm good," Shane said. "Besides, this is meatloaf and mac and cheese night at home and I want to be hungry enough to eat it."

That made Garrett's belly growl again. He tried to think what leftovers he had in the fridge at home and what little there was paled in comparison. Still, he didn't want to look like a hog. Like 'Pig Boy.' "Well, then, someone else can have it."

Jose, the smallest of all of them and who might have topped 85 pounds if you filled his pockets with rocks, shook his head.

Lynn waved his hand in front of his mouth, still trying to cool down. "It's wasted on me. I burned off my taste buds."

That left only Ray and Garrett turned his way. Everything about Ray screamed poor. From the hand-me-down clothes to the dirt and grime that filled in the cracks in his neck and the pores in his face. Ray once commented, in a very matter of fact manner, that everyone in his house was limited to one bath per week because their well was almost dry.

The Mayhugh clan - that's what everyone called them, not a family, but a clan - lived in a hundred and fifty-year-old farmhouse far enough outside of town that they couldn't even get cable TV, so Garrett believed the water story to be true. He also knew that Ray's father was in prison for killing a man in a bar fight a few years earlier, and that his mother had run off when Ray was only two or three years old.

There were rumors that the Mayhugh's made moonshine in the big. partially collapsed barn behind their house, knowledge that made Garrett wary of getting shot when he visited. Heck, he didn't even know the names of the men and women (mostly men) who lived on the property. On any given visit, there seemed to be between eight and fifteen people mucking about.

One of them was Ray's sister, a mentally retarded girl a few years older than them, but she never attended school and usually wandered around aimlessly, never speaking, only humming to herself. Two other residents were Ray's grandparents and Garrett supposed the rest were aunts and uncles and cousins, but they were a rough bunch, and, while he'd have never admit it to Ray, he was always a little scared when he went to the farm to meet up or play.

While the pickings in his own cabinets were slim, Garrett

guessed they were even slimmer at the Mayhugh's. "It's all yours, Ray."

Ray's eyes widened. "You sure?"

"As can be. Like I said, I'm full."

Jose reached across the table and poked Garrett's bulging belly. "More than full. I think he's going to pop!"

From anyone other than these four friends, such an act would have sent Garrett into a depressed, emotional crisis, but this was different. From them, the jokes didn't make him feel like an outcast or a loser. They made him feel accepted. Loved, even, although he wasn't sure if boys their age were capable of love.

He dissolved into laughter and wrapped his arms around his fat gut as if holding it hostage. "Cover your heads, boys! I think it's going to blow!"

That sent them all off and their loud, peeling gales and squeals filled Luigi's and drowned out Phil Collins' groovy love that had taken over the speakers.

"Shrapnel! Incoming!" Garrett shouted.

Lynn, who had been draining the last third of Coke from his cup, snorted and brown cola spurted out both of his nostrils like he was a living water feature.

"Honestly!" The old woman gasped.

Garrett saw her and her husband flee the restaurant and he didn't even care, he just kept laughing.

CHAPTER EIGHT

THE QUINTET PEDDLED THEIR BICYCLES TO THE BOWLING alley. Shane had promised them four bucks each in quarters, and Ray estimated they could make that last at least a few hours. But before they could even park their bikes, Garrett spotted rides that they all recognized as belonging to Nolan Haddix and his makeshift gang. They hightailed it away before getting caught, to the relief of all of them.

Like each of the others, Ray'd had his run-ins with Nolan in the past. In the fourth grade, Haddix had caught him alone in Stepping Stone Creek. Ray'd been gathering crayfish and had half a pail full when Nolan arrived and decided to play his own version of Chinese water torture. That consisted of dunking Ray repeatedly, holding him under from anywhere from thirty seconds to two minutes at a clip, all the while laughing like a lunatic. After ten minutes of it, the cloudy, silt-filled water clogging his nostrils and throat, Ray became convinced he was going to die. Die alone with that sour, muddy taste filling his mouth.

The next time Nolan yanked him out of the water, Ray barfed up almost enough of the brown fluid to fill a milk jug. Some of it splashed onto the bully and Nolan let out a surprisingly high-pitched squeal and released him.

Before he left, Haddix had dumped Ray's crayfish onto one of the smooth, flat rocks that rose up from the creek and stomped them into a pancake of shattered shells and goo. And despite the physical pain and the fear he'd felt during the ordeal, that last part, the senseless killing of the crayfish, seemed the cruelest of it all.

With the bowling alley off limits, they road bikes on aimless routes for hours on end only stopping occasionally to cool off under a tree or grab a drink at one of the convenience stores. None of the breaks lasted more than ten minutes or so before the riding recommenced.

Sometimes Ray felt like he was a half-step behind the others when it came to conversations. By the time he'd worked out a response, the chatter had moved on. It was especially true on days like this were they didn't do anything but talk, all five of them at once, sometimes not even hearing each other. Ray wasn't bored with this, but he'd been working on an idea for a week or more and decided now was the time to share it.

"Remember a couple weeks ago when we watched *Knightriders* in the clubhouse?" Ray asked, the quip appearing out of thin air and unrelated to anything else they'd been discussing.

The clubhouse was their name for a 10 by 10 storage shed Shane's parents had built in the woods behind their house. It was only twenty yards from the Vinyan homestead but gave the boys a dry place to hold sleep outs during the winter, or on rainy summer nights.

Each of the boys had added their own aesthetic. Shane brought in a love seat and easy chair that his parents were going to toss out.

Lynn had unearthed some old carpet from a dumpster while scrounging for aluminum cans and, after a good hosing down and three days in the sun, it didn't even stink. Much.

Ray brought two lamps with garish floral print shades he'd found in the farmhouse attic and Garrett, for some reason none of the others could fully understand, brought a carpet sweeper. Jose donated the 13-inch TV that had previously occupied his bedroom. Sometimes the picture would roll and they'd have to whack it on the side with a wiffle ball bat to settle it down, but beggars couldn't be choosers, as the saying went.

Once the TV was in place, they decided they needed a VCR. After weeks of hitting up every yard sale between East Main and North Center, they found one they could almost afford. The seller, a short, balding man whose hair tufted out on the sides in a way that reminded Ray of a clown, had been asking fifty dollars for it but his sign said, 'All prices negotiable' and Shane offered him twenty.

The bald man unleashed a rough, coughing laugh. "Twenty dollars, kid? Just for that I ought to charge you seventy-five. What do a bunch of kids need a video player for anyhow?"

If Ray had been answering he might have tried to come up with a good lie. Maybe something about recording the soap operas for his grandmother. Something to tug at the guy's heartstrings, if he had any.

But Shane was candid. "We got a clubhouse and a TV, but it can barely pull channel six, even with rabbit ears. Unless we get a VCR, we're shit outta luck."

The seller laughed again, but with less condescension. "That right huh?"

Shane nodded. "Sure is."

"Hell, that's better than being out and getting up to no good. 'Sides, I remember what it was like to be a kid and chumming with my pals."

Ray wondered if the guy, who looked at least forty, really could remember that far back. That must've been practically ancient times.

"I'm selling it because the remote shit the bed. But you got young legs so there ain't no reason you can't walk over to it and press play and stop." He cracked his swollen knuckles, looking at each of the boys. Then he grinned. "Thirty bucks and it's yours."

Shane handed over the cash and their entertainment system was complete.

Jose had been a few paces behind and peddled faster to catch up. "That was the one with the motorcycles?"

Ray nodded. "Yeah."

"That movie was a total shit pickle," Lynn said. "Worst movie I ever saw."

"Yeah, we know, Lynn. You wanted to see zombies. You only said that about every ten minutes. 'Where are the zombies?', 'When do the zombies show up?'" Shane steered his bike closer to Lynn's and used his right foot to push him sideways, toward the gaping ravine that lined the road. "'How long 'til someone gets eaten by a zombie?' What's with your hard on for zombies, anyway? They don't even think. They just eat. How's that scary?"

Lynn wobbled momentarily before regaining control. "They eat people, man! It's not like they sit around and munch pork rinds and nachos, you stupid pud."

"They eat slow people. Anyone that can walk faster than a two mile per hour clip is safe as shit," Shane said.

"Well Jesus Christ, Shane, excuse me if I like watching zombies rip open someone's guts and chow down like it's an all you can eat buffet. To me, that's entertainment." Lynn cut in front of Shane, trying to throw him off balance but failed. "Besides, it was a George Romero movie. Of course, I was expecting zombies. Not fags on bikes."

"They weren't fags. They were knights," Ray said. "And besides, that's not the point."

"You mean you actually have one?" Lynn said.

Ray was beginning to regret bringing it up. Sometimes getting his thoughts across wasn't worth the effort it took. "I don't even know why I bother."

"What about the movie, Ray?" Garrett asked, trying to put the conversation back in Ray's hands.

"I actually get to speak?" He looked to Lynn and Shane who stared at him, but kept their mouths closed. "All right then. What I was trying to say was that the movie gave me an idea for a new game."

"Is it, 'Let's try to find a less shitty movie than Knightriders'?" Lynn asked. "Because we'll all be winners."

"No questions yet. Just meet me tomorrow morning on 219 where the road dead ends, all right?"

His friends stared at him, mostly confused, but a little curious too. It took every bit of self-control Ray had to keep this glorious idea to himself, but he knew that simply describing it wouldn't do it justice. They'd need to see this in person. And they'd have to wait a little while longer.

They were just two blocks from the low-income housing complex where Lynn lived with his mother and older sister. Ray had developed quite the crush on the girl over the past year. Charlene Ohler's face was plain and doughy and not altogether different from Lynn's own. She even had long, but thin blonde hair, just like her brother. But what she possessed that Lynn did not, were two of the biggest tits Ray had ever seen in his twelve years of life. Even when she wore a baggy sweatshirt during the winter months, they pushed against the fabric like overripe melons.

Ray loved staring at Charlene's tits so much that it even made hanging out with Lynn worth the hassle. He took every opportunity possible to visit the Ohler's apartment, to the point where Garrett had once asked him if he liked Lynn better than the rest of them. Ray didn't want to cop to the truth, but didn't want to hurt Garrett's feelings either, so he came up with a lame lie about going there because their place had air conditioning. Garrett didn't mention that it was February.

As they approached the red brick buildings that everyone called The Towers, Lynn turned his bike toward the entrance. "See you later, chuckle fucks."

Ray wanted to follow him, to go to the apartment and see if Charlene's tits were around, but the sun was dipping close the horizon and he didn't want to make the eight-mile ride home to the farm in the dark. And alone.

"Tell Charlene I said 'hi.'" The words slipped through his lips even as he tried to corral them, like his mouth was a worn-out faucet and no matter how hard you turned the knob, it still leaked.

Lynn responded by flipping him the bird over his shoulder. That wasn't so bad, Ray thought. But, when he looked to his three remaining friends, he saw them all staring.

"Really, Ray?" Shane asked.

"I was just being polite." He felt his cheeks blaze red hot and pedaled furiously, hoping the wind would calm them.

"You like Charlene Ohler," Jose said in a matter of fact way that made it clear it wasn't a question.

"I do not."

"You loooooove her!" Shane laughed, his typical hard cackle. A mocking bird.

"Shut up!"

"That's gross, Ray. She's like Lynn's doppelgänger," Jose said. "If you put them in bonnets and wooden shoes they could be those kissing Dutch kid lawn decorations."

Shane caught up to him. "He's right, you know. Doing her would be like doing Lynn. And that's about the most vile thing I could ever imagine."

Ray hated them for catching onto his crush so easily and knew changing their minds was impossible. The more he denied it, the more they'd harass him. He slammed on his bike's brakes and turned to them. "I only like her tits, okay? Are you happy now?"

The three boys looked at him, Shane and Jose with Cheshire cat grins. Even Garrett struggled to hold back a smirk.

"She does have really great tits," Shane said. "But still. Gross."

Ray couldn't fight off laughter that was rising inside him. "She's a total two bagger!"

"Two bagger?" Shane asked.

"She's so ugly that, to screw her, you need two bags. One to put over her head and one to put over your own in case hers falls off." Ray laughed until he thought he might barf up his lunch, but the other boys only stared with blank-faced confusion.

"I don't get it?" Jose asked.

"It's so you don't see her face."

"But then you wouldn't even see her tits," Shane said.

Ray hadn't thought this through. It was just something he'd heard his Uncle Wayne say and which he'd found hilarious because it had come from the mouth of a grown up. But now, the humor was gone.

"Never mind. It was just a joke."

"A mean one. That's Lynn's sister, after all," Jose said, his expression sober and scolding.

"Yeah. And you're no prize either," Shane said and gave him a punch, a hard one, on the shoulder before turning onto Bittner Road. "Adios, amigos." He gave a blind wave and disappeared down the street.

Jose's house was one street up and he too parted ways, but not before shaking his head at Ray. "Not cool, dude."

Ray opened his dumb, broken faucet mouth to protest, but Jose was gone. He looked over to Garrett. "I may as well go home and shoot myself."

Garrett shook his head. "Don't worry about it, Ray."

"You don't think they'll tell Lynn, do you?"

Garrett belched out a chuckle. "Oh, they'll definitely tell Lynn."

"Fuck me."

Garrett reached over and gave the horn on Ray's bike a squeeze. "Race you to Gilmour!"

Ray didn't feel like racing but as Garrett lumbered away on his bicycle, he decided he needed to take whatever small victories he could get and hoped tomorrow would be better.

CHAPTER NINE

NEAR EXHAUSTION AFTER RIDING AROUND AIMLESSLY ALL afternoon with his friends, Garrett huffed and puffed as he coasted down the dirt and shale driveway leading to their trailer. It had been a great day even though they hadn't done anything of note. Just stupid kid stuff, but the kind of fun that also seemed the epitome of happiness.

All day long he hadn't given a thought about Harrison, who'd been gone for almost a week now. But that changed fast and his good cheer vanished when he saw a police car idling beside his dad's truck. The red and blue lights whirled, temporarily dazzling him with their brightness.

He knew his dad shouldn't be home from the gas station yet and immediately jumped to the conclusion that something terrible had happened. He leapt off his bike, letting it crash to the ground. He forgot his exhaustion as he jogged to his home and vaulted up the three metal steps, through the open screen door.

Larry Roberts sat at the kitchen table, dragging on a cigarette that was only millimeters from the filter. He flinched when Garrett's heavy footsteps hit the linoleum floor then settled again when he saw it was only his youngest son.

"This is Officer Hanes." Larry nodded toward the cop.

The policeman turned Garrett's way. He had a broad face with angry, burst capillaries trailing out from his nose and onto his cheeks.

"You're Garrett?"

He nodded. "Yes, sir."

"Have a seat beside your dad here. We've been having ourselves a discussion about your brother."

Garrett scooted across the floor and grabbed one of the wobbly chairs, dragging it out from the table and flopping down in it. It unleashed a soft groan. He tried to read the cop's eyes, but they were empty. Then he looked back to his dad, almost afraid of what he might find lurking there. But, Larry ground out his butt and their eyes didn't meet.

"He's not dead, is he?"

The cop yakked a startled cough. "Jesus Pete, son. I sure as hell hope not. Don't walk yourself down that road." He gave a toothy smile that was supposed to be reassuring but didn't quite pass muster. "Your dad said Harrison wanted to go visit your mother. You know anything about that?"

Garrett tried to slow his breathing. He didn't know why he'd assumed the worst. Or why the notion had scared him so bad. "He's been talking about her a lot. And yeah, he said he wanted to go live with her."

"On a permanent basis?" The cop asked.

Garrett saw the shocked curiosity on his father's face. "I, uh. I don't know." He looked down, but he knew his father would see through the lie. He wondered if the cop could read him as easily.

"But he wanted to go there? To Cincinnati?"

"Yes, sir."

"How about you and me take a look through his room. See if you notice anything's gone missing."

"Okay."

As they passed by his father, Garrett avoided looking at the man.

Harrison's room was one step up from the den of a wild animal. Clothing was heaped in a pile that filled one fourth of the floor. The bed was unmade, revealing sheets stained with sweat and something Garrett didn't recognize yet. Dirty dishes and silverware were stacked on a TV tray and flies dive-bombed the food particles that clung to it.

"Jesus Pete," the cop repeated. "I take it your brother doesn't put a priority on cleanliness."

"No, sir. He's pretty gross."

Officer Hanes chuckled at that. "This might be a lost cause, but can you tell if he took anything? Maybe he had a piggy bank or a shoebox where he squirreled away his money?"

Garrett's eyes jumped across the room. He hadn't been allowed inside for over a year and it was hard to focus on anything besides the wonton filth and mayhem.

"Maybe. But if he did he sure wouldn't have told me where it was."

"You two didn't get along?"

Garrett shrugged his shoulders. "I'm the little brother." That said it all.

"All righty then." The cop pushed aside some clothing with his foot, revealing nothing. "Tell me now, how was your father and brother's relationship? Your dad told me they had a disagreement the night before Harrison went missing."

Garrett debated what and how much to say. He wasn't supposed to lie to a police officer, or any adult, for that matter. But he knew the truth could be a grenade that explodes and takes out innocent people too. "They argued. A lot sometimes."

"Those arguments ever come to blows?"

Another internal debate and the truth won out. "We get spanked when we don't behave, if that's what you mean. Harrison pushes the boundaries more than me."

The cop nodded. "Your dad told me as much. Says he gave the boy a... 'Whoopin.' I think that's the word he used."

The cop gave a pinched smile as if to say, '*Good on you boy for ratting out your dad*' and Garrett resented being asked a question to which the officer already knew the answer. It made him not want to respond to anything else the cop might ask, and to distrust the man's geniality.

"Your brother, he have any hiding out places? Like treehouses or an old shed? Anything along those lines?"

Garrett knew the kinds of places the cop meant because Garrett and his friends had several. He supposed Harrison probably did too, but he didn't know where and besides, any urge he'd felt to be helpful was gone. "Not that I know of, Sir."

"Okay. Okay then."

After the cop left, Garrett set about making supper, but Larry waved his hand. "None for me."

Garrett set aside the pan he'd been ready to use, disappointed. He'd been enjoying these evenings with his dad. These evenings *alone* with his dad. Life was easier and better without Harrison to play the role of the asshole. But it appeared as if the good times were over.

"You all right, dad?"

Larry nodded, but Garrett noticed his can of soda was still full and had gone flat and he picked at the skin around his fingernails. Signs Garrett knew to be nerves. "I'm fine. Just don't have an appetite."

That was never a problem for Garrett and he wondered if it would be rude to eat in front of him. He decided it would be and that he could wait until his dad turned in for the night, then he'd slip back into the kitchen and make a sandwich or two. Or three.

"I'm sure Harrison's fine." Garrett wasn't sure of that at all, but it seemed like the right thing to say.

Larry gave a weak smile and barely perceptible nod. "If I know that boy, he'll be rolling in to Cincinnati right about now. I told your mother as much."

"You talked to mom?" The question exploded out of Garrett's mouth in a shout and he clamped his jaws so fast to silence himself that he would have severed his tongue if it had been in the way. As far as he knew, his parents hadn't spoken in over four years. Any messages they had for one another, not that there were many, were relayed through their sons.

"I did." Larry pulled a cigarette from the pack. He tapped the end against the table two times before raising the butt to his lips and lighting it.

Garrett had never tried smoking, even though Lynn smoked almost regularly and both Shane and Ray bummed cigarettes off him from time to time. One of Larry Roberts' most serious orders was that his sons never pick up his filthy habit and the fear of getting caught, and whooped, stopped Garrett from even trying. Nonetheless, he enjoyed the smell of the fresh smoke and he inhaled deeply as Larry blew out a mouthful. He was still trying to comprehend that his parents had been in contact when Larry spoke again.

"She sounded good, your mom. Worried, when I told her about this nonsense with Harrison, but good."

"Why should I care?" Garrett said.

He'd long been clear about the side he'd chosen in the not so civil war between his parents and assumed that made his father happy, but Larry's brow furrowed at his sarcasm and he pointed his cigarette at him.

"That'll be enough of that. Now she and I have our problems and I know it's been a long time since she was around for you—"

"She never was. And I don't care because I hate her." Garrett muttered the words, eyes cast down at the table, away from his dad's judging glare.

"Goddammit, Garrett!" He roared the words, having turned from

Jekyll to Hyde with blinding speed. With his free hand he grabbed the heavy ceramic ashtray and slammed it down on Garrett's hand, smashing his fingers against the table. Garrett heard a muffled crack as the thick ashtray split in half.

"She's your mother and you only got one of those. And she's still my wife and I'll be goddamned if you're gonna disrespect her to my face!"

This night keeps getting worse, Garrett thought. It was like he'd walked into some alternate reality where up was down and right was left. He wished he'd have stayed out with his friends because there, things made sense. There you could be honest and you didn't have to pretend people cared about you just because you shared the same bloodlines.

That it was his father - the man Garrett had pretty much been caring for singlehandedly - that was giving him this lecture, just added more salt to the old wounds.

"Now, she told me you two haven't talked in going on a year. That's not right and I expect you to remedy that. You're gonna apologize to her. You hearin' me?"

"Whatever." Garrett still refused to look at his father's face. He half expected the man to get the razor strap. He almost wanted that because it would give him a reason to trade in the emotional hurt he was feeling for the physical kind.

Larry reached across the table and grabbed Garrett's chin. He squeezed hard, his grease-stained fingernails digging into the soft flesh as he forced Garrett to meet his gaze. His wild, gray hair gave him the look of an old lion.

"I asked, you hearin' me?" Larry's eyes blazed.

It had been a long time since Garrett had seen this kind of anger hurled in his direction. He was surprised to realize that he wasn't scared as much as he was disappointed. Disappointed because he'd thought he was the good son. The favorite son. He wasn't used to being anyone's favorite and he'd come to like it. Now he realized that was a lie.

"Yes, sir."

Larry released his powerful grip by shoving him backward so hard his chair rocked, then toppled over. Garrett crashed down with it, banging his head off the floor and watching stars flicker in front of his eyes.

"Get to your room."

That's where Garrett wanted to be, and he didn't protest. He briefly considered slamming the door, thought better of it, then pulled it shut with a soft click. Once in the confines of his bedroom, he balled his hands into fists and pounded his thighs over and over again, trying to beat out the pain that had overtaken him. By the time he finished hitting himself he was out of breath and plump tears gushed down his cheeks.

His hand throbbed and when he took a look he realized the skin over the knuckles had been smashed open by the ashtray. Blood oozed out in a slow dribble, already well on its way to clotting, but what had escaped his body tattooed the back of his hand.

Upon closer inspection, he could see the white bone of the knuckle of his middle finger poking through the wound and the sight made him gasp and feel like passing out, or throwing up, or both. He flopped onto the bed, the old springs giving a wheezy, protesting *awwwk* as his heavy body fell onto them.

Garrett wiped at his eyes and told himself to stop being a baby.

He tried to forget about it. To think about nothing except summer and his friends. To hell with his father and brother. He'd spend every minute of June, July, and August with his buddies if it came to it.

Exhausted from riding his bike in the sun all day, he passed out less than ten minutes later. He laid face up on his bed as he slept, not seeing or hearing the figure that crept along the backside of the trailer, outside his bedroom window. He didn't hear the pads of its fingers press on the glass as it tried to push the window up. Didn't hear its flesh skitter across it when it didn't open.

That locked window saved Garrett's life. Maybe the night hadn't been so bad after all.

CHAPTER TEN

GARRETT ROBERT'S GOOD LUCK AND LOCKED WINDOW brought luck of the opposite kind for Maud Merritt, better known to the students of Sallow Creek Middle School as Mighty Mole. She'd spent the better part of the day and all the evening at Hernley's Ranch, a dive bar that loomed large at the end of the road upon which Garrett lived, hoping some guy would be drunk enough or desperate enough to buy her some drinks. That did not happen, so Maud had to settle on buying her own. She was down almost twenty bucks when Earl Hernley, the owner slash bartender, shook his head when she asked for yet another scotch and soda.

"Whattya mean?" Maud asked, managing to slur those simple words.

Earl pointed at an industrial white clock that hung above the bar. "Closing time, Maud."

"Not for..." She narrowed her eyes, trying to interpret the fat, oversized numbers. "Three minutes."

Earl had wiped the bar clean of spilled booze, peanut shells, and other assorted detritus. Pretzels, corn chips, dandruff, drool. By the end of the night it all blended together. Even Dan Milner, who might have been the biggest and sloppiest drunk in the immediate area, had cleared out, leaving only Maud and her over-sized, hairy mole, to give him grief.

At this point of the night, customer relations no longer garnered a spot on his priority list. He was ready to lock the doors and go to bed. Besides, he had decades of experience tending bar to know that she wouldn't remember any of this by the time the sun was again in the sky.

"Come on now, Maud. Skidoot."

"I don' wanna."

"But you gotta and you're gonna, even if it means I gotta haul your sloppy ass out of here in a wheelbarrow."

Maud's eyes widened in shock, but any moment of clarity was brief. "Hell of a way to treat a paying customer, Earl."

Maud slid off her barstool, almost continuing onto the floor. Earl said a silent prayer that she didn't go down because lifting, or trying to lift, Maud Merritt, was even lower on his list of things he wanted to do than clean the bathrooms.

Fortunately, for Earl and for Maud, the woman steadied herself by gripping the slick bar with both hands. She closed her eyes for a good ten seconds, swaying back and forth like she was on the deck of a ship.

Earl jangled the keys inside his pocket, their muffled sing song jingle the only sound in the bar. "Wakey, wakey, Maud." He rested his hand on top of one of hers and gave it a gentle squeeze.

She opened her eyes, and even the purposely dim overhead lights of Hernley's Ranch turned them into mirrors. Earl knew the proper thing to do would be to give her a ride home, but he also knew Maud had a reputation for pissing her pants when she was drunk. And while his old Plymouth was no prize, he didn't need the passenger seat smelling like this old hag's urine for the rest of its days. Besides, she'd driven herself home in worse states. God watches out for children and fools, as his mother, rest her soul, had often intoned.

"I'm awake, Earl Hernley. And don't you go trying to get fresh with me." She pulled her hand away from his.

Earl wondered how long it had been since someone had got fresh with Maud Merritt, then tried to push that image out of his head. That wasn't a visual he cared to dwell upon.

Maud made a staggering circle, turning herself away from the bar and toward the doorway above which a red neon sign that read EX T. The I had burned out a few months earlier and Earl couldn't be bothered to fix it. The way he figured, everyone knew the way in and out, signage or no signage.

"You be careful now, Maud."

Maud waved her right hand without looking back. "Yeah, yeah."

She made it to and through the door without crashing into any of the tables and chairs and, as far as Earl was concerned, that was good enough to convince him that she could take care of herself. And, after he noticed the dark, pumpkin-sized wet spot on the back of her green, polyester pants, that was much-needed good news. He grabbed a bottle of bleach from under the bar and reluctantly began to sanitize the stool upon which she'd sat all night long. Oh, the joys of being self-employed, he thought.

Outside Hernley's Ranch, Maud narrowly avoided a pothole as she stumbled toward her station wagon. At the start of the day, when she was sober, she worried one of the drunks would door ding her two-year-old ride, so she refused to park it in the lot. Instead, she parked on the street. Descending the curb proved the trickiest part of the voyage and she almost lost her balance when she stepped down, but after two clumsy sidesteps, she managed to remain upright.

"Woo," she muttered, blinking her eyes to clear them. She wondered who put that curb there and when, but was distracted from this thought when she saw a man on the other side of the street.

The arc sodium streetlights did little to illuminate the gray night, so the man was nothing more than a shadow. She wanted to get a good look at him, to see if he was worth chatting up. Pickings were slim in these parts, but she never knew when a Prince Charming might come along. In a life where she'd spent the last twenty-eight years slopping cheap food onto plastic trays for ungrateful brats, Maud had managed to remain something of an optimist.

A minuscule, and still somewhat sober part of her mind thought it was late for someone to be out and walking around, but the drunk part was much larger and more convincing, and it told her that she was out, after all, so that wasn't odd at all. Nope. Nothing wrong here.

"Evening." She tried to inject a seductive purr into the word. The figure across the road stopped walking and turned in her direction. "If you're looking for a drink, the bar's closed."

Come a little closer, fella, she thought. Let me see what I have to work with here.

The man did come closer, halving the distance but still remained outside the light. She could tell he was tall and looked fit. Not fat, which was good. She didn't like the fat ones.

"But I gots a bottle of Johnny Walker back at my place. And I heard his good friend, Jim Beam might drop in too." Maud laughed as if this was the wittiest comment she'd ever conjured up and it just might have been. As she laughed, her diaphragm spasmed and a belch as loud as a cheery bomb exploded from her mouth. After the fact, she covered her mouth. "Scuse me."

The man didn't seem deterred. He continued coming closer and in two more steps he was near enough to the streetlights to make out his features.

Much to Maud's dismay, the possible Prince Charming wasn't any more than sixteen. Probably didn't even have his license yet. "Fucker," she muttered to herself. It was bad enough she had to be around these little pricks nine months of the year at the school. Why'd they have to come around grown up places like the bar too?

This one looked familiar. She seemed to recall he always asked for a second helping of mac and cheese, but she didn't know his name, nor did she care to. One brat was no different from the rest.

Maud was over these shenanigans. Time to get home, take off her bra, and get some beauty rest. "Take a hike, kiddo. This place is adults only."

He kept coming.

What was that word Earl had used? She thought it was funny. Something like scoot. She wanted to use it but couldn't quite recall. "Skeedaddle." As soon as she said it she realized that wasn't right, but it didn't matter. Her words weren't working.

The teen wasn't stopping and he was now less than twenty feet away.

"Hey!" She barked the word out, wanting to sound forceful and authoritarian, but it sounded scared. Because, even though she was drunk, she was getting scared now. "I said go away."

Ten feet.

"I'll have Earl call the cops on you."

Five feet.

Maud tried to stare him down, but she couldn't see his eyes which were hidden in shadow. Two obsidian chasms carved deep into his face. She lost interest in his eyes when he raised his hands. As she looked at them, she saw they were full of—

Spaghetti.

Why the hell's he got spaghetti in his hands, she thought. None of this was making any sense and she wondered if she was drunker than she had realized. Wondered if she was hallucinating even. That would make more sense than this.

And then the boy was right in front of her. He swooped his hands at her face like a demented mother playing airplane with her baby's lunch and when his hands came in closer, she realized his hands weren't full of spaghetti after all.

They were full of worms.

But that wasn't right either. The boy's hands weren't holding worms. His hands *were* worms. Dozens, no hundreds, of them writhed from the ends of his wrist. They undulated and pulsed, their slimy bodies, the color of Dijon mustard, glistened under the garish overhead lights.

They were six inches long but growing longer as they neared her. The worms stretched like rubber bands but didn't bounce back. They were a foot long now and Maud could see brown holes at the ends of them. Holes from which opaque, flesh-colored ooze dripped.

That's their mouths, she thought, just before the worms stretched even further and caught hold of her face.

They burrowed through the caked-on foundation, through the epidermis, and into the thicker meatier tissue underneath. She could see them sinking deeper into her, feel their writhing bodies going in and under and through her flesh.

This should hurt, she thought. But she felt no pain and that made her more convinced that it was all some bizarre drunken fugue. That she was probably passed out on the floor of Hernley's Ranch or maybe even fell asleep on the john and this was a dream (*nightmare*). That would be embarrassing, but still better than this being real.

The teen backed away from Maud and she realized that his wormy hands remained behind. His arms ended in two stumps from which a tar-like fluid seeped and then coagulated. She watched him watching her. His expression, if there was one, was vapid.

She opened her mouth. "Why?"

The worms that weren't already wriggling themselves into her face dove for that open orifice. They bored into her tongue, carved into her gums. The worms battered against her uvula like it was a speed bag, triggering her gag reflex and sending five hours with of slow gin fizzes, partially digested pretzels, and stomach acid spewing from her mouth. The noxious concoction didn't stop, or even slow the parasites which launched themselves down her throat like it was a water slide at an amusement park.

Less than ten seconds later Maud could feel the worms writhing through her guts, then as far down as her kitty, as she'd always called it, as in, 'Wanna pet my kitty?' She collapsed onto the street, her skin rolling and rippling as the worms worked their way into every part of her.

Even worse than the feeling of the creatures inside her was the sound. A passerby would have heard not a thing, but Maud's eardrums reverberated from the noise of them pitching and diving through her.

As her body convulsed from the inside out, Maud's eyes drifted across the parking lot as she sought out the young man who had done this to her. But he was gone. Disappeared into the night. And soon the worms had even infested her eyeballs, and she saw no more.

CHAPTER ELEVEN

GARRETT'S SLEEP WAS RESTLESS AND DREAM-FILLED. IN ONE of them it was him running away from home, trudging deep into the woods only to step into a pit of quicksand. He could feel it sucking him down like a thirsty, desperate mouth. As he was drawn deeper into its clutching depths, he kicked with his legs and swung his arms, frantic. But the more he struggled, the tighter the hole gripped him.

He was up to his chin, the thick wetness beginning to enter his mouth, when he came awake. He bolted upright in his bed and when he saw the pitch-black room, he thought he'd been sucked all the way into the pit. It wasn't until he thrust his arm upward, reaching for air, that he realized he was in his bed. Safe, but feeling the fool.

He tossed and turned for hours after that nightmare, half-afraid he'd reenter that hungry pit if he drifted off again. The last time he remembered checking the clock on his nightstand it was 4:47 and just when he thought he'd be awake until dawn, sleep claimed him.

He awoke again and for the last time shortly before sunrise, but heard his father rummaging through the kitchen, probably grabbing some soda and snacks for lunch. Garrett waited until he heard his father leave the house and his old pick up roll away from the trailer, before fleeing the safety of his bed.

Ever the wearer of glasses of the rose-colored variety, he'd half expected Larry Roberts to come into his room and apologize. To tell him he was sorry he'd hit him and hurt him and that he was still the favorite son. When that didn't happen, Garrett thought - hoped - that his dad had left him a note of reconciliation, but a quick scan of the kitchen and living room revealed nothing of the sort. He was alone in the trailer with nothing but his own hurt feelings to keep him company.

So, he did what he always did in times of crisis - he ate. He started with scrambling four eggs in the skillet and topping them off with a diced tomato and some cheddar cheese. When that had been devoured, he toasted two packets of Pop Tarts (Dutch apple) and washed them down with a glass of chocolate milk so cold it made his teeth hurt.

And, for whatever screwed up reason that had led to him weighing two hundred pounds at twelve years old and five feet two inches tall, the food helped make even the worst of times a little more bearable.

CHAPTER TWELVE

"WHERE'S JOSE?" RAY ASKED.

"He had to babysit." The last word, babysit, crawled out of Shane's mouth dripping with disgust and just in case his vocalizations hadn't conveyed his true feelings, he stuck his index finger into his mouth and faked a gag.

As far as most of them were concerned, little sisters were the worst and the idea that Jose's was robbing him from a day of play further cemented that opinion.

Garrett thought Ray looked disappointed, but it passed in an instant when Shane motioned to a pile of what appeared to be the contents of a suburban garage on the concrete roadway. "What's all this crap?"

"Our weapons and armor!" Ray said.

Piled before him were two broomsticks, two metal trash can lids, and some old tennis balls that looked like they'd been chew toys for a dog for the last decade.

"Have you lost your shit Ray?" Lynn asked, exhaling a mouthful of cigarette smoke in the process.

"No. Remember how I said I got the idea from *Knightriders*?" He looked to them as if expecting affirmation which none provided, then went on. "We're going to joust!"

Shane strolled to the assortment and knelt. He took a tennis ball in his hand and examined it. "It's got a hole in it."

Ray nodded. He took the other tennis ball and, using a similar hole, impaled it on the end of one of the broomsticks. "That's so we don't lose an eye." He jabbed the now padded end of the makeshift weapon into Shane's forehead. "See,"

Shane grinned. "Smart thinkin', stinkin'." He grabbed the other broomstick and added the ball to it. "So, these are like swords, huh?"

"Lances."

"Who the hell's Lance. Sounds gay," Lynn said, but he too was moving toward Ray's amalgamation of junk.

"Lances are what you use to try to knock your opponent off his horse. Or in the movie, their motorcycle. Or, for us, our bikes."

Garrett thought, as far as made up games went, this one wasn't bad at all. He grabbed a garbage can lid by the handle and held it in front of him. "And these are our shields?"

Ray nodded, eager and excited. "Pretty cool, huh?"

Shane stabbed at Garrett's shield and Garrett deflected. "Not bad. Not bad at all, Raymond. But there's one part I'm not sure about."

"What's that?" Ray asked.

"Who goes first?"

ROCK, PAPER, SCISSORS DETERMINED THAT SHANE AND LYNN would be the first combatants. They sat atop their bicycles, about thirty yards apart. Broomsticks in one hand, the handlebars of their bikes and the garbage can shields in the other.

Since Ray had created the game, he was the de facto announcer. "To our right, atop his black Huffy, we have Shane Vinyan."

Shane gave an exaggerated bow.

"To our left, riding a piece of shit bike that is more rust than paint, the reigning trash talking champion, Lynn Ohler."

Lynn raised his lance into the air. "Prepare to die, Vinyan!"

"In your dreams, Pussy."

Ray stood about half-way between them. He held up his hand. "On your mark. Get set." His hand dropped. "Go!" He scurried to the shoulder where Garrett waited and watched.

Saddled down with their newly acquired gear, both Shane and Lynn took a few seconds to get up to speed but soon both bikes were moving. Their tires almost glided over the pristine, never-used concrete as they flew down the deserted highway.

Within seconds, they were plunging toward one another and Garrett realized he was so caught up in the spectacle that he was holding his breath.

They were ten yards apart.

Five yards.

Then ten feet.

Garrett saw Shane raise his broomstick first. It wobbled as he tried to aim it. Lynn was doing the same, his stick steady but his bike had begun to sway side to side as he forgot about steering.

They hurtled at each other, weapons raised—

And completely missed.

Lynn dropped his broomstick to the road and reversed his pedals to brake his old bike, which really was a piece of shit. "Son of a bitch!"

Shane circled his bike around and when Garrett saw his face, he was grinning wildly. "That's hard. Harder than you'd think. But hairy balls, it's fun!" He motioned to Lynn. "Try again?"

"Hell yeah."

And they did. They missed each other on the next three tries too, but by round five, both sweaty and breathing hard, Lynn finally made contact. He'd aimed his broomstick for Shane's shoulder, held firm, and rode straight. Shane was too busy attempting to make his own hit to raise his shield and Lynn's stick nailed his upper arm.

Garrett watched as the force of the blow sent Shane off balance, his mouth open in a shocked but excited and silent *Oh!* Shane and his Huffy teetered sideways, then hit the pavement.

Lynn let out a riotous scream and held his broomstick overhead like a scrawny, blond brave who'd just experienced his first victory.

Shane jumped to his feet, still grinning, and walked the bike to Garrett and Ray. "This is goddamn incredible, Ray. You're practically a genius."

Garrett thought Ray's cheeks flushed pink with pride, but his friend didn't take time to bask in the glory, instead turning to face him.

"We're up."

Their first two rounds were misfires. Garrett especially had trouble juggling the stick and shield and keeping the bicycle upright and he was quickly getting annoyed, especially since Lynn was wound up and couldn't keep his taunting mouth shut.

"Look at the gay boys. They're both trying to lose so they don't have to go against me. Bunch of pussies!"

Garrett fired a glance his way, hoping it would quiet him. It didn't work.

"Pussy, pussy, pussy, pussy, pussy!"

Garrett tried to drown him out, to make the world go quiet and pedaled. He had tunnel-vision, seeing nothing but Ray racing toward him. He knew he wasn't coordinated enough to control the lance, the shield, and the bike simultaneously, so he dropped the garbage can lid. It clattered and bounced over the road behind him, but he barely noticed. Every ounce of concentration he had was focused on aiming the broomstick.

His goal was center mass, Ray's chest, and his eyes were so focused on that point of impact that he never even saw Ray's stick coming at his gut. He remained entirely unaware of what was about to happen until it hit him.

Ray was of average build but possessed the strength of a boy who grew up working on his family's farm and he held his broomstick with an iron grip. It didn't give an inch when the tennis-ball covered end made impact with Garrett's belly, sinking deep into the ample flesh which rippled from the blow.

The wind gushed out of him with the force of a hurricane and he seemed to float backward off his bike. It rolled another five feet before crashing around the same time Garrett hit the concrete.

"Holy, Jesus!" Ray screamed and Garrett heard his bike crash too, then the boy's footsteps pounding to him. "Are you okay?"

As he stared into the cloudless, cobalt sky above him, Ray's face came into view. Garrett gasped, chest heaving. "Never." He gulped down a heaping mouthful of air. "Thought." Another mouthful. "I'd be." Shane and Lynn arrived now. All three stared down at him. "So glad to..."

"To what?" Ray asked. "To what?" Panic sent his voice a few octaves higher.

And then Garrett smiled. "Be fat." He laughed, high, almost giddy.

"You ass!" But Ray laughed too, "I thought I might of broke your lungs or something."

Garrett pushed himself into a sitting position, laughing even harder now. "Your lungs aren't in your belly, Ray."

"Screw off. You know what I mean." Ray extended his hand and helped Garrett to his feet.

"Sure, Ray, you probably think women shit babies out their assholes too." Lynn barked laughter like a hyena.

Garrett leaned in to Ray, close enough to whisper. "Do me a favor?"

"What's that?" Ray asked.

"Kick his ass."

Ray grinned. "It would be a pleasure."

CHAPTER THIRTEEN

JOSE LOUNGED IN THE GRASS HALFWAY BETWEEN THE regular and kiddie pools and let the sun bake his skin to golden brown. His mother, JoAnn, sprawled on a vinyl beach chair twenty or so yards away with the other moms, but her skin had only two variations - fish belly white and lobster red. Since summer was still young, she remained a member of the white family.

The only reasons they came to the pool were so she could attempt to get a tan and because it was cheap babysitting. Sure, the season pass was $49 for adults, but Jose fell into the $19 bracket and for his baby sister, six-year-old Donnatella, admission was free.

It was Jose's job to watch Donnatella, which meant his hours actually in the water were limited, but he didn't mind all that much. His baby sister could be a pain, but he liked her. For the most part.

She was spoiled and whiny, yet he also thought she was pretty cool for a little kid. She rarely tattled on him, not even when she caught him playing cards for money with his friends (a huge no-no in there very conservative Christian household) and there was a gentleness to her that made him want to shield her from the more savage aspects of growing up. He hoped he was doing a good job at that part. In a way, he thought protecting her was the most important thing he could do in life.

As she splashed in the six-inch deep wading pool with the other little kids, Jose's eyes were cast toward the regular pool where three dozen or so people swam and dove and laughed. He enjoyed the sightseeing as much as any actual swimming, especially because one of the pool regulars was Laura Lynch.

He'd had a crush on Laura Lynch ever since the second grade. His feelings were so deep that, every February when they passed out Valentine's cards, he always gave her one that said something mushy like, "I only have eyes for you," or "I'll be your Valentine if you'll be mine." All he ever got back were the generic cards, like "Happy V Day, Pal" but he didn't mind because even those cards were signed with her name in delicate, loopy handwriting.

Jose knew, as did all the other boys, that Laura Lynch was the prettiest girl in the whole school. She had strawberry red hair that swooped over her shoulders in loose curls. Her cheeks were dotted with freckles that got darker in the summer months. And this past year, she became one of the first girls in their grade to start to get breasts.

He'd had an inkling that it was happening. Sometimes when she wore a shirt with writing or a design on it, he'd notice subtle curving at the sides. But it wasn't until this summer at the pool that he became one hundred percent certain.

When he first saw Laura in her red and white polka dot bikini, his stomach tightened up so hard that he thought he might barf right there on the lawn. Her top half was only just developing, certainly nothing like Lynn's sister, but those apple-sized mounds still made Jose feel energized and queasy and a little foggy-headed all at the same time.

They even made him forget a traumatic event at the end of the school year. When it came time to sign everyone's yearbooks, Laura had inscribed his with, "To a nice boy I met this year." At the time, that had crushed him since they'd known each other for six years, not one measly year. He was so sick over it that he vowed to himself that he'd never waste his time thinking about her again.

But then came the red and white polka dot bikini and Jose didn't stand a chance.

He watched as she sat at the edge of the pool, chatting with two older boys who were tall and athletic and he supposed good-looking. They would say something, and she would tilt her head back and laugh or she'd playfully shove them in the chest. Taking all this in was a kind of torture, but Jose couldn't force himself to turn his attention elsewhere for more than a minute or so at a time.

Just as Laura stood up, taking a quick moment to pull her bikini bottoms out of her crack, Jose's rapt attention was broken by, of all things, a scream.

It was shrill and loud and unmistakable because he heard that same scream about five times a day. It was Donnatella.

Because her outbursts came so frequently he wasn't alarmed, but he did tear his eyes away from Laura Lynch and direct them to the kiddie pool. Don (as he often called her, much to their mother's horror) was in the process of scrambling out of the shallow body of water. Two other kids, one boy and one girl, both around her age, remained in the water. Something was off, in a bad way. It almost looked like the girl was drowning the boy.

That couldn't be right. Jose knew it was just a trick of the angle from which he viewed them or maybe it was some kiddie game to which he didn't know the rules, but the boy was definitely on his back and the girl was crouching over him and there was a lot of splashing.

What the heck, he thought, and climbed to his feet. The grass tickled his toes as he moved off his towel and toward the kiddie pool. A few others watched, some even approached, but Jose was the closest.

Donnatella, now out of the water, screamed again as she ran to him. Her head swiveled back and forth between the kiddie pool and Jose and she was toddling along so fast that she smacked right into him. When she looked up at him, he saw genuine fear in her face.

"What is it, Don?"

"Snakes!" Donnatella's eyes were red from the chlorinated water but Jose could also see tears forming. "She made him eat the snakes!"

"What?" He looked back to the pool. No one else had reached it yet and he felt like he should do something, even if he had no idea what was happening. "Go to mom," he told his sister and gave her a little push in that direction. He saw his mother had sat up in her folding chair and watched them, placid and unconcerned.

Don did as told and Jose continued to the kiddie pool, although his pace had halved. He wasn't sure why he was nervous. Even if what she had said was remotely true, he wasn't afraid of snakes.

The previous fall he'd found one in the woods and kept it as a pet until it eventually escaped from its shoebox home, never to be seen again.

Part of him kept hoping, praying, someone would beat him there, but no one did.

"Oh, crap!" As far as swears went, 'crap' was about as hardcore as Jose allowed himself to go and he even hated to say that one out loud, but what he saw in the pool seemed positively crap-tastic.

The boy was on his back, his entire body thrashing and flailing, his spastic actions dropping the water level fast.

Jose looked to the other occupant, the girl who wore a white one piece with Smurfette on the front of it. She was on her knees in front of the boy, her face blank and emotionless and he thought she might be experiencing a mild case of shock.

It wasn't until he took a closer look that Jose realized her right arm was missing from the elbow down. There was no blood, like it had been torn off by some invisible baby pool monster. But it also wasn't a healed wound, like the one belonging to his Uncle Henry who'd needed to have three fingers amputated after an accident with an M80 firecracker.

No, this was different from anything he'd ever seen. At the end of the girl's arm, long tendrils of flesh hung like tan streamers, swaying in the midmorning breeze. These tattered remnants of flesh didn't bleed or ooze or seep. And, even weirder, the girl paid no attention to her own injury. She only stared at the convulsing boy.

"Move!" The voice was loud and authoritative and before Jose could obey a hand shoved him between the shoulder blades and he stumbled sideways. A teenager in red trunks, one of the lifeguards, rushed past him and hopped into the kiddie pool. He grabbed the boy under his arms and pulled him out of the water, then eased him onto the grass where his entire body continued to shake, as if he was experiencing an earthquake from the inside out.

The lifeguard looked toward what was now a growing crowd of onlookers. "He's having a seizure. Call an ambulance!"

Jose had heard of seizures before and thought he recalled something about swallowing your tongue when you got one. That made him remember what his sister said. *She made him eat the snakes.*

He looked to the water, thinking he would see something that would make sense out of that remark, maybe even see an honest to God snake, but the water was clear and empty. Serpent free.

That emptiness added to his confusion. While he'd been watching the lifeguard rescue the boy from six inches of water, the girl with the missing arm had vanished from the kiddie pool. He knew someone else must have grabbed her, that someone was helping her too. He was no doctor, but he was pretty sure a missing arm topped a seizure.

He examined the crowd, expecting to see her being attended to, but when he found her, she wasn't receiving first aid. She was clinging to a middle-aged man with a hairy gut and black-framed glasses. The man paid her no heed, his eyes focused on the lifeguard and the boy, and Jose almost yelled out, *'Hey! Your daughter's arm is gone! Do something!'*

But when he opened his mouth to shout just that, he realized the girl had both of her arms. They were wrapped around her father's chunky thigh and each looked as normal as the sun on a summer day.

Jose shut his eyes tight then rubbed them with the palms of his hands. He had to be seeing wrong. He opened them and looked again. Same girl. Same Smurfette bathing suit. And two arms.

A half dozen more people pushed into the scene, surrounding the lifeguard and the boy. Excited, concerned murmurs filled the air like a concert. Over them, he heard a siren wail in the distance.

He was so confused and nervous that he paid no attention to Laura Lynch as she squeezed through the crowd and toward the commotion, until she spoke.

"What happened, Julio?" She looked at him, eyes earnest.

Jose sighed. "I have no idea." He didn't even bother with an up-close glance at her bikini top, instead turning away and retreating to his mother who continued to lounge in her rubber chair. Donnatella sat in her lap, bottom lip puffed out in a pathetic pout.

"You okay, Don?" He asked.

She nodded, her damp hair spilling onto her face.

"Don't call her that!" His mother shot him a *'you know better'* scowl, then grabbed a bottle of coconut oil and added another layer to her milky skin.

Jose leaned in close to his sister. "Snakes?"

Don nodded. "Little baby snakes. She put them in his mouth."

"What are you two blabbing about?" JoAnn's narrowed eyes pivoted between them.

"Nothing, Mom," Jose said.

JoAnn watched them both or another two seconds, then laid back in the chair, which uttered a pained groan. When Jose was certain she wasn't watching, he turned to his sister and held his finger to his lips. He'd talk to her more about this later, but how could he expect a six-year-old to explain it when he hadn't a clue what he'd just seen. He needed to tell someone, but not his parents. He needed to tell his friends.

CHAPTER FOURTEEN

GARRETT AND SHANE SAT SIDE BY SIDE ON THE BERM, watching as the other two boys worked themselves up for the coming battle. Ray paced back and forth, muttering to himself. Lynn bounced on his feet like there were springs in his shoes. He shook his arms, then punched the air. Garrett thought he looked like he was preparing for a boxing match rather than a bicycle joust.

"Damn, Garrett, look at your hand. What did you do?"

The question shocked Garrett out of his good mood and he looked at his hand which was swollen and stained with a purple-yellow bruise. The wound had crusted over but there was a deep divot where the bone had previously revealed itself. "Must've happened when I crashed."

He knew Shane was smart enough to identify that lie. After all, bruises didn't form and cuts didn't clot that fast, but he hoped his friend would have the decency not to call him on it.

And Shane did. Their friendship was the longest and Garrett

couldn't remember a time when they weren't friends, even if he tried. And along with that came the willingness to ignore each other's untruths.

"Nothing on your brother yet?"

Garrett shook his head. "Nah."

"I heard the cops were at your place."

Garrett considered asking how he'd heard but didn't bother. Sallow Creek was a small town, and no secret lasted long.

"You know, if you need a place to stay until this gets sorted out, my folks would welcome you with open arms."

"What?" Garrett had heard him but didn't know how to respond. He felt a little like crying over the kindness of it, especially after his father's anger the night before, but part of him was offended too.

"I'm just saying. If your dad's in any trouble and you need--"

"My dad didn't do anything wrong." That came out louder than he'd intended.

"Yeah?"

"He didn't, Shane. Harrison took off for Cincinnati to see our mom. I heard him sneak out his bedroom window."

Shane held up his hands, submissive. "All right. I was just saying. If you need anything..."

"Okay."

Garrett looked back to the others. Lynn was now slapping himself in the face. Ray was on his bike and ready to rumble.

"Thanks," Garrett said. "Really. Thanks."

"You bet, Bud. I'll always have your back." Shane smiled. "Now let's watch these two idiots fuck each other up."

Round one was a draw. In round two, Lynn's broomstick collided with Ray's thigh but it was a glancing blow and the boy never wavered. Lynn's attempt in round three was blocked by Ray's shield and both Garrett and Shane heard him cursing with frustration.

"Come on, Ray!" Garrett shouted. "Time to show that toe-head who's the boss." He saw Shane give him the side eye and reminded himself that he really needed to work on his shit-talking game.

"Mayhugh?" Shane yelled. "More like May-peeeeeee-ewwwww!"

Garrett could only shake his head at that one.

"Okay, you 'tards. On the count of three," Shane said. "One. Two."

And they were off. Their legs were a blur as they peddled, faster now than any time before. Garrett focused on Ray, as if he could telekinetically empower him to win.

He watched Ray raise the broomstick. Steady it. Aim.

He stole a glance at Lynn who had his weapon ready. When he looked back at Ray, he saw his lance had dipped slightly as he raised his shield to cover as much of his midsection as possible.

"No," Garrett said, not realizing he was speaking out loud. "Pay attention, Ray."

The charging bikes were on top of each other and Ray's broomstick made first contact. But not with Lynn. Instead, the balled end of his lance plunged itself between the front wheel and frame of Lynn's bike. The new addition brought Lynn's wheel to an immediate halt, but forward momentum was too great to stop and Garrett watched with awe and a bit of horror as Lynn's bike somersaulted ass over head, taking Lynn along for the ride.

Everything, Lynn, his bike, Ray's bike, their weapons, hit the concrete with a raucous clatter and, for a moment, the other boys were paralyzed by their surprise. Then Lynn groaned and broke the spell.

"You cheat!" Lynn climbed to his feet, uninjured aside from a bad brush burn on his right forearm.

"How'd I cheat?" Ray asked.

"You're supposed to hit the other guy, not the other guy's horse!"

"Says who?"

"The movies, asshole! So, that means I win."

"Nuh uh. You fell off your bike. And you fall off your bike, you lose. Those are the rules."

Lynn looked to Garrett and Shane for back up. "Tell him he's wrong."

Garrett's cheer had returned and he couldn't hold back a grin. "When he explained everything, he didn't say anything about not taking out the other guy's bike."

Lynn focused on Shane. "It's his game, man," Shane said.

"You assholes." Lynn turned to Ray. "I'm gonna pound you, you cheat."

Before Lynn could do just that, Ray was off and running and Lynn chased after, laughing. He never did catch him, and after they exhausted themselves the four of them flopped under the shade of a silver maple to recuperate. The day was long and there was more jousting to come.

CHAPTER FIFTEEN

THE NEXT DAY GARRETT, SHANE, AND LYNN HAD DOWNED three fourths of a pizza as they listened to Jose's tale about the happenings at the pool. They'd made a few stray comments along the way, mostly about Laura Lynch's budding breasts, but for the most part stayed silent.

After he finished telling them about the little girl's missing and there again arm, the story was pretty much over. Garrett thought it sounded wild and far-fetched and wondered if Jose was pranking them, but the boy's face was serious. Dead serious.

"You're sure her arm was really gone? Maybe she had it tucked behind her back or something." Garrett stood and placed his forearm behind himself to demonstrate.

Jose shook his head. "No. I saw her skin all ripped apart. Like hamburger coming out of a meat grinder."

Garrett was glad Ray, with his easily upset stomach, wasn't there to hear that. If he had been, he'd probably be adding hamburgers to go along with hotdogs on the *'things I'll never eat again'* list.

"You don't just regrow an arm though," Shane said.

"Lobsters do." Being able to share this knowledge delighted Garrett who had a penchant for weird facts and arcane information.

"They do?" Shane asked.

Garrett nodded. "I watched a documentary one time about how they could pop off their legs or claws to escape traps and grow new ones."

"Really? I never knew that." Shane sucked the last bit of soda through his straw making a hollow, slurping sound. "That's fascinating."

"Yeah. And I watched another one on platypus's and how they—"

Lynn banged his hand against the table making the condiments dance. "Shit, guys! *Swamp Thing* did that too! Remember that scene?" He pulled his own arm up into his sleeve and slowly pushed it back out like it was regenerating, adding an *arrueeghhhh* sound effect.

"Hey!" Jose said emphatically enough they all stopped and stared. "She's not a lobster." He looked to Lynn. "Or *Swamp Thing* you idiot."

Lynn frowned and pushed his arm the rest of the way free of his shirt sleeve. "Sorry."

"She was just a regular little kid."

"That's where I beg to differ," Shane dug a wad of bills from his pocket, counting them silently and laying them on top of the bill.

"Regular little kids don't regrow missing arms and give other little kids seizures by force feeding them snakes."

"That's the point!" Jose said it so loud one of the cooks by the cavernous pizza ovens looked over, curious.

Garrett thought Jose was as mad as he'd ever seen him before. Or maybe mad wasn't the right emotion. Frustrated, he supposed, was more accurate. "But no one else saw it? Not even your sister?"

Jose's chin dipped toward his chest. "No. All Don talks about are the snakes."

Shane signaled for the waitress to come and get the money, then turned back to Jose. "Do you know her name?"

"No. But her dad looked familiar. A really tall, fat guy with those old-fashioned glasses. The kind with the thick, black frames. Like out of the fifties."

Shane squinted, thinking. "Mr. Whipkey? Who owns the hardware store on West Main?"

Some of the annoyance left Jose's face. "Yeah! That's where I recognized him from."

The waitress arrived and they all fell silent. She was a middle-aged woman whose droopy breasts were on display as she leaned over the table and slowly scooped up the money. "You boys enjoy yourselves?" She stayed bent over, very aware of the looks Lynn and Shane were throwing down her blouse.

"Sure did, Mindy," Shane said, not bothering to look away. "And you keep the change."

Mindy flashed a broad smile that revealed crooked teeth, but

Garrett knew most of the customers weren't tipping her based on her dental hygiene.

"Well aren't you a big spender? Thanks, Doll." She gave Shane an exaggerated wink. "Come again."

"Oh, we will." Shane said and as soon as she was out of earshot they all burst out laughing.

"She'd totally let you bang her." Lynn grabbed a piece of pizza crust that Jose had left behind and gnawed on it.

Shane's face went red with a blush. "She just likes my big tips."

"Your big something," Lynn said.

"You've been peeping on me when I take a leak haven't you? Perv." Shane gave Lynn a playful, but hard jab in the shoulder and Lynn held his hands up in submission.

Garrett was still laughing along with the others, but he couldn't get Jose's story out of his mind. Apparently neither could anyone else.

"You ready?" Shane asked, looking at Jose.

"For what?"

"To find the one-armed girl."

CHAPTER SIXTEEN

An overhead bell gave a cheery jingle as Shane pushed open the door to Whipkey's Tools & More. He stepped inside and the other three were close behind. Lynn, the last in, closed it with a clatter that made Jose jump.

Shane leaned in close to them and spoke in a whisper. "Walk around and look for Mr. Whipkey. Pretend like you're looking for something to buy but don't look all suspicious or someone will think we're a bunch of kids out shoplifting."

"What are we buying?" Lynn asked.

Shane hadn't thought that far ahead. "I don't know. It doesn't matter. Anything cheap. No more than five bucks. You guys are bleeding me dry."

"How about a box of screws?" Lynn asked again.

"Sure."

"I'll look for a screwdriver," Garrett said, his voice filled with an eager helpfulness that made Shane smile.

"Good thinking, Garrett."

"What kind of screws though?" Worry clouded Jose's face.

"It doesn't matter. We don't really need screws," Shane said.

"But if Lynn gets Phillip's head screws and Garrett gets a straight screwdriver, they'll know something's up."

"What about hex screws?" Lynn was full of questions today and Shane was over them.

"Jesus Christ." Shane shook his head. "Get a hammer and nails then."

Lynn rolled his eyes. "Excuse me for living." He and Jose split off.

Shane and Garrett headed in the opposite direction, pretending to browse shelves. Shane noticed that Garrett was practically tiptoeing along and gave his arm a shake. "Stop sneaking."

"I was sneaking?"

Shane nodded. "Very badly. We're allowed to be here so walk normal. You're just a kid buying a screwdriver."

"Hammer."

"Whatever."

Shane didn't put much credence in Jose's story about the missing arm. He wouldn't have said as much out loud, but if he had to theorize what really went down, he would have said that Jose simply panicked after his sister screamed and he saw the kid having a seizure.

Even though Jose was the same age as the rest of them, he seemed younger somehow. Like, when they rented scary movies at A&H Video to watch in the clubhouse, Jose was the only one who still covered his eyes during the gross parts. And the only one who whimpered in his sleep after watching them. The boy was easily scared, which made it obvious to Shane that there was no girl with a magic arm.

Despite his doubts, he was enjoying this afternoon adventure. It was a welcome break from riding bikes up and down the same streets again and again, and safer than almost killing himself during games like bicycle jousting. Not that he didn't love those things, but this felt more grown up and he liked that feeling.

The first two aisles they traversed were empty. In the third they saw a boy in his late teens or early twenties, home from college and working his summer job.

"Help you with anything?" He asked.

Shane shook his head. "No. We're just browsing."

"I'm buying a hammer!" Garrett blatted out with forced cheer.

"Hand tools are in aisle seven." The worker watched them a little too close for Shane's comfort and he pulled Garrett into the next row.

"Real smooth," Shane whispered.

Garrett didn't respond. When they reached aisle seven, he grabbed the first hammer he saw, but Shane shook his head and pointed at one that was a third of the price. His best friend gave a weary smile and traded tools.

When they got to aisle four they saw Jose and Lynn, the latter carrying a one-pound box of nails, ambling in their direction. Shane mouthed, *'Anything?'* and the others shook their heads.

"Shit." The store wasn't that large and if Mr. Whipkey was in the building, the only other place he could be was the back room where they presumably kept extra merchandise. "You guys go to the counter and check out." He handed them a five-dollar bill.

"Where are you going?" Garrett asked.

"Just go. I'll meet you up front in a minute."

They did as told but Shane noticed Garrett lag, the boy stealing glances his way. Shane made a shooing motion with his hands to get him to move on, and Garrett did, with obvious reluctance.

With that trio out of sight, Shane hurried to the rear of the store where double doors separated the customer area from the *'For employees only'* room. He ignored the sign and pushed through the doors which swung open and shut with ease.

He was familiar with back rooms such as this one because his father's pharmacy had something similar, only it was better illuminated and the shelves weren't taller than his head. It also didn't have the musty and somehow sour aroma that filled his nostrils now.

The room was larger than he expected and he couldn't even see the rear wall from his spot near the double doors. He decided to be bold.

"Mr. Whipkey?" His voice sounded hollow as it bounced through the room. No answer came. "Are you back here, sir?"

Again, no answer. He was certain no one was in the room. Even if someone other than Mr. Whipkey was around they'd have answered because they'd want to know why some kid had entered the persona non grata area.

He went to turn, to exit, but something about that smell made him linger. Must, he could understand. But there was a pungent undertone to it that didn't smell like something that belonged in a hardware store. It was more like the odor you'd find in a bait shop. Or maybe a slaughterhouse.

It drew him further into the supply room, passing by row after row of metal shelving. He saw nothing out of the ordinary. But the smell was still there and it was getting stronger. So strong he started to breathe through his mouth to avoid it.

Another ten feet into the room and he had the sudden feeling that he wasn't alone after all. That someone was back here. It wasn't anything he saw or heard, but a sense, the way he sometimes felt when they played hide and seek and his friends were closing in on his hiding place.

"Mr. Whipkey?"

No answer.

He waited a long moment, then continued, passing by two large skids of steel rebar, banded together and stacked four feet high. The rear wall of the building was less than fifteen feet away and the smell was now so noxious that he felt like he could taste it. He covered his mouth and nose with his left hand and walked on.

Ahead, on the floor, Shane saw a shimmery brown fluid. It was oozing and spreading, as lumpy as poorly made mashed potatoes. Mustard yellow (the French kind) chunks the size of golf balls were scattered throughout it, but they weren't perfectly round. They were oblong and irregular and they made him think of rotting fruit.

"What are you doing back here?"

Shane spun around, hand still covering his mouth. He saw the young employee who'd earlier directed him to aisle seven for hammers and hand tools.

"Didn't you see the sign?" The man shouted as if Shane was hard of hearing and hadn't heard the first question.

"I'm sorry. I was looking for Mr. Whipkey."

"Why?"

Shane had been prepared for this. "He was my T ball coach. I haven't seen him in a while and just wanted to say 'hi.'" The first part, at least, was true.

The employee's eyes narrowed and he looked him up and down. "He's home today. Now get out of here."

Shane was ready to vamoose but he couldn't. Not without satisfying his curiosity. "I have to ask. What the hell is that stink?"

The employee looked from Shane to the spreading pool of goo, then back to Shane. "Sewage backed up."

"Shit," Shane said.

"Yeah. Shit," the employee said. "Now go."

"You bet. Good luck cleaning that up." He thought the guy might laugh or make an obscene joke out of it, but he didn't. Instead he only stared at the phlegmy substance, still and silent as a statue.

Shane knew when the getting was good and that was now. He speed walked out of the room, taking only one fast glance behind him but the employee hadn't moved.

As he neared the counter, he heard Lynn's voice. "Do you sell hooks?"

A woman's voice answered. "We have the type you hang planters from. They're in aisle two."

Shane could see them now. Garrett held a brown shopping bag with their purchases and Jose watched as Lynn leaned against the counter, tapping his fingers on the worn fiberglass top.

"No, big hooks. Like someone with a fake arm would use."

The cashier was a dumpy woman in her twenties. Her mousy, brown hair was pulled into a pony tail and her face was confused. "A fake arm?"

"Like a pirate." Lynn extended his fist, feigning a missing hand. "Arrgh, matey!"

The cashier stared.

"You pay already?" Shane asked, a little out of breath, not from exertion but because his chest was tight with nerves.

They all looked to him. Lynn gave a toothy grin. "Hey, buddy. I was just asking—" He checked the cashier's name tag. "Dolores here about hooks."

"Are you boys making costumes or something?" Dolores the cashier asked.

"Yeah," Shane said. "For the bible school play. But it's okay. We have what we need." He grabbed Lynn's shirt sleeve and ushered him toward the exit.

"Thanks, Dolores," Lynn called out as Shane pushed him through the door, the bell giving a goodbye ding.

The four of them were on the sidewalk and Shane stared at them, gape mouthed. "Hooks? Really, Lynn?"

"I thought maybe the guy's daughter has a fake arm. A... What do you call it? Prophylactic. That would explain why it was gone one minute and there the next. Maybe she takes it off to go swimming."

"But why hooks?"

"For her hook hand. Don't you remember William Devane's in *Rolling Thunder?*" He made a hook with his own hand and slashed at the air miming bad karate.

Shane remembered, but struggled to make sense of Lynn's thought process, if there was one. "But the girl didn't have a hook." He looked to Jose. "Did she? Did she have a hook?"

Jose shook his head. "No hook."

Shane turned back to Lynn. "See. No hook."

"Well, maybe she has a couple different ones. Like a pretty, plastic hand for when she's out in public, like at the pool. And a hook for when she's just, you know, hanging out at the house, pulling weeds or some shit."

"Pulling weeds?"

"With her hook!"

Shane turned to Garrett hoping to find an ally, but saw his friend was as red as a brick and looked about to burst from struggling to not laugh.

"You all suck." Shane forced himself to think about the putrid pool of feces in the backroom of the hardware store to prevent himself from giving in to the bizarre humor of it all.

He hopped onto his bike. "Garrett, take Lynn to the clubhouse so he can't do anything else stupid."

"What about me?" Jose asked.

"You're coming with me to Patriot Street."

Jose climbed aboard his bicycle too, obedient. "What's on Patriot Street?"

"Mr. Whipkey's house."

CHAPTER SEVENTEEN

JOSE HAD NO INTEREST IN GOING WITHIN A FOOTBALL FIELD of the girl from the pool, let alone to her house, but when Shane said to do something, all of them did it, usually without question. Now, with their bikes hidden from view of the house and leaning against a fat oak across the street, he regretted following the leader.

"Come on, Shane, I wanna go home." Jose looked skyward as he said it, because Shane had clambered up fifteen feet of the trunk and now sat straddling a limb that overhung the road. He had his hands cupped around his eyes like imaginary binoculars.

"I think I found her room. Second from the left on the ground floor."

Jose looked to that room. Through the window he could see pink paint or wallpaper, the color making the room look like the inside of a Pepto Bismol bottle. It certainly seemed like a young girl's room, but he saw no one inside. "I don't see anyone."

"I don't either. Keep watching while I go higher."

Jose saw no sense in Shane climbing further up the tree but knew protesting was pointless. His eyes traveled between the bedroom, to the tree. Back and forth. Up and down and up again. Shane was stories high now, thirty feet or more and the younger branches at that height sagged under his weight.

"You're gonna kill yourself," Jose muttered as he watched.

Shane finally ceased climbing and stared at the house. He said something, but he was far enough away now that his hushed voice didn't carry all the way to Jose.

"What?"

More garbled nonsense. Jose thought he might have said 'I can't see anything from here' or maybe 'Do you see anyone there' or even 'There are bees in my hair.'

Jose had given up on whispering. "Come down!"

"Who are you talking to?"

The voice was behind him and Jose's neck snapped around so fast he felt a fiery burst of pain as he pinched a nerve in his spine. His physical misery was swapped for fear when he saw the voice belonged to the girl from the pool.

His gaze immediately went to her arms and there were indeed two of them. And both ended in hands. Real hands, not oversized hooks or plastic fantastic ones. He stared at them.

"Hey, dumb-dumb. I'm talking to you."

Jose looked back to her face. Her furrowed brow created a thin cleave in her forehead, but he thought the confusion didn't carry all the way to her eyes which were blank. Doll's eyes.

You're being stupid, he told himself. Just like at the pool, his imagination, what his father called his *overactive imagination,* was seeing things that weren't really there.

Don saw it too.

But did she? She said nothing about missing arms. All she yammered on about were snakes and for all Jose knew, the two kids could have been snacking on gummy worms and Don got confused. Maybe she had an overactive imagination too.

"You're Donnatella's brother," the Whipkey girl declared, not asked.

Jose nodded. "Yeah."

"You were at the pool."

Softer, weaker. "Yeah."

For the first time there was genuine emotion in her face. A sort of wry amusement twisted her mouth into a grin. "I remember you. You were scared."

Jose tried to swallow but failed because his mouth was dry as a desert.

"You're scared now too, aren't you?"

He forced his mouth open but his tongue was stuck to the roof of his mouth like it was held there with crazy glue. He was scared and it was all Shane's fault for dragging him here. He thought about looking up, somehow signaling SOS, but before he could, there was a loud thud as Shane dropped down behind him.

The girl's smile vanished so fast it was like someone had flicked a switch. "Who are you?"

Shane brushed away a few leaves that had got caught up in his clothing and gave a little bow at the waist. "Shane Vinyan. How do you do?"

The girl's whole demeanor had changed. Maybe that was to be expected since she was a little girl and these were two strange, older boys, but Jose thought it was something else.

"Why were you in the tree?"

"Saw a cat up there. Thought I'd play the hero and rescue it." Shane pawed his hand in her direction and uttered a low *rawr* sound.

"Then where is it?" She looked into the tree, eyes darting to and fro.

"Got away. Hopped to the next tree over. It saw a blue jay or something. Guess it didn't need rescued, only a hot meal."

The Whipkey girl looked back to them, cautious and disbelieving. "I'm gonna tell my dad about you."

"Please do. Tell him I said 'howdy.' He was my T ball coach when I wasn't much older than you. Real nice guy, your dad. He didn't even care that I couldn't field to save my life." Shane gave his most winning smile and it was so darn genuine that Jose almost believed it. Man, he was good.

The girl backed into the street, only one step. If it had been two she might have been creamed by the box truck that was rolling down the road ten miles over the speed limit. The driver blatted his horn and cast all three of them a look Jose recognized all too well. *Damn kids!*

She never flinched. She took another backward step, then spun on her heels and walked to her house. She was halfway there when a large, male figure filled the front doorway.

Jose found his voice again. "Is that?"

"Yeah. Mr. Whipkey." Shane gave a cheerful wave. The man in the doorway didn't reciprocate and Shane struggled to hold his winning grin.

The girl and her father stood there, silhouetted by the hard shadows under the porch, and stared at them.

"Is this as weird as I think it is?" Jose asked.

"Oh yeah. This is weird as shit."

"Can we go now?"

Shane grabbed his bike and that was all the answer Jose needed. He jumped aboard his and pedaled away.

"I hate you," Jose said as Shane caught up to him. "I really do."

Shane nodded. "I don't even blame you."

One final backward glance revealed that the Whipkey's had not moved a millimeter. They stood still as wooden Indians. Watching.

CHAPTER EIGHTEEN

HE FELT LIKE A HOBO, MARCHING DOWN THE ROAD WITH A garbage bag slung over his shoulder. All I need is a cardboard suitcase, Lynn thought, and smiled. He thought that sort of wandering, pointless life sounded appealing. No chores. No school. No one telling you what the fuck to do all the time. You could be in Pittsburgh one day and Los Angeles the next. He'd never given much thought to the future, but that one didn't sound half-bad.

He spotted a green Mountain Dew can crushed on the road, checked left, then right, then left again even though he had a half-mile clearance in both directions, and finally jogged to it. He scooped it up, then opened his trash bag and added it to the collection. The bag wasn't even half-full yet and he'd been collecting cans for almost two hours. The morning was humid and he already had a sunburn on the nape of his neck. It was starting to sing which made all this walking and hoping to stumble across aluminum gold less appealing.

I should go in town, he thought. Maybe he could even get to the dumpsters at the bowling alley before they opened. Summer leagues were in swing which meant lots of beer was getting drunk and that meant lots of cans were getting thrown away. Cans that he could turn into cold, hard cash.

During the summer months, whenever Lynn wasn't preoccupied with playing, he roamed about looking for cans, almost to the point of obsession. On an average week he could make twelve bucks and sometimes twenty or more on a great one. He'd take the bags to the junkyard where Mr. Thompson would pay Lynn the going rate for aluminum. He'd even round up to the nearest dollar, which Lynn thought was awfully generous.

Most grown ups wouldn't do that. Most grown ups weren't kind to kids, especially to ones like Lynn who came from the Towers. Most adults were assholes, but Mr. Thompson was one of the few good ones.

He retreated to the shoulder and picked up his pace. He only had half an hour or so before the bowling alley opened and, once they did, the manager would call the cops on him if he caught him going through the garbage. Like it was any skin off his big nose.

What he really needed was a ride. Lynn thought hitchhiking was about the most damn fun he could have outside of flogging the bishop with one of Shane's magazines as a visual aid. He usually didn't have much trouble getting picked up, but he knew getting a ride with a garbage bag half full of smelly, sticky cans would be easier said than done. Send me a redneck with a pickup, he wished, and less than a minute later he heard a vehicle approach from behind.

"My lucky fuckin' day." He hoped saying it would make it true.

It did not. The vehicle that came rolling up behind him was a Pontiac Firebird with paint as red as a firetruck. It had ben waxed to a high gloss shine that was almost blinding in the sun and Lynn gasped a little at the beauty of it. He didn't even see the driver until he opened his fat mouth.

"Look at this! Garbage picking up garbage!" The voice was jubilant and giddy.

He recognized the face of the teenager driving the car. He'd just graduated and was what Lynn's mother would have called, a 'rich prick.'

"I thought they made the jail birds pick up the garbage. You trying to steal their job or getting a head start on your future?"

Lynn glowered and, when he saw the prick's hyena grin, his own face grew even darker. What he lacked in brains, he made up for in attitude. "How about you put that mouth to use and suck my cock?"

The prick's smile vanished and the absolute shock that replaced it was so sudden that Lynn almost laughed out loud.

"Cat got your tongue, fucknuts?"

The prick opened his car door but the engine was still running and Lynn wasn't scared. "I'll kick your ass for that you inbred shithead."

With his free hand, the hand not holding the garbage bag, Lynn reached into his jeans and pulled out a battered, and quite dull pocket knife. He used it to pry stuck cans out of storm grates and it wasn't good for much else, but the prick didn't know that. "You put a foot on the pavement and I'm gonna carve my name into that pretty paint job of yours."

The prick's eyes narrowed. "Fucking delinquent!"

He slammed the car door shut and revved the engine. It roared so loud Lynn's eardrums hurt and he chucked him the finger. The prick floored the gas pedal, the tires screaming and throwing a tornado of shale and dirt into Lynn's face as the car raced away. Lynn closed his eyes to keep out the dust, but his mouth was open in a broad, triumphant smile. He hated rich pricks.

But his smile and his triumph was short-lived.

Less than five minutes and half a mile later, new tires grated against the ground behind him. Lynn knew immediately they were bicycle tires and a part of him, a small, stupidly optimistic part, thought it might be his friends.

"Take a look at the trashboy" The voice was guttural and mush mouthed and unmistakable. Nolan Haddix.

Fuck me, Lynn thought. His day had just gone from mediocre to apocalyptic.

He turned, not wanting to see Nolan and whatever halfwit, shop class rejects that were riding his coattails on this given day, but he knew he couldn't wish them away and make it reality.

Nolan's face was plastered with something between a snarl and a grin. To his right was Matt Ross, a boy who was a grade up from them. He was even taller than Nolan, but where Haddix's body was lined with wiry, lean muscle, Matt Ross had the build of a linebacker. Behind the two of them, R.J. Petrillo straddled this own bicycle. Unlike his fellow thugs, Petrillo was short and skinny, but Lynn knew he was a mean little bastard and wasn't surprised to see him paling around with Nolan.

"Aren't the towers already full of trash? Why are you picking up more?" Petrillo pushed a mop of black hair out of his eyes and gave a low chortle.

Lynn knew he couldn't outrun three boys on bikes, especially not these three, and decided his only hope was defusing the situation with his charm. "Out doing my good deed for the day, that's all. Keeping the neighborhood green. Trying to keep that Indian on TV from crying and all that shit."

Nolan glanced at Matt Ross, then back to Petrillo, then returned his gaze to Lynn. "We ain't buying that." He stomped down the kickstand of his Schwinn and stepped off it. "Gimme that bag."

No sense getting the shit beat out of him over a couple bucks worth of aluminum. Lynn held it out and Haddix snatched it away roughly, the cans inside giving a musical jingle jangle.

Nolan opened the pinched end of the bag and peered into it. "Christ, this reeks. Now I know why you always smell like hot shit. I thought it was just from hanging out with stinkpot Ray." He overturned the bag and let the contents fall onto the road. "You get your rocks off picking up other people's garbage or something?"

The other boys unleashed their trollish laughs.

"He's like one of those *Garbage Pail Kids*," RJ said. "You know, like the sticker cards. What should we name him?"

"Lyin' Lynn?" Matt offered but the other boys didn't latch on to that.

"Nah. I got it," Nolan said. "Trash Bin Lynn."

Even Lynn had to admit that wasn't half bad. If he came away from this encounter with nothing more than a derisive nickname he'd consider himself a very lucky boy. He should have kept his mouth shut, but that was something he'd always had trouble with.

"Hey, it beats working for a living." Lynn gave his most winning smile.

"Your parents don't give you an allowance?" Matt Ross's question ended with a wet burp.

Lynn was surprised the boy could manage a three syllable word like 'allowance' but didn't have a chance to answer before Nolan interrupted.

"He don't got a dad. And his ma's on welfare. That's why they live in the towers. Fucking trash. Mooch off people who got jobs and pay taxes, like my parents."

Petrillo brayed a whooping, horsey laugh, but Lynn didn't find it amusing in the slightest. His mother worked thirty-two hours a week cleaning hotel rooms at the Budget Inn and another twenty stocking shelves and mopping the floor at the Fisher Big Wheel department store. She might be poor and they might get food stamps and live in the towers, but his mother was not trash. And neither was he.

But, a socioeconomic debate with Nolan was even further down on Lynn's 'List of things I want to do' than a habanero enema. He knew that all of this was inevitably going to end in a beating and, at this point, just wanted to get on with it. Time to speed up the process.

"I didn't know they taxed whores in Pennsylvania." Lynn turned to Matt Ross. "Guess you learn something new every day, huh?"

Too far, Lynn wondered.

Nolan's eyes blazed and his nostrils flared while his already pink flesh turned almost as red as that rich prick's firebird. "I'm gonna rip your sack off."

Yeah, too far.

Lynn watched Nolan's hands clench into fat fists. God, the kid has huge hands. The better for beating you with, he thought and almost laughed but stopped himself because even Little Red Riding Hood didn't have to deal with these bad wolves.

He'd been planning to accept his punishment, but the sight of those oversized mitts changed his mind and, without even thinking, Lynn spun on his heels and ran. Taking a straight course down the road would be pointless, they'd catch him on their bikes. He knew his only chance, and it sure was a shitty one, was the woods.

In a running leap he hurdled the guide rail and almost fell when he landed on the downward sloping ground on the opposite side. He didn't slow down and didn't look back, not even when he heard Nolan Haddix bellow.

"Get that motherfucker!"

CHAPTER NINETEEN

ASIDE FROM HANGING OUT WITH HIS FRIENDS OR OGLING
Lynn's sister's tits, one of the high points of Ray's life was
spending time in the woods with his Papaw. They usually went
out once a week to gather various berries and roots and herbs.
Today, the hunt was for wild mushrooms.

On a good day, they could fill a brown, paper grocery store bag
with their bounty. But even the bad days, when they came up
with barely enough to fill their pockets, or got skunked entirely,
weren't really bad at all because they were together, without the
near constant chaos that was life at the farmhouse.

"Over here, Ray."

Ray wasn't allowed to gather mushrooms himself, because he still
struggled to separate the ones that were good for eating from the
ones that would send you to the hospital, or maybe even the
morgue. He was content with carrying the bag and keeping
Papaw's hands free for the picking. He crossed to the man who

was on his knees beside a dead and rotting oak tree that loomed high above them.

"Find something good, Papaw?"

The man raised his hands, which were black with the rich forest earth, and which gripped two fistfuls overflowing with a tannish gray fungus. It was enormous with a wrinkly, windy texture unlike anything Ray had ever seen.

"Is that a mushroom?" Ray's eyes bulged.

His grandfather's tan, lined face was split by a broad grin, one that revealed his aging choppers which were yellowed, crooked, and broken, but still all his own. "It's the hen of the forest."

That sounded exotic to Ray's twelve-year-old ears and he was even more excited because of the absolute glee on his grandfather's face.

Ray's Papaw's given name was Vyatt Mayhew and earlier that year the family had celebrated his 76th birthday. Ray himself had saved up all winter and most of the spring to buy his Papaw a new silver-plated belt buckle that featured a scene of a man hunting ducks with a shotgun and two beagle dogs. After the party, when it was just the two of them, his Papaw had told him that it was the best gift of all the gifts he received. When Ray asked him if he told all the other gift-givers the same thing, the man paused, gave a sober nod, and quietly added, "But this time I really mean it." Ray hoped that was true, but even if it wasn't, Vyatt made him believe it and that was all that mattered.

Vyatt was tall, over six feet, but stooped by age. He almost always wore the kind of floppy hat that Ray associated with fishermen, but his grandfather didn't fish and underneath it was long, thin hair that he kept pulled back in a ponytail. His grandmother often threatened to cut it off when he slept, "Thing looks like an albino poodle tail," she'd bark, but she never did.

"It's bigger than your head, Papaw."

Vyatt laughed, a throaty sound full of good cheer. "It certainly is. And bigger than our bag too. I think our foraging's finished for the day."

Ray thought it was a swimming start to the day and didn't want it to end. He had never given much thought to heroes, but if he had Vyatt would have been at the top of the list. He idolized near everything about the old man, but most of all the way he made Ray feel. Safe and loved and important.

"We didn't even eat our lunches yet." Ray shook the other bag he was carrying, a smaller, paper sack, as if to prove this fact.

"No. I suppose we didn't. Let's remedy that, Ray."

Vyatt set the fungus, the hen of the forest, carefully on some fallen leaves and then the man and the boy settled on a prostrate ash tree which was soggy with decay. Ray felt the wetness seep through his jeans, past his underwear, and dampen his butt and knew he'd have a spot that made it look like he'd pissed himself when he eventually stood back up, but that was all right. It was just the two of them and even if his Papaw laughed, it wouldn't be in a mean way.

Ray unrolled the end of the bag and pulled out two egg salad sandwiches which were enclosed in plastic wrap. The bag and plastic and food all smelled strongly of cigarette smoke, an aroma that he instantly associated with his Meemaw, who chain-smoked Camel's every waking minute of the day.

He handed a sandwich to Vyatt and offered him a drink of pop from his thermos.

Vyatt smiled and gave his head a slight shake. "You keep the pop, Ray. I got something better." He pulled a battered flask from the back pocket of his pants, took a sip, then another, then closed it.

Ray knew it was moonshine and he knew that's what his uncles and cousins were always up to in the big barn behind the farmhouse. Sometimes he wondered if they actually managed to sell any or if they just drank it all up, but that wasn't his question for asking.

"You having a good summer, Ray?" Vyatt bit away a quarter of the sandwich in one mouthful.

"I am," Ray said. "Real good. We even did bicycle jousting the other day. I came up with that all myself."

"Bicycle jousting?" The words were thick as they came through the food. "You'll have to let me watch that sometime. Sounds fascinating."

"It was so much fun. I—"

He'd been on the verge of telling Vyatt how he'd sent Lynn and his bike flying through the air when an ear-splitting squawk echoed in from their left. Ray was so startled that he jumped to his feet and did an about face in the direction of the sound, like a cadet who'd just been issued an order from his drill instructor. He didn't even notice his sandwich tumble into the dirt.

"What was that?" Ray asked.

Vyatt watched the woods, but didn't seem concerned and took another bite of his sandwich. "I don't rightly know. But how

about you come over here." He patted the side of the tree opposite from where Ray currently stood.

Ray obeyed eagerly and, when he did, he saw Vyatt's right hand
fall to the grip of the .44 magnum pistol he always kept holstered
on his hip. That movement both calmed and frightened him at
the same time. Together, they watched and waited.

CHAPTER TWENTY

Lynn had been running as fast as his skinny legs could carry him through the woods, impervious to the brambles and vines that ripped at his arms, clawed at his face. They were a minor nuisance compared to whatever punishment Haddix and his crew would dish out if they caught him.

The bigger boys weren't far behind if the symphony of their destruction was any indication. The sounds of them stomping branches and bulldozing saplings drowned out the normal noise of the forest. At times they sounded almost close enough to grab him. He had the sense they were never more than a few yards back and whenever he risked a panicked glance to his rear, he could see the bright colors of their clothing blurring through the brush as they chased.

His chest heaved and he felt like his lungs might collapse or catch fire, or both. His legs were rubbery and clumsy and he was all too aware that eventually, maybe soon, his body would betray him and he wouldn't be able to go on.

Hide, he thought. I need to find a place to hide.

Lynn risked slowing his pace to scan the forest. A twenty-feet wide pond stretched out ahead and to the right. It was covered with scum that looked almost thick enough to walk across. Near the center, he saw the puke-green slime rise a few inches, mounding up in a half-sphere, then suddenly burst with a wheezy hiss and smack back onto the water. He'd never seen swamp gas in person, but supposed that had now changed.

I just saw my first swamp fart, he thought and he had to force himself not to laugh because, if he started laughing, he thought he might lose his mind and never be able to stop. Any humor he'd found in the situation was quickly quashed because the thrashing and crashing of Haddix and company was closer now.

Dashing past the pond, veering to the left, he pushed through a dense copse of pine trees, their needles scratching his pale skin and leaving behind thin red lines that looked almost like finger-nail scratches. Another ten yards and he came upon a massive, fallen oak laying prone on the forest floor. It would have to do.

Lynn dove under it, slithering as far under the trunk as possible, then using his hands and feet to dig into the ground and squeeze in even further. He had a narrow field of vision beneath the trunk, toward the area from which he'd just came. He knew his would be tormenters would arrive soon and all he could do was wait and watch.

The raucous crashing sounds of Haddix, Ross, and Petrillo approaching suddenly stopped, replaced with a wet splash. Then a whiny, pissed off voice that he immediately knew was RJ Petrillo's.

"Aw, goddamn it! My fucking Nike's are gonna be ruined!"

He heard another voice, one he was pretty sure was Haddix's, but couldn't make out the words and didn't care because their movement, their chasing, had stopped.

This is my chance. I should take off. High tail my ass the hell out of here while they're distracted.

But he felt safe under the tree and was almost certain they wouldn't find him there. It was quite the dilemma. He debated with himself for a good thirty seconds, almost an eternity to his young, spastic mind, before deciding that hiding under the tree in the stinking, sour ground of the woods wasn't how he wanted to spend the whole day.

Lynn belly-crawled out of his safe place and back into the dusty, green light of the forest. He watched the area from which he knew the bullies had been coming, body tensed and ready to run in case this had all been a trap and they were waiting to lure him out, but no one came.

He backed away at first, slowly, awkwardly, then turned and speed walked. He made it maybe twenty yards when he heard the scream.

It was so loud, so surprising, that Lynn jumped straight into the air. He came down awkwardly, wrenching his knee sideways which sent an electric jolt of pain up and into his thigh. If he hadn't caught hold of a thick rope of grapevine he'd have fallen.

"What the fuck was that?" His own voice startled him and he realized he was shaking all over. The scream was like nothing he'd ever heard. It wasn't even a scream, not like any kind he'd heard before. Not even like the sound his sister had made a few years earlier when she stepped on some kid's yoyo and fell down the steps leading to the apartment, breaking her leg in two places. That sound was horrible and painful, but still recognizable. This was foreign somehow, like retching and crying and shrieking all at the same time. The noise an eagle might make if bigfoot was ripping off its wings. It sounded like violent, agonized death.

Gooseflesh covered his arms and he ran his hands up and down his forearms even though he wasn't cold. Not in a physical way.

Run.

The thought wasn't his own. It was like someone, maybe God, had implanted it inside his head. In that part of your brain that also told you not to walk down certain alleyways at night or not trick or treat at the house where the guy who drove the old van lived all by himself. That primitive, animal part of your brain that kept you from doing stupid shit like standing in the middle of the woods, exposed, and waiting to see what was coming for you. Lynn thought it good advice and despite the ache in his knee, he listened to it.

He ran.

CHAPTER TWENTY-ONE

Ray chewed his bottom lip like it was saltwater taffy and watched as his Papaw aimed the pistol in the general direction from which the noise came. Ray's eyes kept pivoting between the brush and his grandfather, his mind seesawing between fear and admiration. He couldn't comprehend how his grandfather could be so calm. The barrel of the pistol didn't waver a millimeter, his hands, swollen and gnarled with arthritis, didn't shake. He'd often heard the phrase cool as a cucumber and now he was seeing it in real life. His Papaw was one cool dude.

"What is it, Papaw?" Ray swallowed hard, not sure if he wanted to hear an answer to that question.

Vyatt held steady and didn't look back. "Well, I believe we're about to find out, Ray. You just sit tight and, if I tell you to run, you run."

Run? Run and leave his grandfather? If Ray was simply afraid before, he was downright terrified now. He was about to say they should both run when the crashing noise became too close to make that an executable option.

Ray saw his grandfather's finger change placement from the guard, to the trigger. As the noise was almost on top of them, that finger began to squeeze. Ray held his breath.

The brush came alive. The lush, emerald foliage first shaking then thrashing, then parting. Something was coming through it. And coming fast.

A figure burst through the cover, a wild blur of flailing arms and pistoning legs, lunging toward them. Ray looked away from it, toward his grandfather, waiting for the man to shoot this intruder.

But Vyatt didn't shoot. Instead, his finger flung free of the trigger so fast Ray heard his knuckle pop.

Ray was about to holler out and ask him what he was doing when his eyes traveled away from his grandfather and toward the new arrival.

And he realized it was Lynn.

The boy had dropped to his knees. His chest heaved and sounds like a broken whistle spilled from his mouth.

"Lynn? My Papaw almost shot you."

Lynn stared at them, eyes bulging. "Well thank Christ he didn't," Lynn said. "Because this day's really sucked so far and that would have been the turd on top of the shit sundae."

Ray couldn't believe Lynn would talk that way in front of a grown up let alone his grandfather, but Vyatt burst out in hearty laughter and holstered the pistol.

When Lynn filled them in on his day, Ray wasn't surprised to hear about the run-in with Nolan Haddix and the other boys, but he was shocked to hear how far they'd carried it. He realized how lucky he might have been that day at the creek, that the only things that Haddix killed were a dozen or so crayfish. When it came to the scream, or whatever that awful noise had been, Lynn could offer no source. Vyatt mentioned there being wildcats in the woods when he was a boy and said they'd made some godawful sounds, but Ray thought his grandfather's voice lacked certainty when he gave that explanation.

After ten minutes or so, Lynn had caught his breath and there'd been no sign of Haddix and the others. It seemed to all of them that the time had come to move on and Ray grabbed the paper bag of fungi while his grandfather picked up the gigantic sheepshead mushroom.

"What the hell is that?" Lynn gaped at it.

"Hen of the forest." Ray said, even though he himself wasn't quite sure what that meant.

"Is that like chicken of the sea?"

Vyatt laughed again and patted Lynn on the shoulder. "Come on back to the farm with us and I'll cook it up and show you."

CHAPTER TWENTY-TWO

Minutes before the scream, Nolan Haddix was sure they were going to catch the Ohler shit. Catch him and beat his ass into the ground. Mouthy little fucker sure as hell deserved it.

But then they lost him after getting tangled in a huge, wild patch of mountain laurel and when they emerged into the open on the other side, the bastard was nowhere to be seen.

Haddix looked to Petrillo and Ross, held a finger to his lips to be quiet, then they continued on.

After a few minutes of trudging through the stinking woods and getting bit by who the fuck knows how many mosquitos, Haddix was about ready to give up. This was a small town and they'd run into Lynn Ohler again soon enough and, when they did, he'd have hell to pay. Besides, Nolan thought, some more time to think about how I want to make him pay might not be a bad thing. He had a feeling that more than a run of the mill beating was in order.

Before he could tell his lackeys about the change of plans, Petrillo grunted and shouted. "Dammit. My goddamn Nikes are gonna be ruined!"

Haddix looked and saw RJ up to his thighs in a body of water that fell somewhere between a big puddle and a puny pond. It barely looked like water, it looked more like a pool of green snot and the algae had splashed onto RJ Petrillo's jeans, making them look like they'd been splattered with paint.

"I'd say your Calvin's are shot too," Ross said and snickered, as hollow and brainless sound as any Haddix had ever heard.

"Fuck the clothes you dimwits. It's just pond scum. It'll wash off."

Petrillo, his face petulant, pouting, opened his mouth as if to protest, then reconsidered. The boy took a step, or tried to, and made no progress. He cursed under his breath and tried again. No forward motion. "I'm stuck!"

Haddix shook his head and looked to Ross. "Help him."

Ross stared down at his own shoes and jeans, but realized he had no choice but to obey and waded into the water.

Haddix wondered how he managed to get saddled with such idiots. It said a lot about the losers in this town the he couldn't find better friends. Or at least acquaintances with two working brain cells. But, then again, much of their appeal, or their only appeal really, was that they did as told with only a modest amount of complaining. Haddix liked being the boss almost as much as he liked being the muscle, the punisher.

He got both naturally. His father owned Haddix Manufacturing, one of the biggest employers in Sallow Creek and even though the wages were shit, a quarter over minimum wage for most of the grunts, he had people fighting for jobs.

Nolan knew that, one day, he'd be running that company while rejects like Matt Ross and RJ Petrillo worked the line and supposed some things were destined to never change.

"Hurry the hell up," he said as the two of them struggled to free themselves of the muck at the bottom of the pond-lite. They were almost to dry land when Petrillo slipped and went in over his head.

Haddix exploded in laughter, big, horsey brays so hard they bent him over at the waist. "You clumsy fucker," he got out between the hees and haws, then laughed some more.

Matt Ross bent over, plunging his arms through the scum and into the water, his upper body pivoting as his unseen hands searched. "I can't find—" He stopped suddenly. "Never mind. He's he—"

The word went unfinished because Ross went under too. So fast that Haddix thought he might have blinked and missed part of the fall. It was like a magician's act. Presto changeo dissapearo. Ross was gone.

Haddix's hard laughs slowed, then faded to a gradual stop, like turning down lights with a dimmer switch. He assumed they were trying to get one over on him. Trying to make him go into the water since he'd ragged on them for being pussies, but he wasn't falling for that trick.

It wasn't until a few seconds became a full minute that he started believing something was actually wrong.

"Matt? RJ? Stop fucking off."

He watched the surface of the water which was still, not so much as a ripple.

"You dickheads, get out of there!" That was supposed to be authoritative, an order, but it sounded false even to his own ears and it garnered no response. "Fuck you then. I'm out of here."

He turned, took three steps away, and heard a splash. *Assholes,* he thought. *Almost had me, but I'll never admit it.*

"Well look who decided to grow up and—" He turned to face the pond. Matt Ross floated on his back. Not floated. Floated would have inferred he was doing it on purpose. The boy bobbed like an inanimate object.

Behind him, RJ crawled out of the water on his hands and knees. Haddix was twenty yards from them and jogged their way. If this was a prank, it was a fucking good one.

"RJ? What happened? Is he dead?" He looked again to Matt. He sure looked dead. Dirt and mud and slime coated his exposed flesh. His shirt had ridden up and his belly broke the surface of the pond, appearing distended, like he'd just dined at an all you can eat buffet.

"We have to get him out!" Haddix wanted to say *you. You* get him out, but RJ had only now come free of the water and Haddix knew he'd never go back into it alone.

Nolan himself was only a few feet from the edge of the pond and he sidestepped around the perimeter. He'd never admit to being scared, but he was also smart enough to not go in blindly, heroically, without all the facts. He moved to RJ who faced away from him, still on his hands and knees like an animal. He was coughing, retching.

"Hey," Haddix said. "Can you get up and help me?" His eyes snapped back and forth between the others. Ross still bobbed, eyes closed. Only now Haddix realized something else was amiss.

His skin had seemed to separate from whatever held it fast to the tissue underneath. It floated free, untethered, giving him a dreamy, not quite real appearance. A mirage of a boy.

Haddix almost plunged into the pond to investigate further, but stopped himself. Only a fool acts before he has all the requisite information, his father had once advised him.

Matt Ross's skin continued to disengage and was soon a shapeless, formless mass that reminded Haddix of a plastic bag floating on the water.

"RJ!" He shouted. "Get up!"

Nolan Haddix walked backward, quick, deft. He wanted, needed, to put more distance between himself and his dead friend.

He tore his eyes away from Ross and looked to RJ Petrillo. He saw the boy was finally on his feet. Whatever he had puked up oozed down his chin, seeped down his neck, onto his bare chest. It was a green-brown color that reminded Haddix of the foul concoction of pureed vegetables and coffee that his father drank every morning.

RJ stared at him, his eyes red and bulging.

Haddix realized it wasn't only his eyes that were bulging. His body had grown, like a bird puffing out its feathers to stay warm. He was thirty percent wider and rounder than he'd been before.

"What the fuck's wrong with you, man?"

Petrillo took a single step, then opened his mouth and shrieked. The sound was so loud that Haddix covered his ears and squeezed his eyes shut, not sure why he bothered with the latter but needing to block out that horrific sound.

When it stopped, he opened his eyes again and looked at RJ. He was even bigger than before. His dark, olive skin was stretched, becoming almost translucent. He kept expanding, growing. Delicate fissures started to appear, leaking blood. And then—

RJ Petrillo burst.

The previous summer Nolan, along with these two friends and a couple other guys they sometimes palled around with had traded a few cartons of cigarettes for some M80s. They quickly grew tired of blowing up paint cans and milk jugs and decided to ratchet things up.

Nolan bought three whole chickens at the grocery store and convinced RJ to light an M80, shove it up the dead bird's ass, and run. What resulted was almost scarily close to what happened to the boy now.

His stomach went first. It blew out in a spray of ripped flesh and liquified intestines that covered the ground in a two yards wide circle. His left arm toppled sideways while the right pinwheeled through the air before splashing down in the pond. His legs only crumpled to the ground, perhaps too heavy to work their way into anything dramatic, but his head made up for it.

RJ Petrillo's noggin blew twelve feet into the air before slamming into a tree branch, resulting in a hollow *thock!* Then it ricocheted down, hitting the ground, rolling end over end several times before coming to a stop face up and just a few feet away from Nolan. One of his eyes had popped free but the other was open in confused, dead surprise.

Nolan Haddix, the scourge of existence for nearly every boy not yet a teenager in Sallow Creek had lost any will to fight. All he wanted to do now was run. Before he could, RJ's tongue burst free from his dead head, unraveling like a spool of wire and hurtling through the air. The tongue latched onto Haddix's mouth.

Nolan could feel it burrowing inside, pushing past his lips like the world's most perverse French kiss. It wriggled between his teeth, then onto his own tongue. He felt a sharp burst of pain and the warm flow of blood. He tried to scream but that only allowed RJ's tongue better access. It dove deeper into Nolan's mouth, the slimy undulating feeling made his stomach open and his breakfast rocket up his gullet. But the second, unwanted tongue took up too much space and only a trickle of the puke spilled free. The rest sloshed back and forth between Nolan's throat and mouth, a rancid, chunky soup he wanted to spit out but couldn't.

He couldn't breathe. His head felt dreamy and the world in front of him swayed even though he was standing still. Then he blacked out.

CHAPTER TWENTY-THREE

THE BUSINESS WHERE LARRY ROBERTS SPENT NINETY percent of his waking hours wasn't much to look at. Gray, cinder block walls twelve feet tall encased the garage portion, which was barely large enough for one vehicle at a time, plus the assortment of tools Larry used to make repairs. A wooden, clapboard structure had been tacked on to the rear and, inside it was the cash register, a shelf of various automotive fluids, and a cooler in which the bottles of soda and candy bars were housed.

Crouching in front of that cooler was Garrett, his hands digging through the boxes of sweets like they were gold doubloons. He added several to his backpack, then tore open and bit into a Whatchamacallit. His mouth flooded with saliva as he tasted the perfect combination of chocolate, caramel, and peanut butter. As his jaws worked against the chewy and crunchy texture, the bell inside the garage gave a single ding.

"Can you get that, Gar?" Larry Roberts called out from the garage.

The previous violence hadn't been addressed. It was more rough water under the bridge. "Sure, dad."

Garrett left the office, passing through the garage on his way outdoors. He found his father laying on his back, atop a wheeled board labeled a Jeepers Creepers. A Dodge pick up, hoisted into the air by jacks, loomed over him.

As he strode through the open bay door and into the warm, morning air, he saw a Crown Vic police car idling in front of the lone gas pump. The windows were tinted and all he could see through them was the silhouette of the man behind the wheel. He circled around the front of the car, to the driver's door. The window rolled down, slow, and when it was half-way through its descent he saw Officer Hanes.

"Garrett, right?" He gave that same fake, toothy smile.

Garrett nodded.

"Fill it up for me, Son."

"You're gonna have to turn the engine off first."

Hanes nodded. "Course. Course. Safety first. That's good thinking on your part." He turned the key and the engine died.

After removing the gas cap, Garrett grabbed the nozzle from the pump and flipped the lever to activate it. As he started filling the car, the driver's door opened and Hanes stepped out. He turned at the waist, stretching, and Garrett heard an audible pop from his spine. That was followed by a contented *Ahhhhh*.

The cop stood there for a moment, watching him, silent. Garrett felt like he was being examined and when the cop spoke again, he realized he'd been right.

"What happened to your paw?"

The question caught Garrett off guard and his gaze immediately went to the garage where his father was hidden from view.

"I'm talking about your hand, son," Hanes said.

Garrett glanced at his hand which was still swollen and bruised.

"Wiped out on my bike." The lie came quick and easy.

Hanes' eyes narrowed. "Wasn't like that the other day."

"Happened after that. I was out playing with my friends." Garrett tilted his head toward his bicycle which rested lazily against the front of the garage.

The cop took a step closer and Garrett could smell his Old Spice aftershave even over the high fumes of the gasoline. Hanes stole a peek at the open bay door, then leaned in even closer.

"You ask me, I think your pops did that to you. Gave you a... What'd he call it? A whooping?"

The gears in Garrett's head spun into overdrive. Should he tell the truth to the police officer - something he'd always been taught was the right thing to do. Or should he remain loyal to his father, the only consistent adult figure in his life? This was quite the conundrum.

"No sir. I took the turn at Waterloo and Hillcrest too fast."

Hanes gave a single nod and Garrett knew he wasn't buying it. The cop stared him down, eyes piercing, judging. Another five gallons went into the tank before he spoke again. "Supposed to be a fun time. Being a boy, that is. A time when you can leave the adult problems to the adults."

Garrett couldn't understand what the man was rambling about. "Sir?"

"I'm just saying, don't let no one, or nothing, fowl up your child-hood. Especially summer." Hanes' gaze drifted in the general direction of the road but he wasn't really looking at anything.

"By God, I remember the summers. Not a care in the whole wide world. Just might have been the best times of my life."

"I agree with you on that," Garrett said, being honest for the first time in the conversation.

The nozzle kicked and an overspray of gasoline belched from the tank, splashing over Garrett's hand and shoes. He was glad it wasn't the damaged hand because, he imagined, that would have burned like fire.

The commotion brought the cop back to reality. A thin line of fuel trickled over the cruiser's paint, adding a rainbow haze to the gleaming white. Garrett reached into his pocket and pulled out a handkerchief but before he could wipe it away Hanes put his hand on his shoulder.

"Don't worry about that. It ain't gonna hurt nothing."

Garrett returned the rag to his shorts, then the nozzle to the pump. He checked the total. "Eight seventy seven."

The cop already had his wallet out and open. He pulled out a ten and passed it over.

"I'll get your change." Garrett turned to the garage and found his father standing at the edge of the open door. Overhead sunlight cleaved his face in half and the eye that was subjected to the brightness squinted and watched.

"Don't worry about that either," Hanes said. "You keep that for yourself. And don't save it. Spend it. The more foolish the better."

When Garrett turned back to thank him, the cop was already reentering the vehicle. The engine rumbled to life and he retreated to the garage where his father waited, watching the cruiser ease away.

"Here you go." Garrett handed him the ten and his dad deposited it into a billfold that was attached to his belt with a chain.

"He say something to you, Gar?"

"Like what?"

"Don't know. Anything out of the ordinary."

"No. Not really. Just talking about the summer."

Larry peered down at him, watched him for a short moment, then tilted his head toward the road. "You head on out now. Get home and fix us something good to eat."

"I can help here."

"Gar, if I have five more customers before now and closing, I'll consider myself a lucky man. I can hold down the fort. Now get."

After retrieving his backpack and candy, Garrett climbed aboard his bike and did just that.

CHAPTER TWENTY-FOUR

THE SMELL HIT GARRETT AS SOON AS HE STEPPED INSIDE the trailer. It was a fetid, sour aroma that reminded him of the ground in the woods where he sometimes camped out with his friends. The odor that arose when they dug the latrine hole was something like this, only that smell was a small fraction of the magnitude he now experienced.

He tilted his head back instinctually, like a dog trying to pick up the scent of game, but the stench was everywhere and anywhere, permeating the trailer to the core. Seeking it out was going to be an unpleasant, but necessary chore.

But where to start? The bathroom seemed the obvious choice. That was the only place that really made sense. Bad smells always started in the bathroom. And maybe this one had an innocuous reason after all, like a clogged drain or a burst pipe. The notion of stepping into that cramped space and possibly finding the commode overflowing with putrescent, liquified feces both terrified and fascinated him as he tiptoed down the hall, toward the room.

The bathroom door was flimsy and poorly fitted, allowing an irregular prism of daylight to escape underneath it and onto the carpeted hallway floor. Garrett raised his hand to the knob, his fingers inches away, then froze. What if it wasn't just shit inside there? What if it was his father?

The idea was mad, he knew that. His dad would be at the gas station just like every other weekday. But still, there was always the possibility that he'd got food poisoning or had the stomach flu and came home early. And, if his dad was in there, sick and creating this horrendous smell, Garrett didn't want to expose him in the middle of the awful act.

"Dad?" He waited, listened. Nothing. "Dad?"

The second attempt also garnered nothing but silence so Garrett reached again for the doorknob and, this time, took it in his hand. He hadn't realized his palms were sweating until he tried to spin the metal cylinder and it slipped through his slick fingers. Why are you so nervous, he asked himself, feeling silly and a little like a baby. Grow up already.

Then he gripped the doorknob harder and, this time, turned it.

The bathroom was empty. Well, not entirely empty. There was indeed no person inside, certainly not his father, sitting on the commode or kneeling in front of it. Praying to the porcelain God, Shane had once called that posture and remembering that made Garrett smile a little.

Soon, his eyes found a small pile of clothing cast aside beside the shower. Garrett took a few steps into the room and his nose alerted him that the smell, or at least some of it, emanated from that heap. They were covered with mud and muck but through the filth he thought he could make out denim - a pair of jeans probably. The rest looked like socks and underwear, briefs that were so brown it looked like the wearer had experience the worst case of explosive diarrhea known to mankind.

Although the clothes were too filth encrusted to identify colors or styles he didn't think they looked like anything his father would wear (he was a boxers man) and Garrett wasn't about to pick them up to get a better look. His eyes drifted past them, into the shower, and he saw small droplets of water scattered roughshod over its sunburst yellow fiberglass floor. That made him glance up and he saw water pooled on the shower head, a fat bubble of it that magnified the rusty, calcified iron build-up on the dispenser. His eyes were glued to it, watching it grow larger and waiting for it to burst and fall. He was so mesmerized that he didn't realize he wasn't alone.

The water bubble popped and rained toward the shower floor and, as Garrett's eyes followed it, his peripheral vision caught the mirror above the sink and in it, a man's reflection.

He spun around so fast he slipped on the damp floor, his feet skittering under him, the rubber soles of his tennis shoes digging for traction but his eyes didn't care about any of that. His eyes tried to see who was in the bathroom with him. Behind him.

And then he saw his brother.

Harrison stared, silent, a bemused look on his freshly washed face. "When did you turn into such a jumpy little shit?"

As confused relief came over him, Garrett's flailing feet slowed and his calming nerves did the rest. His balance back under control, he was tempted to come back with a smart answer, but he was shaken and comebacks had never really been his thing anyway. He settled with, "Where the hell have you been?"

"That's a long story," Harrison said as he rubbed a towel through his damp hair. "And it can wait until the old man gets home."

The skin over Harrison's bare chest was drawn tight, revealing all the bones that lay just under the thin cloak of skin. There was a concave hollow at his midsection which was hidden in deep shadows thrown by his ribcage. Another towel wrapped his waist, but his legs and feet were bare. Garrett thought his toes looked like those of someone who'd been swimming for an entire day, the flesh almost translucent. He noticed that the big toenail on his left foot was gone, a rectangle of pallid, colorless skin in its place.

With nothing left to see at the bottom, Garrett's gaze went back to the top. He saw the remnants of an eggplant bruise fading on his forehead and a scabby gash in the middle of it.

"You look like crap," Garrett said.

"At least I'm not as ugly as you, fatass." Harrison threw the wet towel, the one he'd been using on his head, into Garrett's face, turned, and left the bathroom.

Garrett watched him disappear into his bedroom and heard the door close. He had questions, dozens of them, but he supposed Harrison was right. They could wait. Besides, he wasn't all that interested in the answers.

CHAPTER TWENTY-FIVE

"THAT SOUNDS LIKE A PILE OF HORSE SHIT, IF YOU'LL pardon my Francais." Shane flopped back in the recliner that sat in the back corner of their clubhouse.

Over the last half hour, Garrett had filled him in on Harrison's return and his story - Shane was sure it was a story - about where he'd been. It started out believable. Harrison had run away from home and was hitchhiking to Ohio. He got a ride less than a mile from their trailer but the guy turned out to be a perv, so he took off running into the woods. That's where it became, in Shane's opinion, horse shit.

"Which part?" Garrett asked.

"Everything after Chester the Molester dropped him in the woods. I mean, come on, Garrett, even if he did run into a tree and give himself a concussion, how does he stay lost in the woods for three damn weeks? This is Pennsylvania, not Montana." Shane could tell by the look on Garrett's face that he was surprised by this opinion.

"But why would he lie?"

"Because he's your brother. That's what he does."

A pathetic whining stole both of their attention. Apollo, the Vinyan's eight-year-old mixed breed dog, had wandered through the open door of the clubhouse. When Shane looked his way he saw a chewed upon tennis ball protruding from the dog's mouth. He grabbed it, ignoring the slick coating of slobber, and chucked it out the door. Apollo gleefully bounced after it.

"I don't know. He was definitely skinnier," Garrett said.

"That's because you haven't been cooking for him. You could fatten up Jack Sprat." He thought Garrett looked crestfallen over that remark and regretted saying that particular "f" word. "It's a joke."

Garrett shrugged his shoulders. "You might be right. But then, where's he been?"

Shane had a theory on this too. He knew Harrison Roberts had been going out with Laurene Draven, a sophomore with a pockmarked, pimply face but an above average ass. He'd obtained this information from one of his magazine customers and, apparently, it was to be kept on the hush hush. Of course, he had told Garrett and all of their other friends and they'd each shared several good chuckles over it.

"Banging Laurene would be my guess."

Garrett wrinkled his nose as if that was the most revolting thing he'd ever heard. "Oh, gross, Shane."

"Come on, Garrett. You think he was dating her for her personality."

"Still." Garrett stuck his index finger in his mouth and faked a gag.

"Your brother's so fracking stupid that he probably knocked her up too. You might be an uncle in nine months."

Garrett held his hands over his ears. "No more." But he laughed and Shane was pleased to see the one eighty in his mood. When he'd arrived he'd been sullen and Shane realized that Garrett hadn't wanted his brother to come home. He suspected Garrett could have lived the rest of his life without ever seeing Harrison again and been as happy as a clam. But, now he'd returned and Garrett would be back to living in a war zone without an ally in sight.

Apollo had returned with the ball but Garrett grabbed onto the mutt before he could make his way back to Shane. He ran his fingers through the dog's wiry fur, petting and scratching and loving on him all at the same time. The dog stood there, in his glory, tail whipping side to side with happiness. Watching this, Shane considered how shitty Garrett's life was. The kid didn't even have a dog of his own. It sure didn't seem fair.

"You know the carnival's coming in next week?"

Garrett looked away from Apollo. "Yeah." His mouth took on a pinched expression that Shane knew to be nerves. "Do you know which night you want to go?"

"Every damn night was my plan."

Garrett didn't respond and Shane was pretty sure he knew why. Garrett didn't have the money for three night's worth of admission. Shane felt a white lie was an appropriate remedy to this.

"Folks that run it gave my pops a stack of tickets this big." Shane held his hands about three inches apart. "All for letting him put some flyers in the store and a poster in the big picture window out front."

Garrett's face un-pinched. "Really?"

Shane nodded. "Yeah. Enough for all of you losers to keep me company all weekend. Maybe this year you can finally knock down all the milk bottles and win one of those fish in a bowl."

Garrett gave Apollo's ball a toss. "And maybe you can finally convince Della to go for a ride on the Ferris wheel."

Shane rolled his eyes but he felt his cheeks heat up. "That was two summer's ago. Ancient history."

"Yeah, sure. I saw the way you looked at her during lunch all year long. Don't try and lie to me, Shane."

"I'll sic my dog on you, boy. Don't tempt me."

Garrett raised his eyebrows and looked at the dog. "Him? Maybe he'd lick me to death."

"That's the most action you'll ever get." Shane pointed at him. "Apollo, attack! Get him!"

Apollo, dropped the ball and leapt toward Garrett. In two bounds it was on top of him, his long tongue painting the boy's chubby face with slobber. Garrett laughed uncontrollably and Shane too succumbed to the kind of feverish good cheer that can only truly be experienced by boys and dogs.

CHAPTER TWENTY-SIX

IT HAD BEEN THREE DAYS SINCE HIS BROTHER HAD RETURNED and life at home was more confusing than ever before. The first night had been about what he expected. His father questioned and accused, yelled and berated. The odd part was that Harrison didn't fight back. He took it all with a kind of acceptance that had previously been Garrett's M.O. The *keep your head down and mouth shut* version of playing their father's violent game. Maybe he knocked some sense into himself, Garrett thought at the time.

The next day and been more of the same, only worse. Harrison's newfound sensibility seemed to ratchet up their father's rage and Garrett came to the realization that his father enjoyed the fights. Or, if enjoyment wasn't the right emotion, then maybe *need* was. Larry Roberts had been a brawler all his life, but to carry on with that he needed opponents and now it seemed like he had none. It was as if being unable to find an excuse to break out the belt and wail away on someone was driving the man crazy.

Garrett had fled the house before things could go full nuclear and before his father decided to try to antagonize him since Harrison wasn't accepting the challenge. He had no idea what would happen after he left, but he had a feeling it could go bad. He almost called the cop, Officer Hanes, to ask him to drive by and check things out, but there was still a part of him that bought into his father's 'Family problems should be kept within the family' BS and he didn't.

Instead, he spent the night in the clubhouse with Shane and Lynn. They played two rounds of Life and, when things got late enough that they didn't have to worry about Shane's mom poking her head inside to see what they were up to, they watched *Porky's* and *Bachelor Party*, both of which featured ample nudity and were favorites of all the boys because of that. Garrett liked them too, although he preferred horror movies when it was his turn to pick. But even throughout the games and movies, Garrett wondered what was happening back at the trailer.

Harrison was asleep when Garrett returned the next morning and their father was already at work. The place wasn't trashed and Harrison looked no worse for the wear, and his anxiety began to fade. He even took the time to fry up enough bacon for the both of them and scrambled eight eggs.

After dividing up the food, and sneaking a few extra pieces of bacon for himself, Garrett tapped on Harrison's bedroom door. "Breakfast."

He listened and heard his brother stir, then the bed creak as he got up. Garrett returned to the kitchen and waited at the table.

Harrison came out fully dressed, even down to the point of wearing shoes.

"You have plans or something?" Garrett asked when he saw him.

Harrison went to the fridge and grabbed the milk carton.

"Thought I might head in town and see if Dean or Wade are around. Maybe head out to the lake and go for a swim."

Garrett hated the lake. Algae that looked like thick snot always floated on the surface and if you managed to get past that and into the water your feet sank into six inches of muck that oozed between your toes and seeped under your nails. Plus, it always smelled like rotten eggs. There was nothing fun about it.

"You?" Harrison took a few long swallows straight from the carton.

Garrett was surprised he bothered to ask. Harrison didn't care about what Garrett did in his free time and he wondered if it was some kind of set up. Like maybe Harrison and his friends were going to track him down and beat him half to death.

"I'm meeting Shane and Ray at the bowling alley, They got a new Cobra Command game in the arcade." That was a lie. Garrett wasn't taking any chances.

"Oh." Harrison reached into his pocket, then pulled out his fist and tossed something toward Garrett.

Garrett flinched and held his forearms across his face to block whatever was incoming. He felt cool metal bounce off his arm and heard a metallic clatter as it hit the kitchen table. He looked and saw it was a quarter.

"Play a round on me." Harrison picked up his plate and started out of the room.

Garrett wouldn't have been more surprised if he'd have woken up that morning with a third eye. He had almost no memories of Harrison being nice to him. Giving him money was unheard of.

Before he could comment, his brother disappeared back into the bedroom and swung the door closed. It bounced off the frame and came open an inch or two, but Harrison didn't bother to shut it. Garrett heard the radio turn on and the bedsprings squeak, but he was still trying to comprehend what had just happened.

He kept pondering the events while he ate his breakfast, which tasted damn good, if he said so himself. He sometimes thought about becoming a chef, but Sallow Creek had only a McDonald's, a Wendy's, and one greasy diner, plus a couple pizza joints so his opportunities would be limited and far from glamorous. The idea of leaving town never really occurred to him. Aside from a couple jaunts to Pittsburgh over the years, usually with Shane's family, he rarely left the town borders, let alone the county. Staying here, even if there was no future, just seemed like his destiny.

When he finished eating he took his dishes to the sink to clean them, then remembered the hovel that was his brother's room and thought the polite thing to do would be to retrieve and clean his plate too. He never expected them to be best pals, but Harrison had been decent, almost kind, since coming home and Garrett felt he should reciprocate.

He went to the room and almost pushed the door open, but the sounds coming from inside stopped him cold. The noise was odd, hitching, but somehow familiar and he strained to make them out over Duran Duran playing on the radio.

Ugnh. Ugnh.

What is that? It sounded deep and hollow.

Ugnh. Ugnh. Ugnh.

Gagging, Garrett wondered. Is that what I'm hearing?

Ugnh.

And then a sloppy, wet *blargh.*

Oh shit, he just barfed. I made him breakfast to be nice and it made him sick.

But he'd eaten the same food and he wasn't sick. And besides, food poisoning didn't come on that fast, did it?

He shuffled to the side to align his face with the inch and a half opening between the door and the jamb. He saw Harrison on the bed, his plate in his lap, and then his brother swallowed.

He's eating so that means he couldn't have puked. The strange noises must have been something else. But what?

Ugnh.

Garrett's eyes locked on his brother. He saw Harrison's Adam's apple bob.

Ugnh. Ugnh.

His neck seemed to spasm.

Ugnh. Ugnh.

And then a puddle of viscous, brown liquid spilled out of Harrison's mouth, landing on his plate. On his bacon.

Now Garrett felt like puking. And as he watched it only got worse.

Harrison reached to the plate and pinched a piece of the barf covered bacon between his thumb and index fingers. He slathered it in the dense goo, coating every bit of it. Then he lifted it to his mouth, the regurgitated fluid stretched between the plate and the food forming a sort of opaque artery. That connective tissue snapped as Harrison suddenly shoved it into his gaping maw.

He didn't chew, his jaws didn't work but Garrett saw his cheeks bulge and flare as his tongue thrashed inside his mouth. Undulating, moist smacking sounds seeped from his brother's lips. It was like he was trying to suck down a triple-thick bacon barf-shake.

Garrett's stomach seized and somersaulted and he pinched his lips between his teeth to keep his own breakfast from making a grand re-entrance. If that happened, he'd be caught spying and as revolting as this was, he needed to see what Harrison was doing.

His brother swallowed down the slimy meat, then wiped a bit of the puke away with the back of his hand. He again looked to his plate and this time leaned over the eggs.

Ugnh. Ugnh.

The sight, the sounds. It was too much. Garrett knew if he stayed in that doorway another second he'd be projectile vomiting. He spun away from his brother's bedroom and goose stepped into the kitchen, then raced for the door. He'd forgotten about his dirty dishes in the sink. He didn't even bother to bring along any snacks to eat throughout the day. He didn't know if he'd ever be able to eat again.

All he cared about was getting away from that house. Away from his brother.

CHAPTER TWENTY-SEVEN

THE SOUNDS OF HIS PULSE POUNDING IN HIS EARS AND wheezing, hitching breathing drowned out the noise of traffic, pedestrians, and nature. Garrett pedaled his bicycle so fast he thought he might die from the exertion, but that fear came in a distant second to telling his father what he'd just witnessed. He never rode his bike so fast in his life and made the eight mile trip from his home to his father's garage in under forty minutes.

The first thing he noticed, even through his near panic, was that the garage door was down. Larry Roberts kept that open every day that the temperature was above 45 degrees and sometimes even when it was colder. Garrett had never seen the door closed on a summer day, but that wasn't even on the same spectrum of weirdness compared to what he'd just witnessed.

He didn't bother with his kickstand and let his bike hit the ground as he circled the building to the rear door. Along the way he passed by his father's pickup. It calmed him somewhat, seeing it there. Because that meant his father was there too, even if the garage bay door was sealed.

The back entrance was also closed, but the door was unlocked. Garrett pushed it open and stepped inside.

The lights were off, and so much dust coated the few windows that barely any sun spilled through. He may as well have been spelunking a cave.

"Dad?" He heard a hollow, metallic scrape.

"Garrett? That you?"

He could almost feel his heartbeat slow at the sound of his father's voice, and noted with irony, that it was usually the other way around. Usually, his father got him worked up, not calmed him down. That realization was just another example of how screwed up his life had become this summer.

"Yeah."

"I'll be out in a minute."

The radio in the garage was on, but it played nothing but static, like someone had been in between changing stations and lost interest. A steady hum interrupted by evenly timed thumps.

Heartbeats

No, just static, Garrett told himself.

He traveled further into the building, passing by the cooler of sodas and candy without giving so much as a single thought. He started at the doorway that separated the sales room from the garage. There was no door there and hadn't been for as long as Garrett remembered, and he was able to see into the shop area.

Florescent tube lights overhead threw dim, vaguely green light downward. In it, Garrett saw his father. Larry's back was turned to him as he wrestled with a 55 gallon drum, moving it from near the garage door toward the back wall. Garrett saw four identical drums lined up in a neat row there.

"What's in the barrels?" Garrett stayed in the empty door frame.

Larry's body stiffened, an action there and gone so fast that Garrett might have imagined it. "Motor oil."

"Doesn't that usually come in plastic bottles?"

Larry turned to him and Garrett saw his usually unruly mop of gray hair was pulled back in a loose pony tail. He had grease smudges on his face that looked like war paint. "This is the used up kind." He let the barrel sit where it was and came toward Garrett. "You go home this morning? Get yourself something to eat?"

Garrett nodded and swallowed hard. "Yeah. And I need to talk to you about that."

They sat in the office as Garrett shared the events of the morning. The only portion he omitted was that he'd barfed up his own breakfast halfway up the driveway. He was surprised that his father listened to it all the way through without interrupting. He'd expected the man to call him a liar or a coward or any other handful of nasty things. But he sat still, head bowed, and let the story be told.

When it was over, Garrett's heart was racing again. His mouth had also gone dry as tinder and even though he still had no appetite, the very thought of eating sickened him - he was dying for a drink. He went to the cooler and grabbed a glass bottle of orange Crush soda. After unscrewing the metal lid, he took a few long swallows and that made him feel a little better.

Upon turning back to his father, he saw the man was still sitting with his head down, like a man in the midst of silent prayer and if Larry Roberts had been the praying kind, Garrett thought it would have been a good time to ask God for some help and guidance.

With nervous, fidgety fingers Garrett began to peel the Styrofoam label off the soda bottle and that tearing sound was the only noise in the office. Except for the thudding static that wafted in from the garage radio, anyway.

Garrett knew the story was hard to digest but he was growing weary of waiting. He wanted to say something, to get his father to look at him instead of the floor, but decided to give it another thirty seconds.

He needed to wait only ten.

"Harrison's been through a lot, Garrett. The doctor who examined him said he had something called a traumatic brain injury, which I suppose is a fancy way of saying he has a concussion. And a bad one."

Garrett struggled to see the correlation and remained quiet.

"On top of the headaches and memory loss, he's been vomiting pretty regular."

"But dad, he—"

Larry held up his hand, his dirt and grease stained palm facing Garrett's way and Garrett closed his mouth. "Now, the doctor guarantees it'll get better but says it will take time. I know I'm a poor one to say this, but we need to be patient with him."

Garrett knew about concussions. Shane had sustained a major

one the summer before when he fell out of a birch tree from almost twenty feet in the air. And Shane had headaches and puked a lot afterward but— "When Shane had his concussion, he didn't barf on his food and then swallow it whole!"

Larry's face may as well have been carved from granite for as much emotion as it showed. He stood, took a step Garrett's way and Garrett instinctively took an equal one back. "You listen now, Garrett. Your brother's been through a lot."

"You already said that." The temerity surprised even Garrett himself. He'd never spoke back to his father quite like this and expected a wallop upside the head and he probably would have deserved it, but saying - no, shouting - these things at his father felt good. Damn good. "I'm tired of you never listening to me. You didn't see what happened this morning, I did! Harrison's not sick. Not in any normal kind of way anyway. He's..."

Larry didn't wallop him. To Garrett's surprise, he didn't do anything but wait for him to finish his sentence. But Garrett had no idea what to say or how to finish because he didn't know what the hell was wrong with his brother, who was acting more like some *thing* than a sixteen year old kid.

A cold, cynical smile came across Larry's face. Garrett preferred the statue look to that.

"He's what, Garrett? What is he?"

"I..." How am I supposed to know, Garrett thought. I'm twelve fracking years old. They didn't teach this shit in sixth grade health class. The closest he'd ever come to anything like this was the movies they watched in the clubhouse.

The movies!

Fireworks exploded behind his eyes because now things began to make sense, albeit in an unbelievable, impossible kind of way.

"He's a monster," Garrett said with complete confidence.

Larry's frigid smirk never wavered. "Oh, is he now? Your brother is a monster?"

It sounded like the title of one of those really cheesy, old movies Ray sometimes rented. *I Was a Teenage Werewolf* or *Uncle Was a Vampire*. The rest of them hated them, but they were good for a laugh sometimes.

He knew it sounded crazy, but he also knew what he saw and that was *crazy*. Crazy and inhuman. "Yeah. He is."

Larry came closer. When Garrett tried to back away again, he hit the wall. Nowhere to go now. "I think you're the monster, Garrett. Making up these bullshit tales about your brother after what he's been through."

Garrett opened his mouth but his father spoke again before he could say anything.

"You used to be a good son, Garret. You get these sick ideas from those friends of yours? Because let me tell you something, them boys only keep you around so they have someone to laugh at and make fun of. You're a clown. A punchline to a bad joke."

Garrett could feel his father's hot breath on his face.

"You think they're your buddies but I don't know how a boy so smart can be so stupid. You aren't their friend, Garrett. In fact, deep down, they all hate you because you're such a goddamn, disgusting, fat pig."

Those words hurt more than any beating his father had ever

given him. He felt fire in his throat and eyes and knew he was going to break down any second, but he wouldn't, couldn't, do that in front of this man. He wouldn't give him the pleasure.

"You get on now and tonight I expect you home. You're gonna apologize to your brother and to me and it best be sincere."

Larry stepped to the side and Garrett wasted no time in running past him and to the back door. He thought he heard the man laugh as he burst into the daylight, but he didn't dare allow himself to react until he'd circled the garage and was back on his bike, riding, fleeing.

Garrett's upper body heaved in sobs and the bike wobbled but he somehow kept it upright. His mind raced from anger to hurt to self pity. His father was the pathetic one. A man with so little control that he beat his children. A man who couldn't keep his wife from drinking herself into oblivion. He probably drove her to it, Garrett thought.

And to say he was disgusting? His dad was the disgusting one, with his greasy hair and shit-brown, nicotine stained teeth.

A realization almost as strong as his earlier lightening bulb moment about movie monsters came to him and he reversed his pedals to bang the bicycle to a halt.

He'd been at the garage for going on an hour and his father hadn't smoked. In his entire life, Garrett couldn't remember Larry Roberts going for more than fifteen waking minutes without a cigarette. Yet now, not a one. And Garrett couldn't even recall the smell of smoke on the man's clothes or on his breath, when usually you could smell him coming five yards away. In a way, his father not smoking was almost as bizarre as his brother barfing on his food before swallowing it like a snake. Almost.

He tried to remember if the ashtray had been on the kitchen table that morning. He didn't think it was, but he couldn't be certain. For a brief, fleeting moment he thought about returning to the trailer to check, but good sense got the better of him. He didn't want to be within miles of his brother or father if he could help it. He wanted to go somewhere safe. Somewhere where he'd be believed.

CHAPTER TWENTY-EIGHT

"Can't you just tell us already? Who knows when those two morons are gonna get here." Shane didn't have to be psychic, or even mildly observant to know something was terribly wrong with his friend. Garrett was pale as a sheet and sat on the edge of the clubhouse's ratty recliner, his right knee bouncing so hard and fast that it made the floor shudder. That, coupled with the building dread, was about ready to drive him nuts. "Seriously, Garrett. What the hell happened?"

Garrett stared past him, toward the clubhouse door. "I'm only gonna be able to get through this once. Everyone's got to be here."

Shane threw a glance Jose's way. The boy gave his shoulders a quick shrug and Shane knew he was going to be of no help.

"Well, shit, then!" Shane grabbed the tennis ball and flopped onto the love seat. He bounced the ball off the ceiling. Apollo, sensing the tension, laid on the floor, head on his paws, not bothering to beg a throw.

Just before Shane's mind could completely snap, the doorknob rattled, but the door didn't open.

"Which one of you cock knockers locked the door?" Lynn said.

Shane rolled onto his side and motioned to Jose. "Get it."

Jose crossed to the door, flipped the lock and opened it. Lynn had been leaning against the door and almost fell inside, stumbling over the big step created by the clubhouse being raised off the ground by concrete cinderblocks. Jose chuckled.

"Dick face." Lynn jumped inside.

Ray was on his heels and pulled the door closed behind him. Shane was ready for Garrett to finally spill the beans, but Ray's physical appearance had been so dramatically altered that he completely forgot about whatever it was Garrett had been holding onto.

Once the proud owner of one of Sallow Creek's finest mullets, Ray now sported a thick, black perm. His hair looped and dangled from his scalp like he had a head covered in caterpillars.

"Oh, sweet Jesus, Ray. What the hell did you do?" Shane asked.

Ray waved his hand in a *shut-up* gesture. "Don't even start on me."

Shane looked at Jose who gawked, his mouth ajar. Even Garrett stared, although he was incapable of working up a smile.

"No. You have to explain that. It would be like me walking in here with a second nose and expecting you not to ask me about it."

Ray scowled, his heavy brow throwing his eyes into shadow. "Screw off. It's a perm. Big deal."

"But you're not a fifty-year-old housewife. Why did you get a perm?"

Ray snuck a look Lynn's way, then gave up. "You know how Lynn's sister is trying to get into the beauty college?"

Shane did. They'd all made their share of jokes about a girl as homely as Charlene Ohler going to beauty school, even Lynn.

"Well, she needed some practice. And I volunteered."

Shane began to laugh. "Did you let her wax your pubes too?"

"He ain't got any." Lynn cackled.

"Obviously," Shane said. "I mean, damn it, Ray. You look like Bob Ross's bastard son."

"I like Bob Ross," Jose piped in.

"But do you want to look like him?" Shane asked.

Jose only shook his head.

"Exactly." Shane turned back to Ray. "I can't even look at you. You need to buzz that shit off. Either that or paint your face like Bozo the Clown and join the carnival when they come to town on Friday because that hair with your face... It's just too much."

Ray wasn't laughing, or even smirking. "Screw off." He looked to Garrett whose leg still quivered. "So, what's the emergency?"

Shane had nearly forgotten about Garrett's news, but now that everyone was here, the story could begin, and Garrett did.

***

It was quite a story, and as far-fetched and made up as it sounded, Shane believed every word of it. Part of that belief stemmed from

Jose's experience at the pool and what followed that at the hardware store and the Whipkey house. But even more was because Garrett couldn't fake the look in his eyes. The fear and shock and hurt. He wasn't that good of an actor. Hell, Al Pacino wasn't that good of an actor.

Upon completion of the tale, Garrett's eyes were wet but he wasn't crying. He managed to hold himself together and Shane thought that was damn admirable. He reached over and patted his friend's knee, sort of like he did with Apollo when the dog seemed dejected. At twelve, he wasn't quite sure what other kind of affection to offer.

"I'm sorry, Garrett." The words sounded pointless and empty considering all he'd been through.

"You believe me though? Because it all really happened. I'm not crazy or making it up, it—"

"I believe you." Shane looked side to side where Jose, Lynn, and Ray sat, all wore the same shocked expressions. "We all believe you."

The other boys nodded and Garrett's shoulders, which had been full of tension, sagged and his shining eyes widened in relief.

It made Shane feel better to see some of Garrett's anxiety leave him, but they still needed to figure out what was really happening. He grabbed a marker and a binder of 11x14 art paper and flipped past some drawings he'd made, mostly comic book stuff, but a few portraits that he actually thought had potential, until he came to a blank page. "We need a plan."

"Thanks, Commander Obvious."

Shane ignored Lynn's jab and scribbled words onto the page, not letting the other boys see until he was finished. Then he turned it toward them. It was a bullet list with the heading: *Monster To Do List*.

The others read over them silently. Shane noticed that Ray's lips moved as he read. It was obvious that Garrett finished first because his eyes left the page and went to Shane, who was suddenly struck by a realization. For him, this was a scary but exciting adventure. For Garrett, this was about his family. He wished he'd have used more candor in making the list.

"I'm sorry, Garrett." Shane found it hard to make eye contact, something that had never happened before with his best friend. "I know this must be extra shitty for you."

He knew Garrett wouldn't yell or punch him or react in any dramatic way. That wasn't his style. But he might give him a good scolding and Shane thought he would have deserved one.

Instead, Garrett shook his head. "I don't think I could say this to anyone but you guys, but now that the shock of it's wore off, I don't think I care."

They all watched him, intrigued.

"Yeah, they're my family, but they're awful too. I wouldn't have wished anything bad to happen, but when Harrison was gone, I was happy. And if my dad just disappeared, I wouldn't mind that much either. Because, I guess, I would be free for the first time."

"But then you'd be an orphan," Jose said, emphasizing the last word like it was the worst thing imaginable. "You'd have to live at the Children's Aide Home."

Shane didn't like this turn in the conversation but felt like he'd created it and now had to let it run its course. "A nice kid like

Garrett wouldn't be there long. Remember Lonnie Carouthers back in the second grade."

"The kid that ate his boogers? And had the boil on his forehead?" Ray nodded as he said it, answering his own questions. "That kid was a world-class weirdo."

Shane nodded. "Yeah. And even he got adopted. So Garrett would be fine." He looked at Garrett and found he was grinning.

"Gee, thanks, Shane."

"Anytime, buddy. Hell, you could even live here in the clubhouse. I doubt my parents would mind. You could bunk with the dog."

"This keeps getting better." Garrett ruffled Apollo's fur, but his expression shifted back to serious. "My dad and brother, they're so damn mean. It's hard for me to feel too bad about this. I guess that makes me sound like a shit."

"No." Shane said, but he thought it did, at least a little. As bad as Garrett's family was, they were still his family. He couldn't imagine being so blasé if something similar happened to his own mom and dad, but then again his folks didn't beat and torment him either.

Garrett looked at Shane then, at all of them, his gaze so earnest it almost hurt to look back. "But if whatever is happening to my dad and brother happened to you, I'd probably go find the nearest tree branch and hang myself. Same for you, Jose, and Ray. And probably even you, Lynn."

Lynn sneered. "Go eat a bag of dicks."

"Not if your sister gets there first." As soon as the words came out, Garrett's hands flew over his mouth as if he could shove them back in. Lynn looked as if he could be knocked over by a feather.

Shane broke out in a wild grin. "Holy shit! Garrett had a comeback. A good— No a fucking great one!" He rabbit punched his friend on the arm and Garrett's face went red. "There's hope for you yet."

They all laughed, the seriousness of the moment, of the entire day, vanquished. And God, that was a relief.

The first objective on the list, and Shane thought the most important, was: *Figure out who's been turned into a monster.*

"Now, the odds that Garret's two and the Whipkey family are the only folks in Sallow Creek to have been turned or infected or whatever the hell's going on are slimmer than Lynn's pecker."

Lynn chucked him not one, but two middle fingers.

"So we need to figure out how many we're up against," Shane finished.

"Where do we even start?" Garrett sounded overwhelmed but excited.

"The carnival."

"And what exactly are we looking for there?" Lynn asked.

"Anyone acting weird."

Lynn turned to Ray, grinning like the Cheshire Cat. "Genius over there thinks he can pick out the monster kind of weirdos from the regular weirdos. And this is our leader?"

Ray shrugged his shoulders. "You got any better ideas?"

Lynn's grin faded away and that was answer enough.

CHAPTER TWENTY-NINE

The calliope blared *Entry of the Gladiators* as the five friends strolled through the gates of the fair. The residents of Sallow Creek had turned out in scores. Farmers mingled with white collar businessmen, housewives shepherded their raucous children from booth to booth. A teenage boy, his face a connect the dots puzzle of zits, carried a stuffed, blue bear almost as big as himself in one arm and had the other wrapped around the waist of a plain girl wearing flannel and cowboy boots.

Mixed amongst the townsfolk, clowns danced while mimes juggled bowling pins and bright, colored balls. Fat barkers beckoned easy marks in to play impossible to win games and scantily clad women who might have been attractive ten years ago sashayed up and down the midway hawking overpriced pretzels and hot dogs and cotton candy.

"Yeah. No one weird here. No one at all." Lynn said, dead serious and the grave quality of his voice made all the others laugh.

"Screw off." Shane gave him a playful shove.

Lynn and Ray started away.

"Remember," Shane said. "Keep your eyes open. Don't just eat crap and go on the rides."

"Yes, bossman." Lynn gave a firm salute. "We'll do as told."

They laughed as they ran off and Garrett couldn't blame them. They hadn't seen anything and even though they said they believed him, he was sure a part of them, maybe a big part, must have doubts.

He hadn't been home in several days and, so far as he knew, his father had made no attempts to find him. He'd already planned, should his father come looking, to call the cop, Trooper Hanes, and tell him the truth about his smashed hand and other past beatings. He'd leave out the supernatural, if that's what they were, aspects though. He might be a kid, but he knew better than to try and convince a grown up of the things he'd seen.

Garrett was wondering if you stopped believing in monsters about the time you grew hair on your pubes, but such hypothesizing was interrupted when Jose grabbed his wrist.

"Ride the Spider with me!" Jose pulled him in that direction.

Garrett watched as its black cars spun and rose and dipped and spun some more over white accents that were painted to look like webs. Even though they'd come here with a mission, it looked like too much fun to pass up. "Okay!"

He looked to Shane who hung back. "Chicken?" Garrett asked.

"You know I can't do the ones that spin in a circle." Shane puffed out his cheeks and mimicked barfing. "Go. Ride. I'll be around."

Garrett and Jose rushed toward the ride, made it two yards, then Garrett looked back. "Be on the lookout for Della Kinsinger!"

Shane chucked him the bird and Garrett giggled as he and Jose continued to the Spider. They flashed their *unlimited rides* wristbands at the operator, who was as tall and skinny as a scarecrow and was only missing a hat and some straw poking out of his shirt sleeves. He gave a low grunt and waved them past the waist high gate that opened into the ride.

"Together or separate?" Garrett asked.

"Together." Jose's eyes were gleeful, but there was a bit of fear in them too. The good kind though, the kind especially loved by boys of a certain age.

They climbed into the nearest car and the ride operator banged the safety bar into place, then trudged away to lock in the next set of riders.

As they waited, Garrett's eyes scanned the crowd. He thought about finding weirdos, but he realized it was impossible here. And maybe the search could wait a little while longer and they could pretend that everything was still perfect and that they were normal twelve year olds. Just one more night, he thought. Then the red lights that were the spider's eyes blazed and the ride lurched into action.

CHAPTER THIRTY

SHANE HATED BEING TEASED ABOUT HIS CRUSH, BUT Garrett was right. His infatuation with Della Kinsinger stemmed back to first grade when his desk was positioned next to hers for the entire school year. During those nine months, she probably said less than nine words to him and that hadn't changed much over the years. She was aloof at best, and kind of a bitch at worst, and for some twisted reason, he found that irresistible.

As he strolled through the carnival, he looked for her. And weirdos, he told himself. But mostly her. For the longest while he thought she wasn't there. That even though there was little else to do in Sallow Creek on a Friday night, she'd skipped the carnival entirely. But then he circled the merry-go-round and found her straddling the unicorn and that seemed pretty much perfect.

Shane waited for the ride to slow before making his way to the exit, timing it so that he just so happened to be strolling by when she walked out and his arm brushed against her side.

"Excuse me," he said, pretending as if he had no idea who he'd bumped into until their eyes met. "Oh. Della. Hi. I didn't even see you there."

"Hi, Shane." She looked past him, toward the crowd.

Probably seeking out her friends, Shane thought. "You having fun tonight?"

"Sure." She still stared away.

He considered moving on. That would have been the cool thing to do, to act indifferent and hard to get. But he had a feeling with Della Kinsinger, out of sight was out of mind. "Want to try the shooting booth? I came within one target of getting one of those giant, stuffed lions earlier."

She finally turned her attention back to him. "Yeah?"

"Yeah." He was feeling more confident now. "Never know, you could be my good luck charm."

Della smiled. Well, not really smiled, Shane thought. It was more of a mildly amused smirk, the kind you get when your four year old cousin tries to tell you a joke and gets the punchline wrong, but you don't want him to feel bad.

Then she wrinkled her nose. "Those things are a pain in the ass to carry."

Shot down again. "Yeah. They are." Salvage whatever pride you have left and leave, he told himself. And he almost did when—

"We could ride the Ferris wheel though."

He stared, certain he'd heard wrong.

"Well? Want to?" Della raised her eyebrows, inquisitive.

"Why not?"

They made the ten or so yard trek to the ride in silence and all the while Shane wondered if Garrett or any of the others were seeing this. Part of him wanted them too, because his years long obsession with the girl had made him the subject of so many taunts, but another part, and possibly a bigger one, wanted this to stay private. Sure, he'd tell his friends about it later, probably that very night, but at that moment, he wanted it to be only the two of them.

They took their spots in the car, sitting a casual distance apart, then were locked in by the safety bar. The ride chugged forward and stopped while more riders got on board, a stop and start action that was repeated five more times before a voice called up from below. "Start 'er spinning!"

As music played they rose higher and higher into the air, which grew progressively cooler the further up they went. The people below looked like ants teeming through a maze of matchbox obstacles. Shane shifted his attention from what was under them, to who was beside him.

Della stared off to the side, not looking at anything but the black sky and he thought that, as far as expectations went, this was rather subpar. They crested the top of the wheel with so much speed that his thin hair floated out around him, then began their descent.

After swooping to the bottom, they climbed again and Shane knew his time with a captive Della Kinsinger was running out. As the saying went, it was now or never.

He moved his hand from his lap, to the vacant area on the seat between them, inching it over until his little finger brushed her thigh. It was a light touch, but she noticed and turned to him.

The cycling rainbow of lights around them illuminated her hair. First green, then blue, then red. She was a pretty girl. Not beautiful, or even exceptional in any particular way, but at that moment, looking at her, Shane's breath caught in his throat and he realized this might be more than a crush.

She hadn't developed much on top yet, but her checkered blouse must have been a hold-over from the previous summer and a few of the buttons strained, the material pulling apart. Through the gaps, he could see the pristine, white lace of her bra.

"You can touch them, if you want."

He'd been staring, not meaning to, but that didn't change anything and now he looked to her face. That same mildly amused grin tugged at her lips.

"I can?"

She nodded and her delicate fingers moved to the buttons under duress. One came undone. More bra was revealed. Another button popped open. Even more bra, and now smooth, milky skin showed too. Skin so private even the sun had never touched it. But he could. She'd told him so.

The Ferris wheel thudded to a halt, snapping him out of his mesmerized daze and he saw they were stopped at the very top. No one could see them. They may as well have been the only two kids in the entire world.

"I want you to." Della said and he noticed her apple-colored lips were full, inviting. He wondered if he should kiss her first. That was first base, after all and you didn't simply run from home plate to second. Yeah he thought, I'll kiss her under the stars, then get a nice handful.

As Shane leaned into her, Della unfastened a third button and the top half of her blouse sagged open. The movement in his peripheral vision made him glance down and he saw—

No, that couldn't be—

Worms—

Her bra, which was indeed pristine and white and silken, had slipped to her waist but where it had been, there were no breasts, not even buds of breasts. There were—

Worms. Hundreds of worms.

Only these worms didn't hang limp and sanguine like earthworms before you impaled them on hooks for bait. These worms stood at attention, like soldiers poised for attack. Their long bodies were the color of rotting kelp, a sickly combination of green and brown and the slime that oozed from their undulating forms was pus yellow. The color of infection.

The worms strained at him, reaching for him. They whipped furiously, the slimy mucous that secreted from their bodies raining through the air like spittle from a man with a bad stutter. Some of it hit Shane in the face and it felt cold and burn-y at the same time. He wiped it away like it was acid.

The insanity of the situation was almost too much to comprehend but he knew this all tied in with Garrett's brother and the girl at the pool. Only they're worms, not snakes, Donnatella, he thought. His eyes followed the worms back to Della, trying to understand.

He'd first thought they'd crawled out of her, like some gaping crevice had opened in her prepubescent chest and bore the creatures, but what he saw disproved that. The worms hadn't come from within her, they came *from* her. They were attached to her and the closer they got to her body, their own bodies changed color and texture, appearing more like the pallid, pale skin of the girl.

They're not worms at all, he thought. They're more like tentacles. Or antennas or—

He didn't have any more time to think because the things were closer, they were stretching and growing longer. They were less than a foot from him.

Shane looked over the edge of their motionless gondola, straining to see the ride's operator.

"Start the ride!" Shane screamed. "Get me down!" His voice had gone high pitched and shrill, the whine of an eight-year-old not the young man he was becoming. If I live that long, he thought.

"Help me!"

He felt hot wetness on his face that first reminded him of the worms' slime, but then he realized it was tears. He was sobbing. "Please get me down!"

But they were 150 feet in the air. No one on the ground could hear him. We're all alone, he reminded himself.

"Quit crying you pussy!" A man collared from below.

Okay, not completely alone.

Shane looked back to the worms, which were six inches away. They strained, pulling themselves straight as rods.

Stretching.

Growing.

He took another look at Della's face which had gone limp, her eyes as dull as clay marbles. Her skin looked like an ice cream cone on a hot day, melting from the top down. Her chin had disappeared under a heavy mound of sagging flesh that morphed directly to her shoulders. If she was fat, she'd look like Jabba the Hut, Shane thought and if he hadn't thought he was going to die within the next thirty seconds, he might have laughed.

He didn't want to die. There was the usual, primal urge to survive, of course, but an even bigger part of him wanted to live through this so he could tell his friends what happened and so they could try to stop it. Because, dude, this was some crazy shit.

Shane's back was pressed tight against the side of the car. He reached behind and pushed himself up. His thin body easily passed by the safety bar and he was on his feet.

The gondola rocked, slow at first, but momentum quickly grew and he thought he might lose his balance. Lights and music and the din of the crowd below added to the dizzying confusion that filled his head.

"Hey!" That sounded like the asshole who'd called him a pussy. "Sit down you dumbass!" Yeah, it was him.

But staying in the car meant certain death. At least out here, away from the worm-tentacle things, at least he had a chance. Not much of one, but he'd take whatever he could get.

He lifted his right foot, pulled it back over the nothingness that was behind him, then did the same with his left. His hands gripped the edge of the teetering gondola. Ten fingers held him fifty yards in the air.

A woman in a car below screamed. Shane's legs flailed, straining for the ride's frame, something solid, and eventually found it. He looked down and saw both his feet planted on a four inch wide steel bar, then carefully crouched down so he could grip that lifeline with his hands.

The whipping, swirling noise of the worms drew his attention upward and when he tilted his head back, he could see the tips of them extending over the car.

They're still coming for me. Fuckers.

"Some kid climbed out of his car!" Someone shouted. More voices followed, a cascade of them down the ride. Shane ignored them all.

He scooted backward, away from the gondola with Della and her tentacle offspring. Progress was slow, but he wouldn't - couldn't - allow himself to stop.

In the middle of his next shuffling step, the Ferris wheel began to turn. The first lurching jolt of movement shook him so hard his right foot slipped off the beam and he tilted sideways hard and fast. Someone else screamed but he blocked it all out. He held tighter with his hands and regained his balance, then replanted his foot on the steel.

Shane risked a glance behind himself and saw a spoke was only a few feet away now. If he could get to that and hold on, he could ride this sucker the rest of the way to the bottom.

He scooted a step, then another, and another.

"You loony! You're gonna die!" That was the asshole again.

Not today, dickhead, he thought. He grinned and realized he was still crying. He wiped away the wetness with the back of his hand and strained to see the man who'd been taunting him below. "I'm not planning on it!"

Shane took another step. And then fell.

CHAPTER THIRTY-ONE

Ray had downed an entire cone of cotton candy all by himself and, as a result, his lips were bright blue.

"You look like you're dying of hypothermia." Lynn's own mouth was half filled with a chili dog. A bean had escaped and clung to his upper lip like an oversized mole.

The sight of the hot dog still made Ray queasy, but he muscled past it and moved on to a funnel cake. The two of them sat at a forest green picnic table, its top littered with trash and peanut shells and it was sticky with spilled sodas, but neither of them minded. The filth was part of the fun.

Ray had broken off a piece of dessert the size of a playing card when he took notice of a middle-aged woman in a bright and busy floral print dress. She stood beside one of the snack booths, the one selling nachos and French fries, but wasn't eating or drinking anything. She only stared ahead in a vacant, looking but not seeing kind of way. Gooseflesh prickled over Ray's forearms.

"You see her?" Ray flicked his finger in her direction, trying to be discrete.

"Who?" Lynn craned his neck, not being discrete in the slightest.

"Flower dress." Ray tilted his head down but kept his eyes aimed her way. She still hadn't moved at all.

"What about her?" Lynn hadn't swallowed his hot dog but nonetheless took another bite, his cheeks bulging out like a chipmunk gathering sustenance for a long winter.

"She looks kind of weird, doesn't she?"

Lynn looked from the woman to Ray. "*You* look kind of weird."

Ray set his funnel cake aside, his appetite on hiatus. "Shut up. You know what I mean."

Lynn took a large swallow of soda to wash down the food. "All right. All right." He looked at her again, this time for a good half a minute. All the while she stood motionless and when Lynn spoke again, the bravado was gone from his voice. "Yeah, she's kind of creepy. Just standing there like the fucking guy in the civil war monument uptown."

"Should we check her out?" Ray wasn't sure what that even meant or how to do it. He wished Shane was with them. This was his plan and, even if it hadn't been, he always knew what to do.

"Like how? Hand her a hot pretzel and ask her if she wants a side order of barf?"

That actually didn't sound half bad. Ray looked to the woman again, only now her face was aimed his way. She was staring at him. "Oh crap!" He crouched down in his seat plastering his elbows against the table, feeling the stale soda sticking to the thin, immature hair on his arms and holding them fast. "She saw me!"

Lynn crouched down too. His back was to the woman and he dared not look. "What's she doing? Is she coming?"

Ray snuck a quick peek. She was gone. "Shit!"

"What? What is it?"

"She's not there now. I lost her." Ray risked taking a better look. He had to sit up further to see, his eyes scanning left, then right, then back again like he was getting ready to cross a street.

The woman in the flower dress was nowhere to be seen.

"Come on, man," Lynn said.

Ray saw he was shaking all over and vowed that, if they got out of this, he was going to totally bust his ass over being such a pussy. Never mind the fact that he was just as scared.

It was while Ray watched Lynn quiver that the gaudy, floral print appeared behind him. It was five yards away, but closing in. Slow and steady, closer and closer.

The horror must have overtaken his face because Lynn's eyes grew wide. "What? What? Tell me."

Ray could feel his feet shuffling under the table. Screw being a hero, he was ready to run. The dress was so close to Lynn that its wearer could have reached out and touched him.

"There you are!"

Both boys jumped in their seats, Ray so far that he banged his knees on the underside of the table. He forced himself to look up, past a cowering Lynn, and to the woman.

When his eyes found her face, he saw a crooked but broad smile. She wasn't looking at him, or at Lynn, but instead past the table. "I thought you was gonna stand me up."

Both boys turned and saw a portly man in a Marlboro shirt and jeans striding in their general direction. The woman moved away from their table and to him and then the two embraced. "Damn lot's so full I had to park half a mile away." The man huffed, out of breath, and then the couple moved toward the midway.

When Ray calmed down enough to remember Lynn, he looked and saw his friend glaring at him. "I fucking hate you."

Ray burped up a nervous laugh. "Are you going to leave that bean there until it takes root." He tapped his own lip.

Lynn's fingers scrabbled at his mouth, quickly discovering the sticky chili bean and pulling it free. A dash of red remained behind, like an old scar. He flung the bean at Ray, who ducked and it whizzed over his head. "Asshole."

"Split my funnel cake and call it even?"

Lynn raised one eyebrow, considering the offer. "Deal."

CHAPTER THIRTY-TWO

THE WHITE SHAVED ICE OF THE SLUSHY TURNED BLOOD RED as the man working the concession stand added raspberry flavoring. "That enough?" He asked.

"A little more, please." Garrett loved the tart taste and watched as the man gave it another two squirts, then accepted it when he handed it over. "Thank you."

"Sure kid. Have fun out there."

Garrett spun away from the stand, his eyes drifting across the crowd until he saw Jose, then went to him.

The small boy was trying to throw metal hoops over stuffed animals. The current toss got hung up on a blue and silver horse's tail. "Darn it!" Jose said, biting down on his bottom lip in frustration.

"I never took you for the horsey type." Garrett giggled.

"Almost had it, pal," the carny running the booth said in a singsong kind of voice. He had tired, droopy eyes and a bulbous nose that was almost as red as Rudolph's. Garrett could see over-sized pores on that schnoz and thought the blackheads filling them in looked like spilled pepper.

Jose handed another dollar bill to the carny and in return the carny gave him three more hoops. He glanced at Garrett. "It's for Don. She's crazy about the things. My parents are getting her riding lessons for her birthday but don't say anything. It's a surprise."

Garrett held his thumb and forefinger to his lips, which were already red with raspberry flavoring, and locked them. Even though he had no interest in having a baby sister, especially one as spoiled as Donnatella Supranowicz, he felt a little stab of jeal-ousy over their relationship and wondered why Harrison never cared about him as much as Jose cared about his sibling. Was it all because he was fat? Did that make him unworthy of being loved, or even liked?

Jose's first toss bounced off the horse's head and the second snagged around its neck. Garrett knew games like this were nearly impossible to win, that's why he saved his money for food, but he wished Jose would somehow defy the odds. He deserved it for being so kind, if nothing else.

His friend was aiming up the third and final hoop when screams down the midway stole their attention. They weren't the high, lilting screams of people scared on the rides or someone feigning terror over one of the roaming clowns. These were real screams. Real fear.

And like sailors to a siren's song, the crowd of carnival goers seemed to ebb in that direction, moving toward the danger rather than away from it.

Garrett was no different and Jose didn't even bother with his third toss. It didn't matter because the carny's attention was also on the out of sight commotion and wouldn't have paid out even if he'd made that impossibly perfect throw.

"Have you seen the others?" Jose asked him and Garrett could hear the worry in his voice.

"No." He felt guilty for buying the slushy, for not paying attention.

The density of the crowd grew steadily thicker. They had to push their way through, bumping into backs, bouncing off arms. The tall adults in the growing throng made it impossible to see anything other than heads and shoulders. For Garrett, this added to the tension. What was up there? What was going on?

The alarmed, scared voices were louder now, a clamoring chorus. Random words rose above others.

Fell.

Kid.

Dead.

This sounded bad. Really bad.

"Garrett!" Ray's husky voice came from behind.

When he turned he saw Lynn and Ray, their faces panicked. His relief in seeing them was short-lived when he realized one of their party was still missing. The four of them huddled together.

"You hear what happened?" Lynn asked.

Garrett shook his head.

"Someone climbed out of their car on the Ferris Wheel when it was stopped at the very top. The ride operator didn't see in time and started it back up. Made it a little over halfway down before they fell."

"Who was it?"

Lynn shrugged his shoulders.

"I think it's Shane." Jose's brown eyes seemed to have grown twice their normal size.

The memory of teasing Shane about riding the Ferris wheel with Della rushed back. But that was a wild coincidence, right? It had to be. "Why? Why would you think that?" He didn't admit that he'd just had the same thought.

"I don't know. Just a feeling."

Shane couldn't be dead. Even the slimmest possibility that it might be true made Garrett feel like barfing up everything he'd eaten that night. And, if Shane was dead, it was his fault because he was the one that dragged him into this. That dragged all of them into it.

"Oh man," Ray said, his breathing speeding up. "This is real bad. If Shane's up there, splattered all over the ground, I think I'll go nuts. They'll have to put me in the state hospital or something because—"

Lynn punched him in the arm. "Shut up!"

"Come on!" Garrett pushed ahead.

They were unable to walk now, the crowd was too thick, so they plowed through the spectators, not caring who they crashed into or offended. Another thirty seconds of shoving and they neared the front where the crowd stopped suddenly as if invisible barricades held them back. Garrett used his heft to break an opening through the front line and they could finally see.

The Ferris wheel loomed high above them, motionless. Its music had gone silent, the lights shut off. To the right of the wheel, the shattered remains of a clapboard booth lay on the ground. The bright, multicolored canopy that had enveloped it was deflated and stomped into the ground. Stuffed animals of all colors and sizes littered the area like spent shrapnel.

A smaller group of people stared, many of their faces vaguely familiar as Sallow Creek residents. The guy who owned the discount grocery store on Plank Road, a janitor from the school, a busty brunette who used to waitress at Luigi's.

And Della Kinsinger. The sight of her made him more convinced that the kid, the possibly dead kid, was Shane. She stared at the carnage with the others.

"You stupid shitass!" A man's voice screamed, his throaty intonation muddied by anger and fear. "You stupid shitass bastard! You stupid shitass almost gave me a heart attack!"

Garrett searched for the screaming man and found him. He was near the destroyed game booth. His back was turned to them, but they watched his arms flail, his fists pound the air.

"I should beat your stupid shitass brains in for this! What the fuck were you trying to pull?"

There came a noise, a hard, wooden sound. Boards and siding being scraped against each other.

"You stay right there, you shitass. You stay right there until the cops get here."

Through the chaos, Garrett saw movement in front of the man. Someone rising from the rubble.

"I told you to—"

It was Shane. Garrett saw him scramble to his feet, then break into a limping run.

"Get back here, you shitass!"

The big carny tried to give chase, and another carnival worker made a lunging grab, but Shane was young and lithe and slipped away without any great effort. He darted into the throng of onlookers, disappearing amid them, and all the fear Garrett had felt vanished with him.

"Let's go!" He shouted to the others and together they retreated through the crowd.

They caught up and regrouped near the bumper cars. Garrett immediately noticed scrapes and scratches all over Shane's exposed skin. A deep gash on his wrist seeped blood. A ragged cut at his jawline had already clotted.

"Holy shit!" Lynn said. "Did you really fall off the Ferris wheel?"

Shane bent slightly at the waist, wincing and catching his breath. "Fifty feet," he said. That number would grow in the coming days, eventually topping out around one hundred as he told and retold the tale.

"Are you okay?" Garrett's anxiety was coming back now that he realized how close his best friend came to dying.

"I'm fine. Mostly. I fell right through one of the game booths. All those stuffed bears, it was like landing on a feather bed." He grinned and even managed a laugh.

Lynn joined in and Ray snickered but Garrett was a long way from finding humor in this. "How'd you fall?"

Shane's grin faded. He looked at them, serious now. "I'll tell you everything but not here." He stared at Garrett. "It's a lot worse than we thought, buddy."

CHAPTER THIRTY-THREE

IN THE CLUBHOUSE, THEIR SAFE HAVEN, SHANE TOLD THEM everything, down to the most minute, gory details. It seemed to him that this was becoming a ritual of sorts. Baring their souls within these plywood walls. And just as when Garrett shared his story, no one doubted that everything that was said was true.

"Fucking aliens!" Lynn banged his hand on the floor sending up a puff of dust and making Apollo flinch. "I should've known it."

"Why do you think it's aliens," Ray asked, his eyes wide and panicked.

"It's got to be, man. Their skin turns into tentacle things. When you put two and two together with Donnatella's eating the snake bit, that means the tentacles get inside you and infect you or some shit. Then you've got Harrison barfing on his food to soften it up so he can slurp it down?" He added a *sluuurrrrrp*. "Fucking aliens!"

Shane had been on the same train of thought. They'd watched hundreds of horror movies in this clubhouse and there weren't any monsters that behaved like this. And while he knew the movies were made up, Shane also believed nothing of this world could behave in the way as what he'd seen.

"She was okay after." Garrett's words came out in a near whisper. He'd remained so quiet throughout it all that Shane had almost forgotten he was there.

"What?"

Garrett swallowed hard. "Della. I saw her there, under the Ferris wheel. She was fine. Normal. Not all melty like you said she was on the ride."

"See!" Lynn smacked the floor again and even Apollo looked annoyed with him.

"Stop that," Shane said to him.

He hadn't seen Della after his swan dive and part of him thought, hoped even, she'd still be a puddle of skin in the gondola. Now that he knew she, or the thing that she'd become, was able to... renew itself... That part creeped him out even more. "Damn." It was all he could think to say.

"Now what?" Ray's panicked expression hadn't dimmed. If anything, it now bordered on terrified. "How do we fight aliens? I mean, they flew all the fuck the way across the galaxy and we're a bunch of dumb kids who haven't been out of Pennsylvania."

"I went to Canada." They all looked to Jose. "When we went to Niagara Falls."

"Oh, I forgot," Ray said. "Did the Mounties teach you how to kill aliens, Jose?"

Jose stayed silent.

"I didn't think so." Ray had been laying on his side, his head resting against a rolled up sleeping bag, but now he sat up, his curls falling into his face. "So, what do we do?"

"Well, I learned the hard way that it's going to be damn near impossible to pick these things out of a crowd. They look totally normal until it comes time to infect you or maybe impregnate you. Or, shit, what if they eat you? I don't know what they do for sure because I got away just in time."

Shane cracked his knuckles, a habit his mother ragged him about, said it was going to give him arthritis when he got old, but he couldn't stop. And, the way things were shaping up, getting old seemed far from a guarantee "So, I say we go to the two places we know the bastards are living." As far as plans went, it wasn't much, Shane thought, but it was better than nothing.

CHAPTER THIRTY-FOUR

SHANE'S FATHER HAD A BOX OF WALKIE TALKIES THAT HE dragged out once a year during hunting season. After putting in fresh batteries, Shane kept one for himself and gave one to each of the others, except for Garrett. They were one short and Garrett didn't need or want a radio because he didn't plan to be more than an arm's distance away from Shane if he could help it.

The mission, such that it was, involved staking out the two known residences of the creatures they now all assumed were aliens. The Roberts' abode and the Whipkey house. Garrett's only request, when it came to the plan, was that he not have to go back to his home and they all agreed that was for the best. "It's like how a doctor can't operate on his own kid," Ray had said and although the analogy was imperfect, it was close enough.

Ray and Lynn would stake out the trailer while Garrett, Shane, and Jose tackled the Whipkey's home. They were to stay there until sun up or until they saw something weird, whichever came first.

Four hours later, Garrett fought to keep his eyes open. He sat with his back against a picket fence, his head lolling on his shoulders. He shook his noggin every few seconds, trying to stay awake. Beside him, Shane aimlessly spun the volume dial on the walkie. Jose was sprawled in the grass and Garrett was almost certain he was asleep.

The Whipkey house was dormant and had been since their arrival. All the lights were off and, as the Christmas poem went, 'Not a creature was stirring.' Garrett found this a combination of boring, disappointing, and a relief.

Shane yawned, his own eyes bleary. "I thought we'd see something helpful. Maybe other people coming and going, getting their worm tanks topped off or something. More people to add to the 'persona non grata list.'"

"I was hoping for UFO's." Garrett looked to the sky where stars twinkled and the moon waxed. "The mothership coming down and taking all the bastards back to planet Kandah or wherever they came from."

"That too," Shane flicked his hand at the house. "Instead... Nothing."

"Who knew aliens had to sleep?" Garrett said.

Shane looked over and there was just enough moonlight for Garrett to see him grin. "Learn something new every day."

Garrett nodded. "The more you know."

They fell silent for a little while. Shane eventually spoke up. "I was so fucking scared, Garrett. I didn't play up that part in front of the other guys but, Christ, I was this close." He held his thumb and index finger mere millimeters apart, "To totally losing my shit. I think the only way I kept it together was thinking about you."

That surprised Garrett even more than the admission of fear. "Me?"

"Yeah. I needed you to know what was going on because, let's face it, Ray and Lynn, they're good foot soldiers but they're never going to win a war single-handed you know. Someone smart has to figure this shit out. Like you." He broke into a wider grin, revealing his near perfect teeth which looked even whiter than usual in the moonlight. "Or me, of course."

"I hate you." The voice drifted in from the grass where Jose laid. They both looked and saw him staring their way. "Couple of egomaniacs. Think you've got all the brains. You're the one who thought Della Kinsinger was gonna let you touch her boobies. How's that for dumb?"

"I was blinded by passion," Shane said.

"Blinded by your ding a ling is more like it."

"Like you wouldn't have done the same if it was you with Laura Lynch."

Jose had no comeback for that one. Shane grabbed a pine cone off the ground and tossed it underhanded at the boy. It skidded by him. "Anyway, mucho apologies, señor."

Jose sat up, fighting off a yawn. "Stick your sorry's up your butt-hole. I'm not even gonna miss you while I'm at camp."

"Will you miss me?" Garrett tried to sound earnest but his grin-ning lips betrayed him.

"Nope. Not a bit. You rocket scientists can go fight aliens while I use my little bird brain to weave baskets and run the three-legged race with Don."

Garrett almost said that he'd rather be with him, weaving baskets, but that would have been a lie. Because, even though when he really thought about what was going on, or at least what they thought was going on, he was terrified, he was also excited.

But right now, he was tired. "Let's go. Jose needs to rest up. He has a busy day of singing hymns and throwing pottery ahead of him."

Jose made a shooting gun motion with his finger, but he was smiling too.

Shane held the walkie to his mouth. "Dumbass Number One and Dumbass Number Two, come in."

A pause, then a static crack. "You're the dumbass, fucker. Over"

Garrett and Shane shared a smile and mouthed *Lynn* simultaneously.

"Any action your way?" Shane asked.

"It's darker inside this trailer than Mike Tyson's asshole. Over." Lynn said.

"Same here. Go home for the night." Garrett's eyes widened with panic and as soon as Shane noticed he whispered, "Not you, moron." Then back into the radio. "Try to come up with some good ideas and get some sleep"

As the three of them grabbed their bikes the radio crackled one more time. "Okay. Over."

Shane shook his head. "Why does he keep saying *over*? All he has to do is stop talking."

"Because they do it that way in the movies," Jose said.

"And he wonders why he's Dumbass Number One."

They were two miles from Shane's house, and the clubhouse, heading south on Patriot Street and passing the only remaining open business on that end of town - Mel's Bar. Unlike the dive at the end of Garrett's road, this establishment served food in addition to booze, but the clientele it attracted wasn't much better.

The rusty, metal door swung open with a *scree* sound and Garrett jumped, his bike wobbling before he regained control.

"You good?" Shane asked.

Although he was still spooked, Garrett nodded. "Yeah."

A woman stepped out of the doorway and tall, broad man in a trucker's cap was close behind. Garrett first assumed the man was pushing her out, like a bouncer kicking a disorderly drunk to the curb, but then realized the guy had his hand cupped over the woman's ample, sagging breasts. He laughed under his breath.

"If they were twenty years younger I'd stick around and watch the show." Shane had parked his bike beside Garrett. "But geriatric porn sounds like something more up Lynn's alley."

Things were heating up fast between the old couple and Garrett noticed the dude's left hand move away from the woman's tit, instead sliding into the waistband of her pants. She groaned in old, raspy pleasure.

"Oh shit." Shane grabbed his arm and shook it. "Do you see who that is?"

Garrett looked closer, most of his attention on the guy, and drew a blank. He looked like any random guy, aside from a tattoo of a Ford logo on his forearm. "No."

"Oh geez," Jose said, his voice a squeak. "It's Mighty Mole!"

"No..." Garrett looked closer. The light was dim, throwing down ghastly green shadows, but now that the thought had been implanted into his brain it was impossible to not see, even with her face hidden. Mighty Mole was there in all her glory, swapping spit with some random dude. And it was hideous.

"Retreat! Retreat!" Shane said, his feet spinning the bike's pedals as it picked up speed.

Jose snickered from behind him and followed. "We'll have to bleach our eyeballs!"

If the boys had waited around even two more minutes, they would have seen Mighty Mole aka Maud pull the dude's face in close to her own. They would have heard his muffled screams. They would have seen the worms. But by the time that happened, they were halfway to Shane's house and Mighty Mole was already nothing more than a memory.

CHAPTER THIRTY-FIVE

Ray split off from Lynn at the entrance to the towers and they promised to reunite the next day. Lynn meant it too, but he neglected to tell Ray that he wasn't going home just yet. As soon as his friend was out of sight, Lynn steered his bike in a wide, looping circle and returned to the road.

He believed the stories Shane and Garrett and Jose had told. As much as you could believe anything you hadn't seen with your own two eyes, that is. Yet part of him struggled to comprehend it. He'd believed in monsters even before these events, but he believed in them the same way he'd believed in Santa Claus and the Tooth Fairy up until he was eight or so. It was an abstract, unproven belief. He guessed it was the same kind of belief Jose had in God. There was no way to prove it, so you just went along assuming it all was real. But his mother always told him, 'You know what happens when you assume, Lynn. You make an ass out of U and ME.'

Lynn didn't want to be made an ass of. He wanted proof this

time. And after he hit the pavement, he rode straight back to Garrett's trailer.

Part of him, and he didn't really understand this but it was still true, was jealous. Why did Shane and Garrett and even baby Donnatella get to see the really weird shit while he and Ray just got the play by play afterward. Sure, they were scared as hell and could have died, but still, they got the up close and personal first class tour. Lynn had never been first class anything in his life and he was ready for that to change.

Although he had nothing more than his shitty, old pocket knife for protection, he wasn't too worried. The alien fuckers didn't seem all that dangerous. Harry hadn't even realized two ton Garrett was spying on him from half a room away. And Della was even closer than that to Shane and failed to seal the deal. They might be intergalactic travelers, but this was Earth, his domain, and if he could escape from Nolan Haddix, two assholes like Garrett's old man and brother wouldn't be much of a challenge.

Garrett lived about five miles outside of town. Not as far as Ray, but still a heck of a long way, especially at night. Especially when there weren't any streetlamps out there in the boonies. Twice he almost pedaled right off the blacktop, only to catch himself at the last second and stay upright. Because of all that, he had to assume a slower pace than usual and it took him almost half an hour to get back to the Roberts' residence.

The lights were still off and nothing had changed since Shane had called off the recon. Lynn leaned his bike against the tailgate of Larry Robert's pick-up, where it would be out of sight from the trailer, then approached.

He didn't bother using a tremendous amount of caution, but he didn't pelt rocks against the metal siding either. When he got to the rectangular box, he went to the window that he knew opened to Garrett's room. He thought he might be able to reach the bottom of the sill from the ground, but even when he gave it his best jump, the kind he used when going for slam dunks at the kiddie playground on Church Street, he couldn't catch it.

"Goddamn it." He went to kick the aluminum skirting, then thought better of it. Walking by the sleeping bear was one thing. Poking it was another. If he was going to take that much of a risk, he may as well stroll right through the front door. And the more he considered it, that didn't seem like a bad idea.

Several times in the past he'd seen Garrett retrieve a hidden key from under a worn through welcome mat and when Lynn checked, it was there. He eased open the screen door, the old hinge unleashing a twangy scree that sounded almost deafening in the otherwise silent night, but he doubted it was even audible inside. Before he inserted the key, he decided to try the doorknob.

It was unlocked. He dropped the unnecessary key into his jeans where it settled in beside the pocket knife, then walked inside.

Garrett had been right about the smell. It was pungent and sour. Garrett said it reminded him of dirt, but Lynn thought it was more akin to rotten potatoes. Or the way the dumpster behind the towers smelled on really hot, humid days. He pulled his shirt up and over his nose and mouth, which made him feel a bit like a burglar, and he liked that feeling. To go along with the look, he took exaggerated, tiptoeing steps as he moved deeper inside the trailer.

Lynn knew from previous visits that there were four rooms back the narrow hallway. The first on the right was the bathroom. The first on the left was Garrett's room. Rear left was Harrison's and rear right was their father's. The bathroom door was open, as was the one to Garrett's. The latter two were not.

A quick peek into the bathroom revealed nothing amiss. No snot covered egg sacs festering in the sink or bodies wrapped in cocoons in the bathtub. He'd actually been hoping for the latter. But, it was just a normal bathroom.

Garrett's quarters were equally mundane and he continued on. When he stood between the two closed doors, he could hear two sounds. The first, and loudest, was snoring. Do alien fuckers snore, he wondered. That seemed pretty far-fetched and any small doubts over this shit really being real that lingered in his mind began to spread like a wildfire.

There was the possibility that Garrett and Shane cooked this whole thing up to get Garrett out of here and away from his dad. Lynn knew that life here sucked ass and he'd seen the black and blue evidence of Garrett's beatings so he wouldn't blame the kid for wanting a new home. But would they go this far?

As he pondered that, the other noise caught his attention. It was low and muffled. So faint he couldn't even tell which room it was coming from. Identifying the noise was impossible. All he knew was that it sounded wet.

He pressed his ear against the door to Harrison's room. The sound was louder. His hand reached for the doorknob and fell onto it. The cool, aluminum slick in his palm. He listened, heard the repetition once more, then turned the knob.

More darkness greeted him. In a way, it was even blacker here than the rest of the trailer. He had a second to wonder why not even the moon seemed to enter this space when the wet sound was interrupted by a loud cracking *shppp*.

Lynn jumped in place, clearing at least an inch or two before landing. The thin floorboards of the trailer swayed under duress, but the carpet muffled the noise he'd made.

"Unit 9. Come in. Unit 9?"

There was a long pause in the voice and Lynn realized it was a walkie talkie radio.

"Unit 9?"

A cop's walkie talkie. But why was a cop's radio in Garrett's trailer? Lynn was tired of being blind and felt beside the door for the light switch, found it, and flicked it on.

The first thing he noticed was that the window was covered in black plastic, the heavy duty kind. That explained the light, or lack thereof. With that mystery solved, his eyes drifted across the room and it took but a second before he wished he was back in the dark.

Sitting on the bed, his head bowed like a man saying his nightly prayers, was Harrison Roberts, or whatever used to be Harrison. The teen was naked and his body coated head to toe in a gelatinous slime the color of bile. It seemed to seep from his every pore and formed a viscous puddle at his feet, or where his feet should have been.

Because, Lynn realized with a kind of disgusted awe, Harrison's feet were gone. His legs from the knees down had stretched and melted into two, long rods of flesh and Lynn's eyes followed them as if they were road signs with blinking arrows.

Those cords of tissue pulsed and bulged and contracted like water rushing through a too small hose. And when he found the end of those horrifically long and distended legs, he saw they were attached to a man Lynn vaguely remembered as being a cop he sometimes saw around town. That took care of his questions about the radio too.

Sprawled on his back the cop looked unconscious, or maybe dead, but Lynn doubted the latter. One of the tubes was connected to the man's neck, the other to his left cheek. Lynn strained to see how they were attached, thinking they must be mouths of some sort, but when he looked closer, he realized they weren't biting, they weren't stuck on, they weren't holding fast with unseen papillae. They had become part of him.

Harrison's legs were like to umbilical cords pumping life into the man who had once protectively patrolled the streets of Sallow Creek. And just when Lynn thought that was about as bad as it could get, the cop's head lolled in his general direction and his eyes found him. They opened in a huge, wide panic that showed white all around the iris. They were the begging, pleading eyes of a man who knew death had come a calling.

The cop's mouth opened and Lynn heard a wet gush of air escape, but no words accompanied it. Instead of vocalizations, what came spewing out of the man's mouth projectile-style were worms. Hundreds of them.

They were a pink-gray, the color of hamburger that had oxidized on the kitchen counter, and when they hit the floor they crawled, writhing and rolling through the peaks and valleys of the shag carpeting.

Their pace was frantic, desperate. They were coming for Lynn.

He'd seen enough. More than enough. He wasn't jealous of Shane and Garrett anymore. This was a club of which he suddenly had no interest in being a member. The worms were only a few feet from his sneakers and closing the gap fast, but he couldn't resist one more look at the man on the floor. All of the worms were still connected to him, the unseen back parts of their bodies hidden away somewhere deep inside his mouth or throat or maybe all the way down in his intestines. They were eight feet long and still coming. Still growing.

Lynn spun away from the insanity—

And collided with the chest of Larry Roberts.

The big man was almost a foot taller than Lynn and through his work shirt Lynn could smell musky sweat and oil and above those expected odors, the sour, earthy aroma that filled the trailer. On instinct he took a step back but as soon as he did, he could feel the worms battering his shoes, searching for a hold.

For a place to *enter* me, Lynn thought, with a new dawning horror that made him want to cry and scream at the same time. Because, when it was happening to someone else, like the cop, it was still a little like watching a movie. But when they were touching him, trying to get *into* him, that made it real.

He stomped his feet and felt several of them burst, but dozens more, hundreds more, still tickled and grasped at him. He could feel them through the fabric of his socks and realized they'd soon slip under his jeans where they'd find bare flesh. And somehow he knew that was all they needed and he'd be toast.

"Fuck you, worms!" Lynn screamed and vaulted himself forward. He collided with Larry Roberts and the suddenness of his action took the man by surprise and they stumbled through the hall, through the open door of Larry's bedroom, and to the floor.

Lynn landed on top, but the texture of what was under him didn't feel like a person. It took him a moment before his mind connected it with the experience of laying on a waterbed the one time they'd visited his aunt and cousins in Cherry Hill, New Jersey. It was like he was floating atop Larry Roberts.

The man's arms came up in a motion Lynn associated with getting hit, but enough light from Harrison's room spilled across them for Lynn to see that Larry didn't have fists. His hands had become more worms. These were flesh-colored and short, no longer than the man's fingers, but growing.

Lynn reared back and punched Larry in the stomach, but met almost no resistance. His hand sunk deeper and deeper until it found something solid, which Lynn was almost positive was the floor underneath him. It had felt like punching a bowl of Jello and he yanked his hand back, staring at it to make sure it was still there.

It was and he looked down and saw a plunging divot in Larry's work shirt where he'd hit him. He had a nauseating suspicion that, had the shirt not been there, his hand would have gone straight through the man's innards, to the carpet underneath.

Larry's hand of worms grabbed Lynn's tee and stuck to it like Velcro. He felt the fabric stretch, heard a stitch in the seam pop. Then another. And another.

Faster now. *Riiiiiiiip!*

Cool, moist air hit his torso where the shirt had been, his entire upper body now exposed. This is bad, he thought. So damn bad.

Why'd I come here alone? Why didn't I go home and eat leftovers with Charlene and get up early and make eggs and toast for mom before she had to go clean nasty rooms at that shitty hotel? They could talk while they ate, not about anything in particular, just the monotony of their lives, but the conversations weren't boring because they were together. He didn't realize how much he loved his family until he thought he might never see them again.

The knife!

The thought came to him like a life preserver to a dying man and his hand dove into his pocket, fishing for it, finding it. Lynn pulled it free and deftly flicked it open, a move he often practiced for fun, not realizing he'd ever have to do it when it mattered. When his life depended on it.

He stared down at the thing that wore Larry Robert's skin and found its mouth gaping open, impossibly wide. It looked like a snake with an unhinged jaw, getting ready to eat a rodent. Only the man's mouth kept opening. Kept widening. Lynn thought at any minute the skin on his cheeks would rip but instead it only stretched further and further until the mouth was bigger than its entire head had been moments before.

Fuck his freaky mouth, Lynn thought. It was the hands that had hold of him. The hands that he needed to be freed from. And to do that, he'd use the knife.

In one harsh, swooping motion he slammed the blade into Larry's left forearm, then yanked it roughly to the side. The dull knife, its blade oxidized with rust, cut through that arm like warm butter. There wasn't the slightest amount of resistance. No sawing through dense flesh. No grinding against solid bone. It went through the arm like a Japanese warrior's samurai sword and, when it escaped the other side, Larry's hand was disconnected from his body.

The worms at the severed piece of it held fast to Lynn's torn shirt, which still clung to his body around the neck and shoulders. The heft of them weighing him down. And the other hand, its convulsing, pustulating bundle of tentacles, continued to pull Lynn toward Larry and his impossibly wide, waiting jaws.

Lynn's hands traded the knife and he sliced again. The results and the ease were the same. Two dismembered hands held Lynn's shirt, but now that they weren't attached to Larry's body, he had more room to move. He shoved the handle of the knife into his mouth and bit down, then slipped off the remains of his shirt. It flopped to the floor with a wet thud and he saw the worm-things scrabbling over it, as if they didn't realize the warm body that had been wearing it was gone.

He took another look at Larry, at the stumps of his arms, and saw there was no red blood, but instead a yellow-green ooze that reminded Lynn of snot, of the loogies he sometimes hawked up when he had a bad chest cold.

Then he saw something else coming from those stumps. Light pink, almost translucent fingers began to grow. Just the tips at first, the nails clear and glistening like they'd been freshly manicured. But, as he watched, all ten of them reappeared. Then the palms. Then the wrists. Lynn felt like he was watching one of those time lapse videos they showed in science class only those were things like butterflies emerging from cocoons or flowers blooming, not motherfucking aliens regenerating limbs.

It *is* like *Swamp Thing*, he thought.

Then he felt the worms on his calves.

Son of a bitch! He'd forgotten about the ones behind him. The ones that had burst from the cop's mouth. They'd trekked up his shoes, summited his socks, and now the bastards were on his skin.

Lynn spun around and saw the river of worms rushing across the carpet and at him. When he turned, several of them dragged sideways and he knew that was because they were connected to him.

He looked at his legs and saw at least a dozen of the things had slithered up his jeans. His first instinct was to grab them and tear them away but somehow he knew that, if he touched them with his hands, they'd stick there too.

His mind reeled as he tried to find a solution to the most fucked up question he'd ever been faced with. How was he going to get out of this alive?

Lynn retrieved the knife from his mouth and bent at the waist, ready to cut the worms that had hold of his legs, but when he did his eyes caught sight of Larry Roberts. The man was on all fours, his new hands acting more like a dog's paws as he came for him. His mouth hung so far open that his bottom jaw dragged across the carpet. Some of the worms slithering about decided to enter that gaping maw, undulating upward until they disappeared down the black abyss of his throat.

Lynn stumbled away, his legs clumsy and slow because the worms weren't letting go, they were acting like tethers keeping him in place until the Larry Roberts creature could gobble him up. He tripped over the tentacles and face planted on the carpet, which smelled like toe jam and sweaty socks.

He felt them dragging him backward, toward the Larry-thing, and rolled himself over. The worms had such a grip on him that his legs criss-crossed at the knees but he managed to work himself into a sitting position. Then, Lynn used the knife again. This time to saw through the ropes of worms. Watery, brown fluid drained from them. It reminded him of diarrhea both in its color and aroma. It reeked of sour sickness.

Another round of cutting and sawing and he was free. He crab crawled backward a yard then pushed himself to his feet. He saw Larry still coming for him. Saw the worms on the floor that he'd just sliced and diced growing again, renewing themselves and slithering his way. Their merciless determination brought about a realization.

I've got to kill them before they spread.

But how? He ran from the hallway, into the kitchen. He rummaged through drawers and cabinets, found utensils and plates and pots, but nothing that could kill. Nothing deadly.

He found a bottle of bleach under the sink, popped the top and returned to the hall which the creatures had almost breeched. He shook the fluid over them, waiting for screaming or sizzling or maybe even for them to burst in some kind of fantastic chemical reaction. But nothing happened. They kept coming.

Larry was in the lead. Lynn knew it was pointless but he grabbed a cast iron frying pan from the stovetop and slammed it down on the man's head. The metal buried itself deep, sinking in almost to the handle, then it stayed there, jutting out like a special effect in a bad horror movie. And he kept coming.

Enough of this shit, Lynn thought. He didn't have to be a hero tonight. It was time to get the hell out of Dodge.

He tried to sprint, but instead limped and lumbered toward the trailer door, thrusting it open. The blue light of the moon never looked so delicious as he stumbled out the door, almost falling down the metal steps, then to the lawn.

Without looking back, he went to his bike and climbed on, pumping the pedals with all the energy he had left and he didn't stop until he was two full miles away.

Exhausted, he stopped at the first street lamp he came to. He leaned his bike against the pole, then leaned himself against it and tried to catch his breath. He was shaking all over, and he began to laugh. It was a shrill, cackling sound that would have sounded mad to any passerby, but he was alone here. He could scream like a banshee and no one would bat an eye.

So stupid, he thought. Almost screwed the pooch. Wait until I tell the guys this.

But first, he had to piss. The urge had hit him before he even fled the trailer but he'd been putting it off and now his bladder felt like an overfull water balloon threatening to blow. Never one to care much about modesty, Lynn unzipped, pushed down his briefs, and whipped out his pecker.

Hot piss shot out, jetting a full yard in distance and steaming against the night air. He sighed at the wondrous relief of the emptying feeling and a firecracker of a fart shot out his asshole. That made him laugh again, harder, and his pecker bobbed and weaved, spraying urine all over the sidewalk and creating a bizarre, abstract pattern.

Half a minute passed before the stream began to lose pressure, like someone slowly turning off the water supply to a hose. It soon became a trickle and he had to watch more carefully at that point to ensure none of it ended up on his shoes.

As he looked down, he saw the four pubic hairs that had begun sprouting on his groin a few months ago. They were wiry and about as white as his hair and he took a strange pride in them. Those thin hairs meant he was becoming a man. He'd heard girls sometimes shaved their pubes off, a bit of knowledge that confused and intrigued him, because he loved his so much.

As the last few drops of piss spilled from his pecker, Lynn realized there was a fifth hair down there. The silky new addition had taken residence to the right of his unit, and the overhead streetlamp lit it up like a shiny, new penny. He was admiring that hair when—

It moved.

No, that couldn't be possible. Just the breeze was all. There was no way—

It moved again. Shimmying. Dancing.

There was no denying it now. This wasn't a fifth, glorious pubic hair that advanced him yet another step on the journey to manhood. It was one of the worms.

Lynn swallowed hard and tried to pinch it between his fingers. It slithered to the side, into the crease between his crotch and thigh. He felt it undulating there, a gentle tickle that stood his hair, his real hair, on end.

He let his pants fall to the ground and used both hands to dig at his crotch, frantic. He felt the worm, tried to grab it again, but again it avoided capture.

One more try. His fingers got it that time. He pulled, but the worm was moist and slipped free.

He grabbed his pecker and his sack, shoving the handful of flesh from side to side, trying to find the worm which he couldn't see any more, but which he felt crawling all over him down there. His hands had gone slick with its secretions and now he could barely even keep firm hold of his own body parts.

Standing there, naked from the waist down, fighting and losing, he felt tears threatening to erupt from his eyes.

Don't you cry. Don't be a pussy. Grab that fucking worm and stomp it to death.

But every attempt ended the same. In failure.

He let go of himself, and wiped his hands on his bare chest. Some of the goo rubbed off but when he pulled his palms away, the substance stretched out the way rubber cement clung greedily to the can when you removed the brush. He shook his hands, trying to fling it off, but it was useless. The stuff was thick as snot and sticky as pine sap.

Lynn looked away from his hands, back to his crotch, and there he saw the worm. Four inches of it rose up and it reminded Lynn of a cobra getting charmed by a guy playing a flute in the movies.

It's looking at me, he thought.

That seemed crazy, but then again, all of this was crazy so why the fuck couldn't that be true? The two of them looked at each other for a long moment and then Lynn made his move.

His hands lashed out, snatching at the worm, but the worm dived and avoided his grasp.

And then it was the worm's turn. The top end of it struck at Lynn's pecker and—

It made a hole in one.

Lynn didn't know what a urethra was, but as he watched the worm disappear into what he called his *pee hole*, all the fight, all the hope, left him.

There was a brief, stinging pain, like getting poked by a pin, and then his crotch went numb. He felt nothing but terror as he watched the worm slither deeper into him. It was long, a foot, maybe 18 inches, and what had been fine, almost delicate moments earlier seemed to fatten up as it entered him. It wasn't a hair now, it was a garden snake, a well-fed one. His twelve-year-old pecker, stretched by this alien invader, looked like a summer sausage dangling between his legs.

Under other circumstances, that would have made him proud. But now, the sight sickened him. He felt movement deeper inside him, a wet, heaviness in his pelvis. Then something moving near his bowels.

I should pull my pants up, he thought, out of the blue. I don't want anyone seeing me like this.

Lynn crouched down, reaching for his jeans, and saw the walkie talkie still clipped to his back pocket. He forgot about redressing and grabbed it.

CHAPTER THIRTY-SIX

THE WALKIE TALKIE CRACKLED TO LIFE. IT WAS LYING ATOP A wooden crate with a stencil reading Fragile. The boys had found it beside the dumpster at the County Market grocery store a year earlier and thought it would make a good table. Now, that crate set about four feet away from both Garrett (on the floor) and Shane (on the loveseat). Apollo, for no particular reason, had been laying awake while the two boys snored. At the sound, the dog cocked his head to the right and looked at the radio.

"Shane? Garrett? Are you there?"

Shrill static that hurt the dog's ears replaced the voice. The dog wanted it to stop.

"Please. I need help."

More static. Apollo gave a low whine.

"Guys? Are you there? I fucked up real bad. I went to Garrett's house and, aw, shit in a shoebox, it's a goddamn madhouse there. It's so much worse than we thought."

Static. Longer this time. The dog tried to bury his head between his front paws to block it out.

"I thought I got away but one got me. It's inside me." He sobbed. "I really need you."

Again, static. But brief.

"Over."

Then came a steady, soulless drone and it bleated on until Apollo gave a rumbling growl. That half-roused Shane from his sleep.

"Apollo?"

He scanned the clubhouse, eyes squinted. Then he heard the static coming from the walkie talkie and rolled off the love seat. He took a shuffling step toward it, not wanting to completely wake up, and picked it up. He held in the talk button. "Hello?"

No answer came.

"Anyone there?"

Nothing.

Shane flicked the radio off and returned to the love seat. Returned to the world of sleep and dreams.

With the static banished for good, Apollo did the same.

CHAPTER THIRTY-SEVEN

THE FIRST DAYS OF CHURCH CAMP HAD BEEN A NONSTOP flurry of games and crafts topped off with inspirational sermons each evening after dinner. Jose would have never admitted to his friends, who never seemed to understand his love of the church and God, but it was the most fun he'd had all summer.

Part of it was the activities themselves, especially water polo which was a new addition this year and which Jose enjoyed so much he'd have played all day long if he'd been allowed, and part of it was the fellow campers who were kind and polite and respectful almost to a fault, but a lot of it, maybe most of it, was that he felt relaxed here at Camp Nobeboski. He didn't have missions where he had to spy on people or put himself in danger, and he didn't have to worry about the darned aliens.

It was wonderful.

The campers had just finished solving the mystery of where the joy, joy, joy, joy was (down in my heart), when Pastor Ted asked who wanted to toast marshmallows. A thundering chorus of

'*ME!*' was followed with giggling and laughter and Pastor Ted and his assistants returned with not only marshmallows, but graham crackers and chocolate bars too.

In between having the time of his life, Jose had occasionally felt pangs of guilt that he was having so much fun while his pals were stuck at home. He felt another as he squished a hot marshmallow and a square of Hershey's chocolate between two crackers. Garrett loved s'mores and Jose realized the boys hadn't made them once all summer. He made a promise to fix that next week when camp was over and he intended to keep it.

Pastor Ted was so old he might have been ancient, even older than Jose's parents. He was probably fifty or close to it and he had an enormous, fat belly that jiggled when he laughed. The man had once joked that he was secretly Santa Claus undercover, but he had no beard so Jose hadn't fallen for it even though a few of the other kids did. Pastor Ted had enormous, fat legs too and had trouble walking so he drove a golf cart around the campground.

Once all the s'mores ingredients had been handed out and consumption had begun, he gave an exaggerated yawn and wished them all a good night. Jose was extremely fond of the big man and yelled, "Goodnight to you too, Pastor Ted!" so loud that a few of the other kids looked at him like he was a weirdo. He didn't mind and Pastor Ted gave him a big smile and a broad wink before he drove off.

Donnatella sat on the other side of the campfire. She was on the far right of a log bench, beside a bunch of the other, younger kids. Jose had seen her a couple times in passing throughout the day, but hadn't said more than a fleeting 'hi.' He noticed she wasn't eating anything and, after he finished his own s'more and licked marshmallow goo from his upper lip, he grabbed the raw ingredients to make another and moved to her.

"Want me to toast you a s'more, Don?"

She shook her head, her light brown curls drooping across her face. She didn't look at him.

"Why not?"

Another head shake. More silence.

Jose sat down on the ground beside her. The bench was quite low and they were more or less at eye level. "Hey, Sis. What's up? You got a tummy ache or something?"

Donnatella finally met his gaze. Her big, baby blue eyes were ringed red and the skin around them puffy. "I wanna go home."

A couple of the nearest kids looked at her, brief, curious glances, then returned to eating and singing and laughing.

"Why?"

Her bottom lip stuck out in a pout he'd seen all too often at home, but it surprised him to see it here. He was having such a great time and assumed she would too. Then he remembered that it was her first time here. Her first time away from home without either of their parents around. She was homesick.

He had been too the first time he'd come to Camp Nobeboski, but that was seven years ago and he'd almost forgotten about it. Now that he gave it some thought though, he did recall crying himself to sleep most nights. And how he'd gone to the mess hall every day expecting a letter from home, only none came. He later found out that his grandfather had told his parents not to write, that letters made the homesickness worse, but at the time, a few scribbles promising that they missed him and would see him soon were much needed. Part of him was still mad at his grandfather for that, but he knew you were supposed to forgive people no matter what they did to you and he tried to do just that.

Jose reached out and took Don's small hand in his own. Her skin felt damp, almost clammy and the feeling grossed him out a little. He hoped she hadn't been picking her nose or sucking her thumb or something. He never was good with the gross stuff. That was something his friends always teased him about.

"It's okay, Don. The first couple days are the hardest." That was a fib, but he hoped it wasn't a sin to fib to your little sister if the intentions were good. Every day was hard that first year and when he finally got to go home, he'd imagined the excitement and relief and sheer exhilaration he felt must be how a man felt when he was sprung from prison after a lengthy stretch of hard time. As he remembered that and watched Don, who looked so small and sad and pathetic, he was surprised he'd ever wanted to come back.

But it did get better. The second year was fun, only a night or two of crying. And every year after was even better yet. She'd see that, in time. But at the moment, he still felt bad for her, even if she could be a brat sometimes.

"I'll hang out with you more tomorrow, if you want." That wasn't what *he* wanted. He wanted to hang with the twelve year olds, but being an older brother meant you had to make sacrifices sometimes.

"You will?" She stared at him, wearing an expression of surprise mixed with relief.

Jose nodded. "You bet." She smiled, her little baby teeth glistening orange in the reflection of the fire, and that made him feel pretty darn good. "Did you know there's buried treasure here?"

Don's blue eyes grew wide, wondrous. "There is?"

"Yeah. Will you help me look for it tomorrow?"

She nodded. Now the curls flew across her face in excited blurs.

"Okay. After breakfast we'll go looking, so make sure to get a bunch of sleep."

"I will!"

She jumped to her feet, eager to rush to her cabin, but he held her hand.

"Remember how dad says," he dropped his voice comically low to impersonate their father, "'Your body needs fuel'?"

"Yeah."

"Well then..." He handed her the three vital ingredients to a s'more and she accepted them, almost ripped them away. She grabbed a pine branch and impaled a marshmallow on it, then thrust it straight into the flames. It would probably catch fire in a few seconds, but he didn't think that mattered much. Don was having fun now and that meant he could continue to do the same, guilt free.

Across the hazy orange bonfire, he caught an older boy watching them. Jose knew his name to be Adam Larew, and only remembered that because a couple summers ago Adam and two of his friends had dumped a bucket of stagnant water on him when he wasn't paying attention during a course on setting up tents. He wasn't Nolan Haddix level of mean, but after that Jose tried to avoid him.

Jose saw Don's marshmallow had indeed been set ablaze and when she pulled it from the fire, he blew it out for her. Its skin was black as coal and it had shriveled to half its size and she looked almost ready to cry again.

"It's all right. Watch." Jose delicately grasped the charred outer layer with his thumb and index finger and lifted oh so slowly. There was slight resistance at first, but then it pulled free leaving a gooey, white mass in its wake. "There."

Don giggled and made her s'more with the remnants of the marshmallow. While she ate it Jose stole quick glances at Adam Larew and every time he did, he saw the boy staring back. He suddenly wished his friends were there, but that wasn't going to happen. Jose was on his own.

CHAPTER THIRTY-EIGHT

FOR THE THIRD DAY IN A ROW, GARRETT SAT AT THE Vinyan's kitchen table and ate breakfast with the family. He still struggled to believe how normal they were, like the parents in a sitcom. Good, kind people and they'd been treating him like he wasn't some random friend of their son's intruding on their picturesque life, but almost like an adopted son.

Their unwavering acceptance was exactly what Garrett needed, but it also made him apprehensive. If life had taught him anything it was that, just when things seemed to be going good, there was an anvil waiting to fall on your head.

Shane's mother, Sara Vinyan, held up a serving plate with the remnants of bacon, eight or ten slices remained uneaten. "More bacon, Garrett?"

Garrett almost reached for it, but stopped himself. He'd been extremely cautious about how much of the Vinyan's foot he ate, scared that if they saw him acting like a pig they'd send him on his way, or if nothing else, silently judge him. "No thank you. I'm full."

Shane cackled. "Full of crap maybe."

Sara shot him a stern glare. "Shane! Enough of that!"

But Garrett smiled. "It's okay, Mrs. Vinyan."

Steve, Shane's father, peered at the goings on over the top of a newspaper. "If the boy's not hungry, I'll take it."

Sara shook her head. "Not with your cholesterol you won't." She set the plate at the opposite end of the table, out of her husband's reach.

Garrett thought even their bickering was perfect. He'd never been as jealous of Shane as the last few days.

Steve Vinyan folded his newspaper and set it aside. "You boys were at the fair last week, right?"

Shane looked about as calm as bathwater. "Yeah. Garrett lost two bucks on the ring toss. Sucker."

Garrett avoided talking by wiping up some egg yolk with a piece of toast and shoving it into his mouth.

Shane's father nodded. "There was an article about some stupid kid on the Ferris wheel climbing out of his car and almost dying. Caused quite a ruckus."

The bread caught in Garrett's throat. He tried to swallow but it wouldn't go down. He fought back a hacking cough and saw Shane looking at him, his friend's face calm but his eyes saying, 'Keep your shit together!'

"Must've happened after we left," Shane said. "Wish I'd have seen that. Sounds like a hoot."

Garrett's eyes welled up with tears as he tried to breathe but not cough, not hack up the barely chewed toast. Shane again cast him an annoyed glare.

"A hoot?" Sara Vinyan said. "With all the illness and tragedy to be had in life, there's no need to bring on more of it through carelessness and stupidity."

Shane rolled his eyes, then he seemed to grasp the seriousness of Garrett's situation and he shoved his glass of orange juice at him. Garrett grabbed it and drank, draining it in three long swallows that, thank God, forced the bread down his throat. He set the glass aside and tried to catch his breath without being obvious about it.

"Let's go, Garrett. Before mom decides to educate us on the preciousness of life." Shane bounced out of his seat, then to and through the French doors which opened to the patio.

Shane's parents both stared at Garrett who, as much as he wished they were his parents too, wanted to be far away from them at that moment.

"Can I go too?" Garrett asked.

"You don't have to ask permission, Garrett," Steve said, then made a shooing gesture with his hand.

Garrett fled.

CHAPTER THIRTY-NINE

Breakfast was three of the best pancakes Jose had ever eaten (although he'd never admit that to his mother), two links of sausage, two strips of bacon, and a glass of milk so cold it made his teeth hurt. By the time he finished eating, his belly was so full that it popped out in a small, hard pooch, but it was worth it.

"Hey, Jose!"

He looked and saw Clint Baker, a boy his age who he considered a camp friend. He had several of those here. Friends that lived as far away as Pittsburgh or Harrisburg and that he only saw seven days out of an entire year. Their friendships were different than what he had in Sallow Creek, more superficial, but they were still plenty of fun to hang out with.

Clint pointed to the exit where wooden barn doors opened to the lake. "Want to practice for the swim?"

The swim was a rite of passage amongst the boys at Camp Nobeboski, and some of the girls too. Five laps from one end of the lake to the other were approximately one mile, or so they'd been told. Making the swim before you were a teenager gave you something of legendary status around the camp and they even carved your name into a wooden placard that hung outside the canteen (a small shop where you could spend your quarters on everything from crackers and gum to patches and postcards). There had only been eight names added to that list since Jose had been coming to camp.

Anything in the lake was high on Jose's priority list and he almost responded with a 'Heck yeah!' when he remembered Don. He lost his grin. "I can't this morning."

"Why not?" Clint asked.

"I've got to cheer up Donnatella."

Clint nodded, knowing. "Homesick."

"Yeah. Besides, I just ate." He rubbed his engorged tummy and, as he did that, he was surprised the idea of swimming had come up at all. They all knew better than to go in the water after eating. If they did, they'd get cramps and drown. That nugget of knowledge was as ingrained in their heads as stopping, dropping, and rolling should they ever catch on fire. "Didn't you eat yet?" Jose asked Clint.

Clint shook his head. "Nah. Guess I ate too many mushrooms last night."

"Yuck!" Jose didn't eat mushrooms. The knowledge that they were grown in manure made them impossible to stomach.

"Marshmallows, I meant." Clint barked a laugh that sounded odd somehow. Like the kind of laugh he'd give if he was performing a role in the annual play.

"Oh." Jose stared at him. Those seemed like two strange things to mix up, but maybe Clint was still tired and mush-mouthed. "Yeah. I ate a bunch too."

Clint puffed his cheeks out like they were crammed full, then worked his jaws. That made Jose giggle and Clint laughed too, a more normal laugh.

"Okay then. Maybe this afternoon? After basket weaving?" Clint asked.

Basket weaving was one of the activities Jose enjoyed the least. He'd made six lopsided baskets for his mother over the years and each one of them ended up in the garage filled with random junk. "Sure."

Clint flashed him a thumbs up, then dashed outside. Jose wanted to follow, but brotherly duties called. He didn't know why, but as he watched Clint flee, he tried to remember his friend eating marshmallows and s'mores the night before. No matter how hard he tried, he couldn't pull up that memory. Jose shook his head and told himself not to be so weird.

He found Don at her table, an empty plate in front of her. If it hadn't been for an amber smear of maple syrup, he would have thought she'd skipped the meal.

"I ate my fuel," she said, smiling and prideful.

Jose laughed a little. "That's good, Don. Because this search is going to be long and hard and tiring. But, if we succeed, we'll be rich beyond our wildest dreams!"

After retiring to his bunkhouse, The Egret, the night prior, Jose had spent an hour drawing a crude map of the camp. When he finished, he crinkled it into a tight ball and rubbed it against the dusty cabin floor. He un-balled it, then dribbled some water over the map and spread it out to dry. The result wasn't exactly an ancient treasure map, but he thought it was good enough to fool his baby sister.

He waited until they were out of the mess hall, and away from any potential pirates, before showing it to her. Don's eyes again grew wide and he appreciated that she was so easily impressed. That was, in his opinion, one of the best parts of being a big brother.

"I think this is the trail to the archery range." He pointed to a pathway on the map and his sister nodded in agreement. "You're sure you're up for this, Don?"

"I am. I want the treasure!"

Jose held his finger to his lips. "Quiet. We can't let anyone else know. This is our secret. You've gotta promise not to tell anyone"

"Yeah! Our secret!" She drew an x over her heart, grinning.

"Hope to die," Jose said in response. Then, they disappeared into the woods.

CHAPTER FORTY

INSIDE THE CLUBHOUSE, SHANE GLANCED AT HIS LIST, which seemed useless now. The second step had been "Figure out what we're dealing with." If they were right, and it was aliens, that part was over. Step three was simply, "Destroy them." But there were no silver bullets or wooden stakes for aliens. At least, none that he knew of. Step 4 was, Become Heroes. Step 5, Celebrate. Those last two still sounded good, but getting there would be harder than he'd expected.

"What was the movie where the cop was the doctor from *Halloween III*?" Shane asked, trying to remember. "The one with the little aliens that looked like slugs and crawled in your mouth and made you all zombie like?" He raised his hands up in front of him, stiff-armed, and swayed back and forth. Miming the walk of the undead without actually walking.

"*Night of the Creeps*," Garrettsaid.

"Yeah." Shane nodded. "They burned them in that, right?"

"Uh huh. He got a flamethrower from the police station." Garrett smiled a little. He'd liked that part.

"You got any flamethrowers we can use?" Shane asked.

Garrett held up his empty hands. "Fresh out."

"What good are you?"

"Not much."

Shane tossed the list to the side, annoyed over the brick wall they'd hit. "You know what we should do?"

"What?"

"Kidnap that little Whipkey shit. The one that Donnatella saw go all Snake Plissken at the pool."

Garrett's brows rose, his eyes bulged. "Why?"

"To torture her. Make her talk."

"She's like six. If we got caught, everyone would think we were a bunch of pedos."

"A good reason not to get caught. Besides, she's a goddamn alien."

"I don't know. It still seems kind of pervy."

Shane thought about it and gave a reluctant nod. "Yeah. Probably."

Everything seemed to be in a holding pattern since Jose left for camp. Ray'd only bothered to come by the clubhouse once and Lynn not at all and Shane was annoyed with all of them. Serious shit was going down in Sallow Creek and those three losers were off going about life as usual while he and Garrett had to come up with all the answers.

He often joked about being the smartest of the bunch, although he'd admit that was a toss up with Garrett, but at times like this he hated it. Because it made him feel responsible and he was only twelve and saving the town, maybe even the world, from alien invaders shouldn't be the burden he carried on his shoulders.

"Shane?"

Garrett's voice snapped him out of his self-pitying daze. He looked up and saw his best friend laying on the couch, one arm draped over Apollo. "What?"

"I think we should tell your parents."

Shane had ben slouching back in the recliner and now shot forward. "No way in hell."

"Why not? They're so nice and understanding. And they listen."

"Look, Garrett, I know to you they're like Dr. And Mrs. Cosby and I'm not going to make them out to be assholes or anything because they're not, but they're adults. And we're kids. Unless we can bring them an alien's head on a stick, they're not going to buy what we're selling."

"Well then, let's do it."

"Do what?"

"Bring them an alien's head on a stick."

Shane thought he might be joking but the look on Garrett's face was dead serious. "Oh yeah? Whose?"

"My father's."

CHAPTER FORTY-ONE

"I think we should make a left here." Jose pointed to his self-created treasure map where he'd drawn a gnarled, old oak tree.

Donnatella double-checked and nodded in agreement. "We're close."

The trek into the woods had taken about twenty minutes. He'd hoped to keep the entire excursion to under an hour and that plan was going swimmingly.

They traipsed left at the tree, heading down a smaller, narrowed path. It might have been invisible had Jose not traversed it, stomping down the weeds and breaking through the underbrush, earlier that morning to hide the treasure. They were indeed close now. Very close.

Another ten yards and Jose pretended to study the map. "Look here, Don." He pointed at a scribble of a fallen tree with cross-bones making the spot. Then he stared ahead where a similar sight lied before them. She took the hint.

"That's it!" The girl gave a quick hop and threw her arms up and down. "That's it, Jose! That's it! That's where the treasure is!" She ran to it.

"Careful. There could be booby traps."

She froze midstep, foot hanging in the air and he bit his tongue to ward off a laugh.

"Let me go first, just in case."

Don acquiesced, allowing her brave older brother to put his life at risk to protect her own. In five steps, he was at the tree and he turned back to her. "It's safe."

She ran to him, eyes darting across the tree trunk and its surroundings. He'd made little effort to actually hide the treasure, camouflaging it with nothing more than a few handfuls of dry, fallen leaves. She spotted it in less than thirty seconds.

"There!" She squealed and hopped again, like one of those fancy rabbits they sold in the pet stores at the mall. "Can I get it?"

Jose nodded. "You found it. That makes it yours."

Don dove for the treasure chest, which in reality was a dented gray lunch bucket he'd borrowed from one of his camp friends. When she opened it, she uncovered an assortment of colorful beads he'd filched from the arts and crafts area, a handful of change that had been jangling in his pockets when he arrived at camp, and a string necklace with a wooden cross charm he'd whittled.

"Wow-ee!" Don said as she rummaged through the items, as excited as she was on Christmas mornings. Jose didn't know if this would hold her homesickness at bay for the duration of bible camp but he was happy to have taken her mind off it for the time being.

DONNATELLA WORE THE NECKLACE, THE SMALL CROSS bouncing left, right, left, right, as they marched out of the woods. She'd kept the beads too, her tiny pockets almost overflowing with them, but she'd given Jose all of the change except for a quarter she deemed lucky because it had the same date on it as the year she was born.

As excited as Jose was to rejoin his camp friends and see what the day had in store with them, he was a little blue that this excursion with Don was coming to an end. The kid wasn't bad at all and, when they were separated from her parents, she acted more mature, or at least less babyish. He liked her this way and thought he might need to come up with another adventure for the two of them to have before camp was over.

As they emerged from the forest, adventure found them.

It was a strange, yet somehow familiar sound that caught Jose's attention. A steady, droning hum.

Prrrrrrrr

He stopped walking, so suddenly Don ran into his back.

"Why'd you stop?"

"Shhh."

He listened.

Prrrrrrrr

Still unable to place the sound, he moved toward it. Slow and cautious. "Wait here," he said to Don.

"No!"

Whatever. He wasn't going to argue. The sound grew louder as they continued. Another ten yards and it hit him. Pastor Ted's golf cart.

Relief washed over him and he picked up his pace. He was eager to tell Pastor Ted about the treasure hunt and he knew Don would be excited to show off her bounty.

The purring of the cart's motor was nearby, just past the log cabin that served as the first aid station where, the previous summer, Jose had received three stitches in his thumb after a clumsy fall.

When they rounded the corner, Jose saw the golf cart first. The cab was empty. But through it, on the opposite side, he saw something. Movement at ground level.

"Pastor Ted?"

There were other noises, but they were impossible to decipher over the idling motor. He saw more movement. Was that an arm, he wondered as he saw an arc of flesh swing in a semi circle.

He had a heart attack, Jose thought. Had a heart attack and fell down and now he needs help.

The thought that what was occurring on the opposite side of the cart had anything to do with the alien goings on in Sallow Creek never crossed his mind. Because, even though Camp Nobeboski was only eight miles from town by road and far less in a straight line, to him, this was a different world. This was church camp. That was home. Those may as well have been different continents to his twelve year old mind.

So, when he rounded the cart he was unabashedly positive that what he'd find would be normal. Scary, maybe deadly (his father always talked about 'the big one'), but normal.

He was wrong.

Pastor Ted was on the ground. Jose'd had that part right but that was as far as right went. The rotund, jubilant pastor was splayed on his back, arms windmilling in a struggle against—

Worms

Tentacles that had attached themselves to the Pastor's face. There were five of them and when Jose followed them back to their source, he found Clint Baker sitting on the ground Indian-style and looking about as calm as if he'd been attending an afternoon picnic. Everything about Clint looked normal, except for his right hand. Five tentacles, each more than two yards in length, grew from his palm where his fingers had once been. His one time fingertips had burrowed into Pastor Ted's chubby, ruddy cheeks.

The tentacles pulsed and Jose could tell that something was flowing through them, into the Pastor.

"The snakes!" Don shrieked.

He'd forgotten she was there until the shrill yelp got his attention. It also drew the attention of Clint Baker who looked at them for the first time. His expression was blank as a mannequin's. Jose thought he saw something flutter behind the boy's eyes, but it was there and gone in an instant.

Clint rose from his sitting position and shook his hand. His fingers broke free and the tentacles raced toward Pastor Ted, burrowing deeper and deeper into his face until they were just excited, wriggling tails. And then they were gone.

While the pastor convulsed on the ground, Clint strode toward Jose and Don, his movement steady and deliberate but not rushing.

Jose heard Don whimpering, felt her hands clutching his shirt, pulling it away from his body. She's going to rip it, he thought with dismay because this was his official 1989 Camp Shirt and the first day he'd worn it and he didn't want it getting ruined.

Clint was closer and Jose could see his hand was already regenerating new fingers. He thought about Swamp Thing and thought to himself that he'd have to tell Lynn he was right.

If he survived.

The realization that he could die shocked him into action, not because he was fearful of his own mortality, but because he had to take care of Don. If something happened to her, his parents would never forgive him.

Jose grabbed his sister's hand so hard he thought it must hurt, but she didn't cry or pull away. And when he dragged her to the golf cart, she went along.

He jumped behind the wheel, then lifted Don by one arm and slung her into the seat beside him.

"Put on your seatbelt!" He said.

"Are we stealing Pastor Ted's car?" Her wide eyes now carried more shock than fear, but she did as told. "Is that a sin?"

"We're just borrowing it."

Their father had let him drive a golf cart a few times when Jose went with him to the local public course. Jose didn't understand the purpose of golf, he thought it pretty pointless really, hitting the ball, going to it, hitting it again, but he loved zipping up and down the dirt pathways that led from hole to hole. He wondered if that was part of God's plan, preparing him for this.

Jose took one more look at poor Pastor Ted whose wild gesticulations had slowed to lazy, rocking, side to side motions. The man's face had swollen up to three times its normal size. The skin had taken on a purple, semi-transparent look and he could see things moving inside it, like he was peering into a dirty aquarium. He felt his eyes sting as tears welled up, but then Clint Baker appeared in his sightline and he knew there was no time for crying.

"Hold on!" He wasn't sure if he said that to Don or himself, but his foot slammed onto the gas pedal nonetheless. The cart lurched forward, slow at first, but rolling quick and picking up speed.

Clint made no attempt to move and Jose didn't swerve. The cart slammed into the boy and Jose half-expected their new ride to be totaled. That the front end would crumple or the motor would come flying into their laps.

But that didn't happen. Almost nothing happened. A shuddering, jarring vibration passed through the cart and he felt his hands quiver against the wheel, but forward motion didn't even slow. Instead, Clint Baker's body burst like an overfull water balloon.

Arms and legs flew to the sides. The boy's head tumbled end over end, then hit the ground with a wet splat that smashed in half the face like it was a rotten, mushy jack o'lantern. Like there was no skull inside it for protection.

When Clint's torso blew, gallons of mustard-colored fluid the consistency of phlegm exploded in every direction and a considerable amount of it splattered against the golf cart's plastic windshield.

It's like we just hit the biggest, juiciest bug in the history of the world, Jose thought and managed a smile, but that was short-lived.

"Jose! Look!" Don again grabbed his shirt.

He glanced to the side, saw her pointing ahead and to the right, and discovered Adam Larew heading their way. The boy was coming at them in a full run and would be on them in seconds. Jose jerked the wheel hard to the left, not considering that they were going downhill, and there was a sickening floating feeling as the golf cart rose up onto two wheels.

Don screamed again and Jose gave a short yelp of his own. *Ack!*

Before the cart could roll, the terrain shifted and they dropped back onto four wheels with a bone-jarring thud. That disaster had been avoided, but Adam Larew was closer than ever.

The cart had lost all of its momentum. It was like starting all over again and even with the pedal tight against the floor, the going was slow.

Adam Larew caught up to them, latching hold of the metal safety cage with his hand and holding tight even as the cart finally, and too late, got to cruising speed. He was on the back of the cart. Jose couldn't see him but he heard wet, tearing sounds coming from behind them.

"Don, what's he doing?"

Donnatella turned in her seat and screamed.

That's not good, Jose thought.

"He's ripping his mouth off!" Don said.

Yeah, definitely not good.

The path ahead was clear so Jose tried to sneak a peek. Don's description, while accurate, didn't quite capture the obscenity of what was happening at the rear of the cart. Adam Larew held onto the cart with one hand and, with the other, gripped his own bottom jaw. The skin around it stretched like taffy, then small tears appeared, bloodless holes that allowed him to pull the jaw further and further away from where it belonged.

And then it came free.

As soon as Adam's jaw was severed from his face it seemed to lose form and turned into a malleable, gelatinous boomerang. He took aim and hurled it at Don.

Jose jerked her sideways an instant before the thing that had been a jaw could strike her. He knew that if it had made contact, it would have stuck to her. Penetrated her.

The mound of gooey tissue smacked into the windshield and fell to the floor where it writhed, alive. It slithered across the floorboards, heading toward Jose's feet which were clad in tennis shoes but bare above the ankle.

He kicked at it. Missed. Kicked again. That one connected but only served to send it skittering toward Don's feet. She squealed and pulled them up, hugging her knees against her chest.

A thud in the rear of the cart shook their seat. Jose glanced back and saw Adam had climbed into the section where golfers would stand their bags. He was within arm's reach and his arms had stretched and melted into thick cables that were coming for them.

Ahead, Jose saw the lake. It was fifty feet away and empty of other campers. And, he thought, it was their only hope.

It was all downhill from here.

"Take off your seatbelt," he said to Don.

She stared at him with big, wet eyes. "But we're still moving."

"Don, take off your seatbelt!" He'd never yelled at her like that in his life and he saw her bottom lip puff out. He half expected her to throw an epic tantrum, but instead she obeyed.

"Now wha—"

Before she could finish the question, Jose shoved her out of the cart. In his peripheral vision he saw her fall, somersaulting end over end, then heard pained crying that made him feel about as low as dirt. But he'd saved her life and that was worth some bruises and maybe even a broken bone or two.

One of Adam's tentacle arms whipped into the front seat, where Don had been. The end of it flopped like a fish out of water, sending up sprays of the thick, poop-colored mucous that coated it. Meanwhile, the thing that had been Adam's jaw clambered over his shoe. He could feel the weight of it against the canvas, the strength of it as it flexed and moved.

The water was twenty feet away. Jose tried pressing the gas pedal further into the floor but it was maxed out. With nothing else to do, he closed his eyes and prayed.

CHAPTER FORTY-TWO

GARRETT EASED OPEN THE OFFICE DOOR TO LARRY ROBERTS'
garage and dipped his head inside. A quick survey revealed the
small room was empty. He glanced back at Shane who crouched
behind him and gave a *come on* wave. Then, the boys entered the
building.

Sunlight spilled through the small, high windows, catching dust
particles that floated through the air and creating a shimmering
haze that dispersed as they stepped into it.

They'd been unable to reach Lynn and assumed he was out
collecting cans, but Ray showed up on his bike, meeting them a
quarter mile from Larry Roberts' garage. When they told him of
the plan, his face which had already been pink with exertion
from pedaling nonstop, turned tomato red.

It took some convincing to make him believe the plan was not
crazy, but after twenty minutes or so, he agreed to go along with
it. While they searched the building, Ray waited outside.

The cooler hummed tunelessly and when Garrett took a quick

glance at the contents, they appeared unchanged from the last time he'd been there, more than a week earlier. He was so scared that even the candy bars didn't tempt him.

Garrett reached the doorway between the office and garage first, hesitating under the jamb and letting his eyes adjust. The garage was even darker, with only two small windows in the closed bay door admitting light. It was about as useful as a match inside a cave, but Garrett began to make out first shapes, then entire objects.

He saw the same pick up his father had been working on during his last visit propped up on jack stands. He saw tools and toolboxes scattered about. He saw there were now five big, steel drums lined against the back wall. What he did not see, was his father.

When he finished his inspection, he came to face Shane who waited in the office.

"Now what?" Shane mouthed.

Garrett shrugged his shoulders. His father's truck had been outside. It made no sense that his truck would be here and he wouldn't.

"What's in the barrels?" Shane asked.

"He said it was used oil, but he never had them before. He just put the oil in gallon buckets and dumped it in the swamp behind the station."

"Then maybe we should look." Shane moved toward them.

Garrett hesitated, his fear keeping his feet frozen to the floor. He pried them up and forced himself to move.

Shane pressed his body against a barrel, using all his weight to try to knock it over and failing. "Shit, this is heavy."

Rather than trying to topple it, Garrett flipped the latch mechanism and freed the band that held the lid fast to the barrel.

"Show off."

Garrett grinned. He grabbed the lid with both hands and lifted, raising the cover toward himself and obscuring his own view. He hadn't done so on purpose, but when he saw Shane's face, he realized it might have been the right move.

Shane's skin took on a sickly pallor. Even his freckles seemed to go green.

"What is it?" Garrett was already moving the lid aside to see for himself.

"I have no idea but it's gross as shit."

Garrett leaned the lid against the wall, the thin metal giving a rumbling thunder sound. Before he saw the contents of the barrel, he smelled it.

It was dank and sour and reminded Garrett of the liquid that leaks out of trash bags and pools in the bottom of the can. The way that brew smelled after several days sitting outside in the summer heat. It was a high, rotten aroma and he didn't want to see what something that smelled so awful could look like, but he had to see.

Garrett leaned over the top of the barrel and stared into it. It was filled to the brim with globs of what looked like raw fat and sinew. The leftover bits after breaking down a whole chicken. Only it was obvious this stew wasn't leftover bits of chicken. All of these bits floated in a watery-brown fluid that looked and smelled like diarrhea.

The awful concoction didn't sicken him. Maybe because he'd been expecting something even worse like the worms the others had described. Squirming, heaping piles of their bizarre, alien forms ready to pounce and eat and infect.

Or maybe something even worse. Like human bodies. Victims of his father and brother. Because that's what he'd been thinking. That his family was out there murdering people and the shame of it was almost too much to bear.

Just as he began to feel relieved--

"Hello, Garrett." His father's voice.

It came from behind him. Behind both of them. Garrett spun, his feet hitting a patch of old grease and crashing first to his knees which yelped as they collided with the concrete floor, then to his ass. He felt wetness soaking through his shorts, through his underwear, and hoped it was oil or gas, anything but the contents of the barrels.

His father stood a foot on the garage side of the doorway, a large wrench clasped in his right hand. Shane backed away, closer to Garrett.

"Haven't seen you in a while, son. Thought maybe you skipped town like your brother."

"We know what's going on," Garrett said, trying to sound brave but the tremor in his voice belied that.

Larry grinned and took a step nearer. "Do you now?"

"Yeah," was all Garrett could get out.

"Yeah," Shane joined in. "We know everything. And we're gonna put an end to you fucking alien losers."

"Well, you sure have me scared. I'm shaking in my boots. See?" Larry's entire body trembled. He looked like a man laying on a vibrating bed, one that had been set to extra fast.

"It's happening!" Shane shouted.

Garrett saw it too. Larry's arms and legs were stretching. His uniform shirt pulled taut against his torso. His flesh rippled. Garrett stepped backward once, twice, then collided with a barrel.

"It breaks my heart to see you like this, Gar. Such a pussy." Larry laughed, a deep, hollow sound that echoed against the walls of the garage.

The words ripped through Garrett like a buzz saw, but also gave him a small amount of courage. He grabbed the barrel lid and strode toward his father. "You know what, dad?" Garrett didn't wait for an answer. "I might be a pussy but I'm not a fucking asshole like you!" He swung the lid and the broad side connected with Larry Roberts' face with a dense, wet splat. He felt no recoil, no bones breaking. It was like he'd smashed the lid into a pile of rotting fall leaves.

Garrett let go of the lid and it hung there for a moment, like it was fastened to his father's face with ticky tape. Then it slowly, so slowly, slid downward. It fell, clattering against the floor, a thunderclap this time. But Garrett's attention was locked on his father's face which was now flat and broad and round as a pizza. All of the man's features had been smashed inward and forced into two dimensions.

Then, Larry's head began to tilt backward, as if his neck

contained a hidden hinge. Only the hinge was broken and his head toppled all the way off.

It hit the floor with a sound unlike the metal lid. This sound was like dropping a strawberry pie. Gooey and moist.

When it landed, the thing that had been a head splattered unravelling dense cords of tissue which rolled out toward the boys. The tentacles were connected in the middle to a central, pulsing mass. They lashed and whipped, crawling and growing as they came at Garrett and Shane, desperate.

They'd been staring at the goings on, awestruck, but that brought them out of it.

"Ray! Now! Do it now!" Shane screamed at the garage bay door.

Through the small windows, Ray was visible, comically large eyes dominating his face.

"Pictures! Take pictures, Ray!"

Ray's face disappeared, replaced with a Polaroid OneStep. Light burst as the camera flash went off. There was a long pause, then another flash. The cycle repeated again and again.

Garrett stared at his father's body which was still stable and upright despite its missing cranium. From his neck grew more tissue which rose up and began to take form, filling in a way that reminded Garrett of pouring sand into a bowl. But there was no bowl holding this together. It was happening all of its own volition.

His head was growing back.

Even though he'd known his father was one of these things, seeing it like this, in its raw, awful glory made it so real he felt on the verge of passing out, like his head was an untethered balloon that was floating off his body. And that reminded him of his father's own head falling off and the dreamy yet nauseas feeling multiplied by ten.

Something grabbed Garrett's wrist. He yanked his arm away, a scream rising in his throat as he spun and discovered—

Shane.

His friend grabbed him again. "We got what we came for, Garrett. Now let's get the hell out of here."

That seemed like a good idea and Garrett let himself be dragged away. He high stepped over the tentacles that thrashed and fought to catch him, ignored his father whose head had now regenerated from the nose down, then ran toward safety.

CHAPTER FORTY-THREE

RAY HELD FOUR POLAROID PHOTOS, TWO IN EACH HAND, AND shook them almost violently. When Garrett and Shane took off, so did he, hopping on his bike and putting fifty yards between himself and the garage. He couldn't believe what he'd seen. What Garrett's father had done, and what he'd become. Hearing about it second hand definitely didn't compare to seeing it up close and in person. He was just thankful that he'd had the garage door separating himself from the craziness going on inside.

Bicycle tires crunched against the gravel road and he looked up as his friends approached. "Holy shit, guys! Holy shit! What was that?"

Their tires skidded to a stop near him. Shane hopped off first. "Yeah, it's something, huh?"

"Something? I ain't never seen anything so fucked up. His goddamn head fell off and turned into an octopus!"

"I thought it looked more like a squid," Shane said.

Both boys looked to Garrett to settle the debate.

"Octopus," Garrett said. "Squids are more triangle shaped."

"Told you!" Ray still shook the photos but Shane grabbed the two in his left hand.

"Aw, fuck!" Shane stared at the photos.

"What?"

Shane held them up. They were two nearly identical images of a dirty white bloom of light. Ray couldn't believe it. He looked at the photos he still grasped in his right hand. They were the same. He blinked his eyes like that might somehow change the image on the paper, looked again. "Shit..."

"What'd you do?" Shane threw his photos on the ground.

"I did what you said! I waited until he was all monster-like and took the photos. I didn't do nothing wrong!"

Garrett crouched down and examined the photos on the ground.

"You photographed the door, Ray! Were you even looking through the viewfinder?" Shane was furious, an emotion Ray had never seen come from his usually relaxed friend before.

"I did! I aimed it right at Mr. Roberts. I did, Shane. I really did!"

"You're such a fuck up!" Shane turned his back on him.

That hurt Ray more than a punch in the face. He'd been so proud of himself after taking the pictures, knowing that he'd carried out his part of the plan even though he was so scared he thought he might turn his tighty whities brown as a Hershey bar. Even though he really wanted to run for his life. And now it was all for nothing and it was apparently his fault. He felt his eyes burn and knew tears were coming.

"He didn't," Garrettsaid.

Both Ray and Shane looked to him.

"What?"

"What?" They spoke at the same time.

"Ray didn't mess up. It was the camera flash." He held up one of the pictures pointing to a particularly bright spot in the center and showing how it trailed off at the sides. "It reflected against the glass in the window." He turned to Shane. "We didn't think about that."

Shane looked from the photo to his feet. "Damn it."

Silence hung in the air for a few seconds and Ray used every ounce of self-control he possessed to not say *I told you* so because he knew that wouldn't help anything.

It was Shane that spoke first. "I'm sorry, Ray. I was a dick." He held out his fist and waited. "Don't leave me hanging, man."

"Yeah, you were. But it's okay." Ray tapped Shane's fist with his own. "Now what do we do?"

They stared at each other and decided to wait until the five of them could be together again before trying to figure that part out.

CHAPTER FORTY-FOUR

Blue.

Gray.

Blue.

Gray.

Jose's head was a confused fog. All he could focus on were the colors. And now it was gray.

Gray.

Gray.

He gasped in a startle breath of air and came away with nothing but metallic-tasting water that filled his mouth and throat and chest. He coughed and puked at the same time and he watched as small, partially dissolved slivers of bacon floated up and around him and intermingled with the gray.

The lake, he realized. I'm in the lake.

It came back in a rush, all of it. And then a hard jolt shook his body and sent brown particles into the gray, joining the barfed-up bacon. He was in the golf cart and he'd just bottomed out.

No. *We.*

We were in the golf cart.

He looked into the back for Adam Larew but the boy wasn't there. He must have fallen out when we hit, Jose thought.

But his thoughts were getting dim again and he realized now wasn't the time for solving mysteries. It was time to get to the surface and breathe.

He pulled himself out of the cart. Above he could see the brightness of day and he kicked his legs with all the strength he possessed. It got brighter and brighter until—

Jose burst through the surface. He took a greedy gasp of air and was halfway through another when—

He was yanked back into the water. His shirt tightened around him, the material stretching and dragging him deeper. When he looked below, he saw the hazy mirage of Adam.

Tendrils of flesh floated up, around his face, the remnants of ripped skin from where his jaw had once been. His tongue lolled and bobbed in the water, longer than it should have been and getting longer still.

What had been his arms were now ten feet long and they both latched onto Jose's shirt, reeling him in to the Adam-thing.

Jose kicked and fought. He made it a few feet back up but the creature that had hold of him was stronger and he had a feeling it could hold its breath for a long time, or longer than he could anyway. But drowning might be the better option.

He thrashed his body, trying to spin sideways and upward simultaneously. His shirt ripped and he didn't even care.

The pressure, the weight that had been holding him, evaporated as his shirt slipped free of his torso. Jose wasted no time, pumping for the surface, then swimming for shore, not bothering to breathe now, arms cycling, legs kicking. It wasn't a perfect stroke, or a stroke at all really, but it got him moving and soon he was in water shallow enough to stand. Then he ran.

A dozen or so campers were approaching but he only cared about one. All he had to do was follow the crying and he saw Don rushing toward him. They met ten feet from the shore and he scooped her up in his arms and held her tight against him.

More campers, all of them, everyone from Nobeboski, was coming now. Their excited, panicked voices were so loud Jose had to press his lips against Donnatella's ear to be heard.

"We can't tell anyone what really happened. Let me do the talking."

Jose hated to lie, especially to grown ups. And especially to grown ups he liked, which was all of them here at church camp. But he also knew that they'd never believe him, a kid, if he told what really happened. Adults always told you to tell the truth, but there were times they didn't really want to hear it.

This was one of those times.

CHAPTER FORTY-FIVE

THE CLOTHES AT THE GOD'S ATTIC WERE THE CHEAPEST IN town. Even on a regular day they charged less than the Goodwill or the Salvation Army and today, Wednesday, was paper bag day. For exactly one dollar Ray could stuff as many clothes into the bag as would fit without it bursting.

He'd been browsing the racks for almost twenty minutes. The bad thing about God's Attic was that most of the clothes were old people clothes. Dresses and suits, ties and shawls. The selection for kids clothes was small and had been picked over pretty hard for summer attire, but he'd still managed to find two t-shirts, a pair of shorts, and a pair of blue jeans. The jeans were a few inches too long, but he knew his Meemaw could fix that. He'd also taken a couple girl's blouses for Sissy, his older sister. He wasn't sure about the sizing on those, but had room in the bag and figured why not.

Ray was on his way to the check out counter where an elderly woman with her hair pulled back in a tight bun sat behind the counter and read a religious pamphlet. That was the other bad thing about God's Attic. Every time he came in to buy some clothes, he also had to sit through a little sermon and answer questions like, 'Have you been saved?', 'Does God have a home in your heart?', or 'When was your most recent visit to church, young man?'

The first time he'd gone there he'd answered the last of those questions honestly. Never. The woman's eyes got as big as half dollars and he thought she was going to fall right off her chair. She started telling him about her church and inviting him to it and telling him all the fun activities they had for children, but when she asked him about his family and he said his last name was Mayhugh, her lips pinched shut tight in a way that reminded him of a butthole.

It pissed him off the way everyone judged his family, even supposedly good people like that woman. It wasn't his fault his daddy was a killer or that most of his uncles and even some of his aunts had taken their own vacations to prison. And even if some of them were bad, it didn't mean they all were. But trying to explain that wasn't worth the effort. He'd learned that lesson about the time he learned how to write his name in cursive.

As he walked he fished quarters out of his pocket so they'd be ready when he checked out. The less time for questions, the better. While this wasn't the woman who'd acted so offended by his last name, he didn't want to spend the afternoon conversing with her. Not when Luigi's Pizza was next door and the smell had his stomach rumbling.

Before coming into God's Attic, Ray had checked Luigi's to make sure none of his friends were inside. If they had been, he would have skipped clothes shopping. He knew they wouldn't make fun of him, but he also knew Shane and Jose's families shopped at the nice department stores. Fisher's Big Wheel and Jamesway, or sometimes even Hess's. And Garrett and Lynn got most of their clothes at the Goodwill where they carried brands he'd actually heard of, not the no name, outdated styles that he could buy at the Attic for a buck a bag.

His friends were good guys and never picked on him about the important things, like being poor or stinking sometimes because the well at the farm was almost dry and he didn't bathe regularly, but he always worried that they might do something worse than laugh at him. He was afraid they might feel sorry for him. That would be the ultimate insult, even though they wouldn't mean it as one.

But, Luigi's was friend-free so he'd planned to fill a bag, then head over for a slice of pizza. If he got plain cheese, it was only fifty cents and he thought that was a bargain.

Ray set his bag of clothes on the counter and the old woman looked up. Her face was small and somehow bird-like and she flashed a bright smile that revealed her dentures.

"Just the one bag, dear?" She asked.

Ray nodded and handed her four quarters. "Yes, please."

She punched the total into the old cash register and waited for the receipt to print. "God's given us another glorious day outside today, hasn't he?"

Ray nodded. Oh, no. Here comes the sermon.

"When I woke this morning, I looked outside and heard the birds serenading me and thought, 'Thank you, Lord for seeing me through the night because I wouldn't want to miss this day.' So many people only think of God when it comes to miracles or grand events, but God's a part of every sunrise, every creature, and every one of us of course. He's—"

The receipt dropped from the register and Ray snatched it up. He reached for the bag but the woman, who had been halted in mid sentence, held it back. She inserted her pamphlet into the bag, and only then handed it over.

"Have a wonderful day, young man."

"You too." Ray was already rushing away as he spoke. He exited the store and descended the four metal steps to the sidewalk, then went straight to Luigi's which was only ten feet away. Yet even before he traversed that small distance, something else caught his attention.

Valerie Arden, the classmate he'd seen projectile vomit a barely digested, and barely chewed, hotdog onto the floor of Miss Zimmer's classroom a little over a month ago, was standing in the alley that separated God's Attic and Luigi's. And she was smoking.

He'd never seen a girl smoke before. Women, yes. It seemed like his own grandmother woke up with a cigarette in her mouth, but never a girl his age. Even though he smoked sometimes with Lynn, the idea that a girl would smoke, and in plain view of anyone passing by, was confusing and somehow exciting. What else might she be willing to do?

Instead of climbing the steps to Luigi's, Ray wandered closer to Valerie. She saw him and ignored him. She must be waiting for someone, he thought. A girlfriend. Probably Fredrica Bowers or Nikki Sarver because those were the girls she usually hung around with in school. Or maybe she was waiting for a boy. Ray decided he wanted to find out.

"Hi, Valerie."

"Hi."

She didn't really look at him and Ray wondered if she even knew his name. He sort of doubted it, but that was okay. At least she never made fun of him like some of the other girls who called him Pigpen or Stinkpot. He'd rather be anonymous.

"That a Marlboro?"

She shook her head and held up the cigarette. "Newport."

"Oh. I only smoke Marlboros." In reality, he only smoked whatever Lynn gave him and those were usually generics that tasted like stale ass. He didn't even like smoking much. It made his head feel sort of foggy. But it also made him feel cool.

"Yeah?" Valerie asked.

"Yeah." Ray closed the distance between them to around four feet. "So, how's your summer going"

"Boring."

Ray almost wished he could say the same. Part of him wanted to tell her everything that had been going on, that he was fighting real monsters, but he knew she was as likely to believe that as if he'd told her he'd spent June climbing that big mountain in Asia. Instead, he settled on, "Yeah."

She dropped the half-smoked cigarette to the pavement and crushed it under her Reeboks. Then she looked to the street again, surveying it.

"You waiting for someone?"

Valerie looked at him, the first time that was more than a glance.

Her face changed from disinterested to annoyed. "What's it to you?"

"Nothing." He said, trying to conjure up the same irritated sound in his own voice, but failing. "I just saw you alone and thought I'd say 'hi.'"

"Okay then. You said hi. Now go buy some more gross, old clothes or something. Just leave me alone."

Ray took a step backward as if her words had wounded him. In a way, they had. He was trying to come up with a response to that when she spun away and headed into the alley, away from him.

"Excuse me. Bitch..." He muttered.

He thought about resuming his old plan to eat a slice of plain pizza, but high, girlish laughter peeled down the narrow walls of the alley. He wondered who was with her in there. Who else was probably laughing at him. His curiosity got the better of him.

Ray stepped to the edge of the corridor and took a quick peek inside. He saw the backs of two girls as they turned the corner between another row of buildings. He followed.

When he reached the end of the alley, he made another cautious peek in the direction the girls had traveled but they were gone. A scratching noise to his right stole his attention. Ray turned toward the sound and found a grossly obese rat scurrying toward him, dragging a pizza crust along as it ran. So much for pizza for lunch.

The rat was only a few feet away and Ray kicked some shale at it so it wouldn't get too close. The gravel rained onto the rodent which dropped the crust from its mouth and unleashed an angry squeal.

"Screw off, rat." Ray sent another spray of rocks its way. The rat bared its yellow teeth and for a moment Ray worried it might charge him, but then it bit down on the crust and fled in the opposite direction.

With the rat, the girls, and his appetite gone, Ray was at a loss for what to do. He turned, retracing his steps to exit the alley. He didn't make it half-way before the door to one of the apartments behind the pizza shop opened. Ray froze, startled, as a man emerged.

He was wide and imposing and wore a Ford baseball cap. Ray noticed a matching Ford logo tattooed on his arm and thought the dude must be one hell of a fan. Ray also realized he was standing in the middle of the alley, blocking the man's way.

"Sorry." Ray stepped aside.

The man didn't pass by. He only stood and stared.

"You got some big assed rats back here. I saw one that looked like it ate a large with all the topping." Ray smiled, expecting to get one in return. He did not.

That was enough attempts at pleasantries and Ray turned. He made it three steps away when he felt hot, moist air on his neck. Breaths.

Oh shit, this day just keeps getting worse.

He had no idea how bad it was about to get.

Ray turned 90 degrees, just enough that he could see what was going on behind him. The dude stood inches away, his chest heaving like he'd finished a marathon. The air coming from his mouth was cloying and rancid. Sweet, dead meat. Roadkill on an August afternoon. His mouth gaped open and, as Ray stared into the cavity, he saw movement. He saw long, featureless things in that black hole. He saw them making their escape.

The man groaned, a sound like door hinges that hadn't been used for a decade coming open.

Rrrrrrrrrr

Ray backed away. One step. Two. Three.

Rrrrrrrr-ggggggggg-

Ray's feet danced as he scurried in reverse. He knew he'd go faster if he turned around and ran but he couldn't put his back to this man. He had to see what was happening, even though he had a damn good idea what to expect.

Gggggg-hhhhhhhhhhhh—

And then it happened.

Half a dozen long, cigar-shaped masses flew from the man's gaping maw.

Not cigars, Ray thought. Hot dogs. He's throwing up hot dogs just like Valerie Arden. Oh, my God.

Only these hot dogs moved. They hit the ground with wet splats. One of them burst, flayed open by the shale and bits of broken glass that littered the pavement. It oozed piss-yellow snot that bubbled and fizzed in a way that reminded Ray of pop rocks.

The other five things crawled like inchworms, humping themselves up in the middle, moving forward, humping, forward, humping. It seemed like a cycle of motion that should take forever to get anywhere but they were coming fast. They were only a few feet from Ray.

Behind them, the dude lumbered forward like Frankenstein's monster. His mouth remained ajar and smaller bits of flesh and tissue fell out. Some moved when they hit the ground, alive and hungry, while the smaller chunks only festered.

That was enough of the freaks for Ray. He spun, took one sprinting step, then another. When his foot came down for the third, it landed on one of the hot dogs. As it burst, his foot slid out from under him like he'd stepped on a stray banana peel rather than an alien's larva, and he careened sideways.

He dropped his shopping bag of second-hand clothes and got his hands up seconds before his upper body hit the brick wall. That slowed some of the force, but not all and his head bounced off the crumbling bricks hard enough to make him see tiny, white explosions.

Behind him, he heard the dude's footsteps. Heard more atrocities falling from his mouth. And Ray knew the inchworm hotdogs had to be closing in too.

He shook his head to clear it because that's what they did in the movies, but it didn't help. It made his disorientation worse.

The worms were almost at his feet. The dude less than a yard behind them. Then, further back, at the apartment door, Ray watched a woman emerge. She looked oddly familiar and it took only a moment for his dazed mind to solve the mystery.

"Mighty Mole," Ray muttered as the lunch lady joined the attack party. She looked different, without the hairnet, but the mole was impossible to mistake. On someone like Cindy Crawford, that was a beauty mark. But on Maud it was an obsidian scar that spawned wiry hair and clung to her face like a furry, black stain. Why doesn't she at least pluck the hairs, Ray thought.

The woman tilted her head back and sniffed the air, like a hound hunting a fox. Then her face broke into a leering grin.

"I know that stink." Her voracious eyes locked on Ray. "Funny place to run into you, Pigpen."

Ray spun away from her. At the end of the alley he could see cars passing. They were twenty feet from him. Freedom – safety - was less than ten yards away.

One of the hot dogs was on his foot. He felt the weight of it on his shoe, looked down, and found it was almost at his sock. Inches away from bare skin. He knew that if it touched him, he could catch whatever perverse disease it was spreading. He kicked his foot but it stuck like it was attached with Velcro. He kicked again, that time kicking the wall to create extra impact, and the thing came free. He stomped it, then ran.

As he neared the end of the alley he felt sticky wetness on his face and almost lost his mind. His hands flailed against it, certain that something from the aliens was on him. But, when he pulled his fingers away he saw they were covered in his own blood. He felt his face again and discovered a three inch long gash where his head had met the wall. It stung and burned, but in a way that was amazing and normal.

He burst from between the shadowy alley as if being birthed from it. He raced to his bike, hopped on, and peddled like his life depended on it. Because, Ray knew, it really did.

CHAPTER FORTY-SIX

It had gone far enough, Garrett thought. Ray was a blubbering mess, his hand me down t-shirt stained with blood, his forehead scarred by a ragged wound that had already begun to clot over. But Garrett knew that, had he zigged rather than zagged or even paused a second to think, he could be dead. Or worse, he could be infected with the same alien disease that had taken over his father and brother.

Shane was helping stock shelves at his father's pharmacy and, if Garrett knew is best friend, was also grabbing several issues of the latest adult magazines for resale. Shane's mother was at work leaving him alone at the house, until Ray had arrived and filled him in on the morning's events. When he saw how scared his friend was, he knew it was time to tell someone else about what was happening, and not another kid. This had ceased being a kid's problem. They needed to get grownups involved.

After getting Ray cleaned up and giving him one of Shane's shirts, Garrettpulled a worn card from his wallet and used the phone in the Vinyan's kitchen to call the number listed on it.

After less than a minute long discussion, the baton had been passed and their well-intentioned, but poorly-conceived notion that they could be heroes, was over. What he didn't know was that he'd just summoned the help of their enemy.

It took some convincing to get Ray to join him for the meeting, but the boy's terror was ebbing like the morning tide. Besides, A&H Video was one of Ray's favorite places in the world so they boarded their bikes and rode into town

As with most weekdays, especially in the middle of the day, the video shop was empty save for Skip Haywood, the owner. He glanced up from a paperback novel as they stepped inside, setting off a motion activated bell that *ding dong-ed* mechanically. The man was in his forties with a big, bald head and a mustache that hovered somewhere between Tom Selleck and Yosemite Sam.

Skip gave them a nod. They were good customers and always brought the tapes back on time and rewound. And they liked him because he let them rent R-rated movies, no questions asked.

The only time the man had ever given them grief was on one occasion when Lynn had slipped through the beaded curtain that separated the mainstream movies from the Adult section. Lynn had been staring, awestruck, at the explicit box covers when Skip caught him and banned all of them from the store for a week. None of them ever dared go into that room again, both over fear of a longer ban or maybe even getting blacklisted entirely from A&H, but also because, when Lynn described the covers he'd seen, they didn't sound appealing or sexy in the way that Shane's magazines were. They sounded pretty damn gross.

The two boys bee-lined to the horror section where the walls were lined with empty VHS boxes. There was another rental store in Sallow Creek, Video Den was its name, and they carried a few horror titles, but only the most mainstream fare. Skip was a genre enthusiast and he stocked the store with movies they'd never even read about in *Fangoria*.

Head Hunter, Black Roses, Evil Ed, Demonwarp, Deadly Dreams. Usually the boxes were the best part. Like *The Nest* with a woman in a bikini being attacked by a giant roach or *The Unnamable* with its albino, fanged monster. They'd seen every horror title A&H stocked, many multiple times, and the highlight of most weeks was showing up each Tuesday to see what new releases had arrived.

"*Flesh Eating Mothers!*" Ray said, pointing to a box with a crazed housewife standing over a pot of stew and a kid's sneaker in the ladle. He snatched the numbered tag off the rack, as if he thought someone else was going to beat him to it and rent it first.

"That looks cheesy," Garrett said.

"I like the cheesy ones."

"I know." Garrett preferred the serious, really scary movies, but under the circumstances some laughter to go along with the cringes might not be a bad thing.

They were looking for a second title when the bell *ding dong*-ed again. Both of their heads snapped toward the door.

Officer Hanes came through the doorway, taking his wide-brimmed trooper's hat off as he entered. His head swiveled right, toward Skip who stared curious.

"Anything wrong, Officer?" Skip asked.

Hanes shook his head. "Not at all. Just looking for some young friends of mine. Saw their bikes parked out front."

Skip pointed toward the horror section but Hanes had already located them. Garrett raised his hand in a meek wave and the trooper smiled and moved toward them.

"Hello, Garrett."

"Hi." Garrett pointed to Ray. "This is Ray. My friend."

"Nice to meet you. Any friend of Garrett's is a friend of mine." He gave a toothy grin.

The side of Ray's lip curled up at the lame remark. "Um. Okay."

Hanes looked around the store, as if verifying it was empty, then glanced back at Skip. "Mind if we use the back exit?"

Skip shrugged his shoulders. "Help yourself."

Garrett followed as Hanes stepped toward the door but Ray lagged behind. Garrett shot him a look and tilted his head in a come along gesture.

Ray held up the rental tag for *Flesh Eating Mothers*. "I got to pay for the movie first."

"Whatever."

As Ray went to the counter, Garrett exited the building.

He squinted as his eyes adjusted to the bright daylight. They were alone behind the store, with only Skip's red Toyota Starlet and a rusty dumpster keeping them company. After the small strip of pavement, there was an empty gravel lot that had been abandoned long enough to spout a bumper crop of weeds and, behind that, the turnpike.

Garrett thought there was an enormous difference between the front of the store and the rear. In front, you were in town. There were cars passing on the street less than ten feet away. People shuffling by on the sidewalk. Here, behind the store, it was like they'd stepped into a forgotten, uninhabited world. He felt the baby hairs on his forearms rise to attention and hoped the cop didn't notice. Why did he have to be such a pussy?

"What did you want to see me about, Garrett? More trouble with your dad?"

Garrett had almost forgotten why he'd requested this meeting, but that momentary confusion was fleeting. "No. I mean, sort of, but not exactly. It's really complicated."

"I'm fine with complicated. How about you start at the beginning?" Hanes put his hat back on, casting his face into dark shadow.

That would be a hell of a long story, Garrett thought. Even though it was only a few weeks he didn't want to travel back quite that far.

"Well, after Harrison came back, I thought he was acting funny. He wasn't eating with me and my dad and he just seemed... off." No sense dragging this out, he told himself. Get on with it. "One day, I went to his room and I saw him barf on his food, then eat it. It was like, he had to barf on it to be able to eat. To soften it up or coat it so it slid down, or something I guess."

He tried to see the cop's eyes, to get a read on whether he was buying any of this, but they were lost in the shadows cast by the hat's brim.

"But that was just the beginning. After that, my friends started seeing weird sh— Stuff too."

"Weird, how?"

Garrett looked to the closed rear exit, wondering when Ray would get here. If Ray would show him the scratches, that would give them something akin to proof, not just words. "Weird like seeing people's arms turn into tentacles. And those tentacles crawling into other people. Like they're—" Don't say it, he told himself. He'll think you're crazy if you say it. He'll take you straight to the funny farm. Don't say it, Garrett. Don't you dare say it out loud. "Aliens."

Shit.

He waited for a reaction. Disbelief. Frustration. One of those *why is this stupid kid bothering me with this* looks he and his friends so often received from adults. But the cop's face was impossible to read.

"Sir?" Garrett asked.

"You're a clever boy, Garrett."

"Thank you."

The cop crouched down so their faces were more or less at the same level. There was an unkindness in his eyes. "Let's say what you told me is true."

"It is!"

"Okay, then it is. So, tell me. What's so special about your life that you're willing to fight for it?"

"What?"

"Your life sucks, Garrett. And when people say, 'It gets better' they're lying. It doesn't, not for kids like you. You've got a loser father who beats you. A loser brother who hates you. A couple loser friends whose futures are about as bright as fifteen watt bulbs. At best, you'll end up flipping burgers or bagging groceries. And that's if you don't eat yourself into an early grave."

Garrett took a step back and bumped into the metal siding of the video store. "Why are you saying this?"

"Because it's about time someone told you the truth." Hanes pointed at Garrett, his index finger as long and thin as a Ticonderoga #2 pencil.

Garrett reached behind himself and fumbled for the door handle but couldn't find it.

Hanes' finger grew, stretched. "It's easier to give in, Garrett. Go with the flow, as they say."

"As who says?" Garrett's hand brushed the handle, caught hold, grabbed it.

"Humans."

Hanes's alien finger, now a full foot and a half long, whipped at Garrett but the boy yanked open the door and spun away. The finger slapped against the door, sticking to it. As Garrett dashed into the store, the finger curled around the door, stretching toward him, reaching for him.

Garrett slammed the door closed, severing the finger. The half that was inside the store dropped to the floor, oozing viscous pus. Garrett watched as the thing twitched, spasmed. Then, sprouted legs like a centipede and scrabbled at him. He overturned a display rack of previously viewed movies which clattered onto it, then ran to the front of the store.

Ray and Skip stared at him as he rushed their way.

"What was that noi—" Ray was stopped mid word when Garrett grabbed his shirt and dragged him toward the door.

"Stay out of the back room, Skip," Garrett said. "There's an alien finger back there."

"A what?" Skip asked but the boys were out the front door and in the wind.

CHAPTER FORTY-SEVEN

JOSE, GARRETT, SHANE, AND RAY WERE CRAMMED INTO A wooden eagle's nest play set that they hadn't used in a couple years. It was Donnatella's domain now, but Jose was grounded until his parents could agree on a punishment.

"They have to pay for the golf cart," Jose said. "It's gonna cost like a thousand dollars."

"But you were fighting for your life. And you saved Don," Ray said.

"They don't know that!"

"Oh, right."

The story he'd concocted was simple. He and Don found Pastor Ted having a heart attack so they jumped into his golf cart to get help. Jose panicked, lost control, and drove it into the lake. The fact that neither of the boys who were actually aliens were going to disagree made it easier to sell. And a search for Pastor Ted turned up nothing, leaving everyone to assume that he'd wandered into the woods and probably died.

Jose's dad was understanding and, Jose thought, even seemed a little proud that his son had attempted to be a hero. His mother was less enthused. "Why couldn't you just run for help?" She'd asked, to which Jose shrugged his shoulders and muttered, "Because it was an emergency."

The boys filled him in on the local events and, by the time all the tales had been told, each of the boys were worried, tired, and frustrated. It wasn't the best audience for saying what he needed to say, but putting it off any longer wouldn't make it easier.

He swallowed the lump in his throat and got on with it. "I hate to do this guys, but I'm out." He kept his head down, not wanting to see their reactions. "The five of us acting like the *A Team* and trying to fight aliens or monsters or whatever they are. It's impossible."

"If we don't, who will?" Shane asked.

"Yeah," Ray added. "Those things will take over if we don't stop them."

"What are we doing to stop them? I hit one of them with the golf cart and made it explode and a couple hours later it was back and walking around."

"We'll figure something out," Shane said. "We have to."

"Maybe you will, but I'm sorry. You're not going to change my mind. It's already made up." He finally met their gaze, feeling more confident because he believed what he was saying to be the truth. "It was a stupid plan anyway."

They called him a chicken and a pussy and told him how important it was. They pleaded to his sympathies and his insecurities. Only Garrett remained silent and Jose thought that might have been even worse, but his decision was final. After fifteen minutes of browbeating failed to move the needle, they left him there, alone in the eagle's nest, wondering what he'd done.

CHAPTER FORTY-EIGHT

GARRETT AND SHANE RODE THEIR BIKES IN SILENCE. RAY had departed for the farm, leaving them alone for the ride back to Shane's house. It was a short trip that felt like it lasted hours and all the while, Garrett couldn't shake the feeling that this was his fault. That he was partially responsible for this fracturing of their friendship. Everything they'd seen, everything they'd witnessed, it all coincided with Harrison's vanishing act and gross reappearance. That made Garrett guilty by association, or so he told himself.

Upon arriving at the Vinyan residence, they found Shane's mother had prepared chef salads for each of them. Even though Garrett wasn't a fan of rabbit food, the motherly care she'd put into it made him willing to take one for the team and eat it.

They decided to dine in the clubhouse and moved to the back yard where Apollo trotted toward them, tail tucked, ears flat against his head. He'd come from the direction of the patio.

Shane gave him an absent-minded pat on the head, but Garrett crouched down and met him at face level, ruffling the fur on the dog's face. "Hey buddy. Why aren't you in the clubhouse?"

Apollo's head swiveled toward the building, then back. That was the only answer he gave.

"Sometimes the doggy door gets stuck," Shane said.

They continued on, but the dog remained behind. Garrett tried to cajole it into joining, but Apollo trotted back to the patio, crawled under a glass table, and laid down.

Shane reached the clubhouse first and pulled the door open.

"Hey, fuckers," Lynn lounged on the loveseat, his head on a pillow, feet crossed.

"Where the hell have you been?" Shane asked as he stepped inside. Garrett followed.

"Around." Lynn said. "Made over fifty bucks off cans."

"Yeah? Well, while you were playing trash collector things got intense here."

"How so?"

They filled in Lynn about what had happened the last few days, culminating in Jose abandoning them and calling them stupid. Lynn laughed at that part.

They discussed how to kill the aliens. Cutting them to pieces was no good. Guns were equally worthless. Lynn, ever helpful, suggested nuclear weapons and Shane told him to call George Bush and ask if they could borrow some. Garrett still liked the fire idea, but lack of access to a flamethrower made the implementation a challenge.

As they talked, Garrett struggled to choke down the remainder of his salad after picking out the ham and cheese. He reached for the salt shaker and doused the flavorless lettuce in sodium for the third time. When he set the shaker down, it fell into a groove in the table and toppled to its side. A small pile of salt spilled out before he could turn it upright.

"Dude, really? We've already got more than enough bad luck." Shane reached into the spilled salt, pinched a few granules and tossed it over his left shoulder.

"When did you become a ninety-year-old Italian woman?" Garrett asked.

"I'm just saying—"

The salt rained onto Lynn's face, the granules tumbling into the deep hollow of his eye socket. He gasped and sat bolt upright on the couch.

Shane glanced back. "Sorry man, did I get you?"

Lynn didn't respond. He rubbed at his eye furiously, fingers clawing, scraping. Garrett thought it looked like he might dig his eyeball out if he wasn't careful.

"Shit! Do you need some water or something to wash it out?" Shane rose from his chair, took two steps toward the exit, but Garrett caught his wrist.

"Wait. Look."

Garrett didn't want to believe what he was seeing was real. He wanted Shane to look and tell him he was crazy. Because what Garrett thought he saw was Lynn's hand dissolving from the fingertips back.

"Oh shit," Shane said.

"He's one of them!" Garrett shouted. "What do we do?"

Shane had no idea what to do and only stared.

Lynn's hand had become an opaque jelly which dropped away from his eye to reveal the entire side of his face was undergoing the same deconstruction. His eyebrow sagged down, stretched, then dripped off in a wet splatter against the floor. Lynn's eyeball had become transparent, revealing a sack filled with yellow mucous inside it. Then it too fell out of his head.

The boy who'd been their friend, the fifth Musketeer, they sometimes joked, was melting. He stared at them, his remaining eye wide and pained and accusing. His mouth opened but not to expel words. Instead, thick, gelatinous goo the texture of lumpy gravy and the color of rotting meat, poured out of him.

"Oh shit!" Shane said again.

Sometime, while watching this, the boys had embraced and clutched each other tight. "You already said that," Garrett said.

"I know. But it's pretty fucking spot on isn't it?"

"Yeah! It is!"

Lynn's head caved in and his now sightless body began to stumble. It crashed into a radio that broke as it hit the floor. He took out a lamp, then knocked over a shelf of Shane's GI Joes. All the while the body continued to go to pieces, His right arm came loose at the elbow, the bottom half falling on the floral print quilt Shane's mom made him use so he wouldn't get cold during sleep outs. An explosion of gore saturated it. Then, the rest of his arm broke free at the shoulder.

The body staggered forward, moving straight for—

"Not the TV," Shane sad. "Come on, man."

Lynn's body hit the TV which wobbled once, twice, then toppled over, the picture tube popping with an explosion of glass.

"Goddamn it," Shane said.

After hitting the TV, Lynn pinballed back in their direction. As Garrett looked from him to the piles of flesh and body parts that littered the floor like bird droppings, he realized something.

"Shane, there aren't any tentacles," he said.

"What?"

Garrett pointed. "Look. They aren't growing or sprouting anything. No tentacles. No worms. Before, it was like every piece of it was alive. But not now."

"It's dying?" Shane said, half-way between a question and a declaration.

Garrett nodded.

They returned their attention to Lynn, who was now gone from the chest up. Great globs of oozing, phlegmy tissue fell at a faster rate. A solid one fourth of the cabin was covered in it. His legs took a clumsy, frenzied step and the foot came down on one of the larger piles.

What was left of Lynn fell, and when the body hit the floor, the skin suit holding it together ruptured sending volleys of the alien flesh into the walls, over the furniture, even splattering the ceiling.

Garrett and Shane were saved from the worst of it as they

huddled against the cabin doors, a few yards away. A chunk hit Shane's shirt, leaving behind a mustard-colored welt of snot when it fell, and Garrett's shorts caught two globs, but that was the worst of it.

They surveyed the clubhouse, where pieces and wads of the thing that had been Lynn were everywhere. The remains bubbled and fizzed like spilled Pepsi. The smell though, was that of death.

"You realize the clubhouse is ruined, right?" Garrett said.

"Oh, hell yeah. There's not enough bleach in the world to clean up that freakshow."

CHAPTER FORTY-NINE

As soon as Ray hung up the phone he planned to find his papaw. His first stop was the kitchen, where he'd heard pans clanging earlier that afternoon. But, when he burst through the doorway, he instead found his Meemaw occupying her usual spot at the head of the table.

Her face had more wrinkles than anyone Ray had ever seen before. There wasn't a smooth spot to be found. As always, a cigarette clung to her bottom lip like it was held there with super-glue. She didn't remove it when speaking or drinking or eating. When he was younger, he'd once snuck into their bedroom at night because he thought maybe she kept a cigarette in her mouth when she slept too. She did not.

A heaping bowl of snap beans sat on the table before her and she was in up to her elbows. "Why are you running in the house?" Meemaw asked, her voice bordering on annoyance.

"I'm sorry, Meemaw. I was looking for Papaw."

She looked to her right, then her left. "Well, he ain't here."

"Okay." Ray made to leave the room but she stopped him.

"Ray."

"Yeah?"

"After supper I'm cutting that hair of yours. You look like a pansy."

He knew his perm looked ridiculous but he'd come to like it. Plus, he was afraid it might hurt Charlene Ohler's feelings if he changed it. He made a mental note to avoid Meemaw after they ate, hoping that by the next day, she'd forget all about it.

"Bye, Meemaw."

She puffed on her cigarette and snapped more beans.

With the kitchen Papaw free, Ray's second guess was the barn. On his way there he crossed through what passed for a living room in the farmhouse. Two of his uncles and one male cousin were sprawled on the couch and recliner, drinking or smoking or both as the evening news played on the black and white television set.

The men ignored him and that was fine with Ray. When they spoke to him it was usually along the lines of, 'Ray, get me a beer' or 'Ray, make me some nachos' or 'Ray, you make a better door than a window so get the fuck out of the way of the TV.' The men shared his blood, but he didn't understand them and had little desire to be around them more than necessary.

He skirted the walls, staying out of their line of sight, but before he could escape the room he saw Sissy in the corner playing with a ratty baby doll that looked like it had been scavenged from Mr. Thompson's junkyard. Over half its hair was missing and the skin was about as black as coal. Sissy hummed a tuneless song while she tried to put a dress on the doll and Ray crouched down beside her.

"Hey, Sissy."

She didn't acknowledge him. He wasn't offended. Sissy lived in a world of her own making and she lived there alone. Her clumsy fingers struggled with the buttons on the dress and Ray reached out and took over. His sister was twenty, nearly twice his age, but that was a meaningless number.

He finished buttoning the dress and handed it back to her. She accepted it, but didn't look at him. "I might be gone for a couple days. Me and my friends are going to save Sallow Creek. Maybe the whole world."

Sissy hummed and her fingers now worked to undress the doll.

"I think it's gonna work, but if it doesn't, I want you to be a good girl, okay?"

No response from Sissy, but his Uncle Vince chucked a can at them. "Shut the fuck up! I'm trying to listen to Peter Jennings."

Warm beer rained on them. Some of it trailed down Sissy's cheek and Ray wiped it away with the back of his fingers. He thought about saying something else, but he knew it wouldn't mean anything to her and would only draw further ire from his uncle, so he left the room without another word.

Next stop was the barn. Much of the building was off limits to Ray but the north end, where his Papaw putzed around on his old Dodge pick up, was one area where he was allowed.

As Ray entered the structure, bright, afternoon sunlight drifted through the wood siding, turning spiderwebs into glistening works of art and painting parallel lines across the earthen floor.

Under the green Dodge, there was a metallic clatter followed by a jovial, "Son of a bitch."

Ray moved toward the vehicle. Two booted feet extended from under it.

"Who goes there?"

"It's me, Papaw. Ray."

"Ah. Afternoon, Raymond. I thought you'd be out playing with those friends of yours."

"I was, earlier. I'm home now though."

Another clatter. "Hand me that can of WD40, Ray."

Ray saw it setting amongst a variety of tools and greases and spare parts. He grabbed it, then crouched beside the truck and stuck his arm blindly under it. His grandfather took the can and there came three quick hisses as it was put to use. Then Ray heard a soft groan after which, "Good. Good."

Vyatt Mayhew's feet shifted as the man scooted out from underneath the truck. When he emerged, he was hatless, a sight that never failed to shock Ray. He didn't like seeing his Papaw without his hat because it made the man look much older.

"Did you fix it?"

His grandfather looked to the old truck. "I put a Band-Aid on it. At this point, stopping the bleeding's the best that can be expected." He wiped his hands on a dirty rag.

"I need your help, Papaw."

The old man smiled. "That's what I'm here for." But when he

looked closer at his grandson, that smile faded. "Are you in some sort of trouble, Ray?"

"Maybe."

His grandfather reached across the divide between them and rested his gnarled hand on Ray's knee. "Well then, tell me what I can do."

"You know how you shoot the rock salt at the deer when they start getting into the corn?"

Vyatt nodded.

"Well, me and my friends need to borrow your shotguns and shells."

"May I ask why?"

Ray considered this and decided, as much as he hated lying to his grandfather, the truth wouldn't work. "There's a family of coons sneaking into the clubhouse. They've got a hole up near the roof and they get in and tear everything apart."

"All right then. You took your hunter's safety course and I trust you, Ray. You're welcome to 'em. How many guns do you want?"

"Three. One for each of us."

"I thought there were five in your group."

Memories of Lynn flooded his mind and he fought them away so he wouldn't get emotional. But he didn't want to get into what happened with Lynn or even the dispute with Jose. "Just three now."

"All right. And how many shells do you want?"

Ray swallowed hard. "All of them, please."

Vyatt stared at the boy with eyes squinted so hard that his eyeballs almost disappeared among the wrinkles. "Raymond, I don't believe your being entirely truthful with me."

Ray looked away, turning his attention to a clod of dirt on the floor. He couldn't bear to look the man in the face and tell another lie so he decided to remain silent.

"But I suspect you have your reasons for that." He stood, the bones in his back snapping and popping as his spine straightened. "Come with me."

CHAPTER FIFTY

Jose's mother was halfway through mixing up a batch of cinnamon rolls when she realized she was out of powdered sugar. With the oven already preheating and his father at work, sending him to the store was her only option.

"But you're still grounded, so straight there and back. No stopping anywhere along the way. No visiting with those friends of yours either."

"I don't think they're my friends anymore," Jose said.

JoAnn Supranowicz had her nose in the cookbook. "What?"

"Never mind."

She glanced up to him. "Straight there and back, right?"

"There and back." Jose said with a nod.

He did go straight there. The closest market was a bit over a mile away, a small country store run by a Mennonite family. To get there he had to peddle his bike past the pond of liquid manure that was located beside the barn where the Shaffer's housed their cows.

The smell emanating from what Jose and his friends called *the poop pit* was so rank he pinched his nose with one hand and steered one-armed. He peered into it as he rode by. Flies teemed along the surface, feasting on the poop, only disturbed by the occasional methane bubble that floated to the surface and burst.

"Gross," he muttered.

He bought a two pound sack of powdered sugar and added an oatmeal raisin cookie that he paid for with his own pocket change. It was a nice break from being grounded.

As he returned, he thought about his friends. He still felt everything he'd said was true, that they were stupid for ever thinking they could fight the aliens on their own, but he also knew he'd let them down. Jesus talked about all kinds of impossible stuff in the bible and his friends still stuck with him. Not that Jose considered his friends on the same level as Jesus Christ, but those four guys were the only real friends he'd ever had and that should count for something.

He tried to figure out a way he could still help them, even while being grounded. His folks still hadn't picked a length of time, but he had the feeling it would be lengthy. As he pedaled and pondered, he didn't notice Nolan Haddix and his two friends hunkered down behind a wooden road sign advertising *Yoder's Market! Fresh Produce, Seasonal Fruit, Dry Goods & Scratch and Dent Discounts!* until he was beside them. Until Haddix had shoved a tree limb in front of him and sent Jose crashing to the road.

The bag of powdered sugar burst in a white haze that blew in front of his face and clouded his vision. Through the fog, he saw the three figures approaching.

"Looks like we're having Mexican for dinner." Haddix said and when he emerged through the fog, Jose saw his face had contorted into a leering, deformed smile. Heavy hunks of flesh sagged from his cheeks like jowls that flapped to and fro as he walked.

Jose looked past him and saw RJ Petrillo, his right arm so long it dragged on the ground. Matt Ross brought up the rear and, at first, Jose thought he was still normal, but when he studied him closer he saw the teen now had a pendulous, swaying gut that would have put even Garrett's to shame. It jiggled and reminded Jose of Pastor Ted, the memory bringing with it a stinging stab of sadness.

The trio was within feet of him now and Jose knew time was not on his side. He grabbed his bike and turned it upright only to realize the front wheel was bent at a thirty degree angle. If he couldn't ride it, he'd weaponize it.

Jose shoved the bike at the bullies and it smacked into Haddix's shins which folded backward bonelessly. He stumbled, stopping forward motion while his legs reformed their traditional shape. Without waiting for that process to come to fruition, Jose ran.

Ahead, there was nothing but open road and fields of soybeans. There was no one around to help and nowhere to hide for a quarter mile. They were behind him, their progress steady but they couldn't keep his pace. But he also knew the story of the tortoise and the hare and he dared not waste time looking back.

He made it to the Shaffer's barn and dashed around the corner. He knew the bullies would have seen him so he headed into the barn and up a row of stalls. The cows were all in the field, but the barn still reeked of their presence and he danced around cow flops as he ran.

Jose came to a stall filled with hay, both in bale form and loose and scattered about. He thought that might be his best, or only hiding spot and dove into it. He pulled heaps of hay over him, burying himself in it.

Buried alive, he thought. I hope this doesn't end up being my actual grave.

He waited, unable to see anything but bits of light that managed to find their way through the maze of hay atop him. But he could hear. Hear the nattering of the flies that shared the stall with him. Hear the sound of his own heartbeat in his ears. Hear the muffled footsteps of the incoming bullies as they trudged across the dirt.

They were close. Haddix's breathing was loud and raspy through his Halloween mask of a face, impossible to conceal. Jose held his own breath.

The sound of their movement stopped. He was sure that happened outside his stall. He wondered if he'd left footprints or made an even more egregious error like hiding with his foot exposed. He shifted slightly, trying to discern by feel whether any bits were poking out.

Rambling prayers raced through his mind. God, I know I haven't been the best boy lately but I'm begging you, please protect me right now. I'll try hard to be nicer and more honest. Please forgive me and protect me.

This was worse than camp. At camp, he had Don to worry about. Even if he wasn't feeling brave there, he had to act brave for her. In this stall, in this stink of the barn, he was alone and no matter how hard he tried to fool himself, he knew he wasn't brave. He was a coward.

The footsteps resumed. At first he thought they were continuing past him but he realized soon enough that they were entering the stall. They were coming straight at him.

I'm begging you, God. Please, please, please protect me. Please help me get out of here alive.

"I spy, with my little eye..." Haddix said. "Something starting with..."

Jose exploded from the hay, throwing heaping armloads of it at the bullies. It created a kind of miniature dust storm and the air became clogged with dirt and hay and dried cow poop and whatever else had settled into the stall.

It was blinding and Jose used the brief distraction to race forward. He hit one of them in the chest, assuming it to be Haddix or Ross due to the height, then ricocheted off that chest and bounced into the stall wall.

"Get him!"

That voice was definitely Haddix's and Jose wanted to be as far away from it as possible. He felt a wet splat against his back as something whipped him but ignored it as he spun and ran from the stall.

In the rush he lost his bearings and took off in the opposite direction from the barn's entrance. He glanced back and saw all three bullies had resumed the chase. A smaller opening stood at the other end of the barn. Another door, he thought. His best hope. His small arms and legs pistoned as he ran for his life.

Jose came to what he'd thought was a door. Only it wasn't a door at all. It was a chute. And when the smell hit him, he knew where it led.

The poop pit.

Oh, Jesus, he thought, and not in a praying way. I can't do this. There's no way.

He surveyed his other option, which was the stampeding bullies. RJ's arm now looked like an elephant's trunk. Matt Ross's belly was the size of a beach ball. Taut skin, ready to burst, poked out from under his shirt. And Nolan Haddix's awful face had grown to three times its normal size. He looked like a living, breathing, enraged bobblehead.

He faced forward again. The aroma this close was what he imagined Hell must smell like when the Devil was having a particularly cruel day. It was rotten eggs on top of spoiled meat blended together with barf and, of course, poop. So much poop. Thousands and thousands of gallons of poop.

Jose closed his eyes and dove down the shoot.

The ride was short. Too short. He didn't even have time to cover his mouth or pinch off his nose before he hit the pool of manure. Only manure was too clean a word for what this was. This was diarrhea that had been aging in the sun all summer long. As it filled his mouth, flowed up his nose, he thought being turned into an alien might have been the better choice after all. But it was too late. He was in. And he was sinking.

It was camp and the golf cart all over again, but at least this time Jose didn't have a monster dragging him down. He pumped his legs and did his best fish impression as he pushed his way to the surface, breaking through the crusty top layer and into the light of day. He thought that must be what it's like to be born, but no birth canal could be that hideous.

As he floated in the liquid poop, the first thing he did was throw up. He proceeded to do that a second time and he never thought the taste of barf in his mouth could be so appealing. Then he blew his nose, shooting out brown tendrils of snot mixed with manure. He could feel chunks of awfulness clogging his braces and spat repeatedly.

Manure ran down his face, into his eyes, but his hands were also coated in the stuff making wiping it away impossible. He needed to get out and he fell into an awkward breaststroke that propelled him to the shore.

As he crawled to solid ground, he felt the poop pulling and sucking at his clothes. He lost both shoes and one sock and only a last-minute grab saved his shorts.

"What in the good gracious are you doing?" A voice shouted.

Jose looked for the source and found a burly man in overalls jogging his way. He raised a weak arm, pleading, plaintive.

"My Lord, boy. Oh my Lord. How'd you end up in there?"

The man was ten yards out and Jose wondered if he'd get to him before the bullies. He turned back to the barn, to the poop chute to see how close they were. They were gone.

When he looked back, the farmer was less than ten feet away.

"Are you all right, son? My Lord, I ain't never seen anyone fall into one of those. I can't even imagine it. Don't want to either." The farmer crouched down in front of him. He pulled a handkerchief, stiff with dried snot, from the pocket of his overalls and began wiping manure off Jose's face. "Are you all right?" He repeated.

The relief, coupled with the disgust and fear and disgust and exhaustion (and disgust) was too much. Jose laid face down on the ground and sobbed. "My mom's gonna be so mad at me."

CHAPTER FIFTY-ONE

Neither Shane nor Garrett had fired a shotgun before, but Ray taught them the basics. It was simple enough, Shane thought, since all of the guns were double-barrel models that held just two shells at a time. They were also of the sawed-off variety with barrels short enough to conceal in their backpacks.

"How hard does it..." Garrett trailed off, unsure of the correct verbiage.

"Kick?" Ray asked.

Garrett nodded. "Yeah."

"Not bad with the rock salt in the shells. It's not like the movies where it'll knock you down. Just hold it tight against your shoulder and you'll be fine."

Shane wasn't worried about the recoil. He was worried about possibly killing someone who didn't deserve it. "Say we go to the Whipkey's. We know the dad and daughter are aliens, but what if the mom's not and we blast her in the chest. I don't think I could live with something like that."

Ray grinned. "That's the best part!"

Shane found that quite disturbing until he explained.

"The salt won't kill anyone. It'll sting like heck, especially if they get shot close enough to break the skin, but it's less dangerous than BBs. The only things it'll kill are the aliens."

"Well, that's good to know."

They'd gathered beside the corn field on the Mayhew property to share all of this information and try to not chicken out.

"You know, Ray," Shane said as he turned one of the guns over and over in his hand. "I appreciate you getting us these guns and the bullets. But don't you think it's overkill?"

Ray's eyes narrowed with confusion. "Why?"

"Well, and again, please don't be offended. We can always just throw salt on them. You know. Underhand, overhand. We can even knuckleball it in if we want too. It doesn't exactly take an explosive amount of force."

"Oh." Ray said, then fell silent.

Shane thought he might say something else, but he didn't. He knew he'd doused his friend's excitement, stomped on his pride, and felt bad for doing so. He glanced at Garrett who stared at him and Shane didn't need to be a mind reader to know Garrett was sending him *What were you thinking?* vibes. "But the guns will still work great. Especially when we don't want to get too close. It was a real solid idea."

"It was?" Ray's eyes lit back up.

"Yeah, Ray. A great one." Shane looked to Garrett. "Right, Garrett?"

Garrett nodded. "You bet. I never would have thought of it." He held his gun overhead with one hand and mimicked Bruce Campbell. "This is my boomstick!"

Ray laughed and the tension Shane had created was diffused. He decided to keep his mouth shut for a little while. Not an easy feat for him.

In reality, Shane wasn't sure any of this was a good idea. Lynn had already died. That hadn't really hit any of them yet. He wasn't just away for a long weekend or visiting his grandparents. He was never coming back and maybe they were partly responsible for that.

If they went forward with this plan, maybe Garrett or Ray would be the next to go. Maybe him. Maybe all of them. The latter actually seemed the most plausible when he thought seriously about what they were up against. They had no idea how many residents of Sallow Creek had been turned into aliens, but it was three boys against the whole of them and Shane knew those were really shitty odds.

As Garrett and Ray worked out a plan to do something of a test run, Shane scribbled a note to his parents. It was rambling and probably didn't make a lot of sense without the context of everything he'd seen and experienced, but if the plan failed, he wanted them to know what was going on so that maybe they could get out before it was too late. He'd completed it and was shoving it into the back pocket of his jeans when a rustling noise nearby stole his attention.

All of the boys looked toward the sound. Ray raised a shotgun. Garrett reached into a box of kosher salt and grabbed a handful.

Shane figured they had it covered. They all tensed, ready, waiting.

A figure pushed through the cornstalks, little more than a specter amid the lush green. The corn bent and separated as the person came closer. Whoever it was was within a few feet now. Shane could make out random bits of clothing through the corn but couldn't see the person's face. He glanced at Ray, saw his finger on the trigger and waved for his attention but Ray's eyes were glued to the incoming figure.

The shape pushed through the last row of corn and the second it emerged Garrett wailed a handful of salt its way. It flew through the air like hail, pelting the face of—

Jose squawked, his hands immediately going to his eyes. "Ow! Oh my God!" He shouted. "What did you do to me?"

Tears streamed down the boy's face. Not slime or pus or mucous or melting flesh. Good, old-fashioned tears.

"Oh crap!" Garrett shouted as he ran to him and grabbed Jose by the shoulders. "I'm so sorry! I'm so sorry! I thought you were, you know, one of them."

"Did you throw acid on me or something? I can't see. Am I blind? I don't want to be blind!"

"It's just salt." Shane grabbed a canteen they'd been sharing and went to the boy. "Sit down and tilt your head back."

Jose did but kept his hands covering his eyes, rubbing them, still crying.

"You gotta move your hands. I'll wash your eyes out."

Jose did. His eyes were blood red and the lids swollen. Shane unscrewed the cap of the canteen and poured water over them. Jose gasped and flinched as the cold wetness hit his face but for the most part he held still and let the water do its job.

"I really am sorry," Garrett said again, looking on the verge of tears himself.

Jose blinked, squeezing and opening the lids repeatedly. After a few tries, he was able to keep them open. He looked like he'd just spent a day watching something like *Old Yeller* on repeat, but his tears had mostly stopped.

"Are you okay?" Garrett asked.

Jose gave a weak, almost imperceptible nod. "I think so."

"Could've been worse," Ray said and held up his shotgun. "I could've shotgunned you in the face."

Jose stared, mouth ajar. He saw the firearms, the boxes of salt. "Why do you have guns? And what's going on with all the salt?"

"It's a lot to explain," Shane said. He sat on the ground beside Jose. "But first you have to tell us why you're here. I thought you were out."

"I'm back in."

"That didn't last long." Shane grinned and wrapped his arm around Jose's narrow shoulders, pulling him in close. "Holy balls, you stink!"

Jose smiled, then burst out in almost manic laughter. Shane wasn't sure if he was welcome to join in, but did anyway.

THEY SHARED THEIR STORIES IN THE DISJOINTED, SOMEWHAT incoherent way boys conversed. Jose was in disbelief over what happened to Lynn and had another good cry over that. The other boys became weepy too and Garrett thought, for the first time, that Lynn's death seemed really real. Maybe it was because they were all together and his absence was especially strong. Or maybe the original shock of it had finally worn off. Whatever it was, accepting his death was painful.

It was Jose's recitation of his exploits in the poop pit that somehow managed to lighten the mood again. Even though it was horrifically gross and made them all cringe and gag, it also made them laugh. Even Jose.

"I don't think I could've done it, man," Ray said through giggles. "They could've turned me into an alien. I couldn't go swimming in all that shit."

"I didn't think it would be as bad as it was," Jose said. "When I got home, my mom made me stay in the shower for almost an hour. I thought my skin was going to fall off. I used a whole bar of soap and half a bottle of shampoo."

"And you still reek," Shane said, cackling.

"I know! I'm still grounded too but mom told me to go outside and find you guys. I think she was afraid I'd stink the whole house up. That she'd never get the smell of manure out of the curtains and carpet or something. She even told me to stay at one of your houses tonight."

"How kind of her," Shane said.

"I guess it worked out though, huh?" Jose looked to the guns and salt. "Because four's better than three."

"You really want to do this, Jose? You're sure?" Part of Garrett hoped Jose would change his mind. That he wouldn't put his life at risk, because Garrett didn't want any more of his friends to die.

Jose picked up a blue box of Morton's. "They took your family. They ruined our clubhouse. They made me jump in a pond of manure. And they killed Lynn and Pastor Ted." He took a handful of salt and let it filter through his fingers, the way normal kids their age might do with sand at the beach on summer vacation. "I'm sure, Garrett. Let's get those alien f—"

Garrett thought he might say it, might actually drop the f bomb for the first time in history.

"Freaks," Jose said instead.

And Garrett loved him for that.

"Yeah," Ray said.

"Yeah," Shane agreed.

Garrett nodded. "Yeah. Let's do it."

CHAPTER FIFTY-TWO

THE FOUR OF THEM STOOD OUTSIDE THE APARTMENT FROM which the dude and Mighty Mole had emerged to attack Ray. Garrett and Shane were closest the door. Jose was a few steps behind. The three of them all held containers of salt. They'd loaded up their backpacks with the stuff and the clerk at the discount store had looked at them, cautious and confused, when they bought every box and can of salt they'd had in stock. 'You know that stuff'll give you high blood pressure,' she'd said. That was the least of their worries.

Ray was at the back of the pack, shotgun in hand, his itchy trigger finger resting responsibly on the guard. "So, what's the plan? As soon as the door opens, I shoot?"

Garrett wasn't sure they had a plan, but it definitely was not that. "We're in the middle of town, Ray. You shoot that thing, every cop in Sallow Creek will be here in five minutes. And we already know at least one of them's an alien. He could've turned the whole force."

"Oh," Ray said, dejection clouding his voice. "Shit."

Garrett turned to Shane. "What *is* the plan?"

"I thought maybe we'd kick the door in and storm the place like a SWAT team."

"A little melodramatic, don't you think?"

"It sounded fun." Shane shrugged his shoulders. "Then, what do you suggest."

"We knock."

"Lame," Shane said, then did just that. Four hard raps.

Garrett felt his body tense as they waited. He'd seen first hand what the salt had done to Lynn, but what if that was some kind of fluke? What if Mighty Mole and her Don Juan were immune or something? What if—

The door opened. It was the dude. His Ford hat was missing, revealing a helmet of flattened, orange hair plastered to his skull. He was shirtless and, to Garrett's dawning horror, pants-less. His flaccid pecker swung side to side like a clock pendulum. When he saw the boys, it grew. Not into an erection, but stretching toward the ground, becoming a tentacle.

The dude's tired eyes narrowed. "You picked the wrong door to—"

Garrett whipped a handful of salt into the dude's eyes. His hands flew to his face and he belched out a pained groan. A few granules dropped onto his chest and bored tiny holes into the facade of skin. Yellow pus leaked from them and dribbled down his chest, saturating the thick tufts of wiry hair that covered his torso.

More pus seeped out from behind the dude's hands and he

collapsed to the ground, his entire body convulsing, his skin bloating, then popping as he melted from the inside out.

"Oh, gross!" Jose said, his voice echoing through the narrow alley.

Garrett assumed he was talking about the dying slug of a man, but Jose was staring past him, past all of them, into the apartment.

"Mother of God" Shane said, his voice haunted.

Garrett followed their gaze through the door and saw Mighty Mole naked as a hairless rat, only far less attractive.

Her pendulous breasts sagged almost to her groin, the torpedo-shaped tits undulated as she came toward them. Her crotch was dotted in sparse, gray hair that allowed pale flesh to shine through. Olive-colored goo, the consistency of runny pudding seeped from her lady parts and he tore his eyes away before they could be forever ruined by the sight of it.

Garrett looked north, to her face. Her black-hole of a mole looked bigger than ever and the hairs that jutted from it had come alive. They were thicker and longer and looked like electrical cords growing out of her face, whipping hysterically, reaching for the boys. In seconds, they'd grown in length to two feet.

On the floor, the dude's body burst and his liquified, phlegmy insides gushed out in all directions. Garrett backed up a step so as not to get any on his shoes.

That brought his eyeline lower again and he saw Mighty Mole's lumpy gut wobble and jiggle. It looked like a sack of rotten potatoes and Garrett couldn't help but remember her snide crack when he bought two half pints of chocolate milk. As if she had any room to talk.

He thought about telling her just that, even though he knew this wasn't really Maud the lunch lady. It was some *thing* wearing her skin as a suit. But it didn't matter. He hated the both of them. He reached for another fistful of salt, but Shane beat him to it.

He threw it by flicking his wrist sideways, almost casually. The motion made Garrett think of feeding bread to pigeons in the park. It was so relaxed.

The salt hit Mighty Mole in the torso, which was the last thing Garrett wanted to see again. Festering sores opened up all over her boobs and belly.

"What have you done?" She cried as her body dissolved underneath her. Tentacles sprouted from her mauve nipples. They flailed in desperation or pain or both.

Shane reached out and slammed the door closed. "That's enough of that. I don't know about you, but I'm never going to be able to unsee that. I'll be laying in bed fifty years from now and when I close my eyes, there she'll be. Mighty Mole in her birthday suit. Jesus."

Garrett couldn't disagree with any of that. He only hoped they all had another fifty years in them.

"Why was she naked?" Jose asked, his voice barely a whisper. "Do the aliens, you know, do it?"

"I can't think about that, man," Ray said. He'd set the shotgun down and was bent at the waist. He looked ready to hurl.

"Come on, Ray," Garett said. "You'll be okay." The sight had indeed been awful, but they were only getting started.

CHAPTER FIFTY-THREE

Dusk had turned to night and, after taking out Mighty Mole and her dude, the quartet headed to the Whipkey residence. They were two full blocks away when they saw the Whipkey family moving down the sidewalk, in their direction.

"Let's get 'em!" Jose said.

They almost did just that, but as the Whipkey family walked, they were soon joined by an elderly man.

Jose was reaching into his bag for either a sawed off shotgun or salt. Garrett put his hand on top of Jose's wrist.

"Wait."

Two teenage girls fell into step with the others. Then a tall, gangly middle-aged man Garrett recognized as—

"Principle Ambrose!" Ray said.

All of them marched forward as efficient as soldiers. They didn't converse with one another. Didn't react when a new party joined their group. Didn't glance at passing cars. They may as well have been robots.

"Do you think they're hunting?" Shane asked.

Garrett wasn't sure what was up, but hunting in packs didn't make sense when compared against what they'd seen and experienced so far. "I don't think so."

"What's it matter?" Jose asked. "We can take out a bunch at once. Why are we waiting?"

It was a good point. All they needed to do was duck behind the bushes or behind a tree and wait and they could destroy seven of the things in a matter of seconds. But he felt, no, he knew, that something else was brewing. Something bigger.

"Because we need to see where they're going."

The other boys looked to him.

"Are you sure?" Shane asked.

Garrett wasn't sure about anything. "Yeah."

The destination became clear about fifteen minutes later. By then, seven had become twenty-two. Men and women of all ages. All silent, stalking drones. And the four boys followed them to the Sallow Creek Middle School.

"Where do you think they came from?" Ray asked as they watched. "The aliens, I mean."

"I'm pretty sure they came from Uranus." Shane strongly emphasized *anus*.

The joke soared over Ray's head. "Why do you think there? And not like Saturn or maybe even another galaxy?"

Shane shook his head. "Ur-anus, Ray. They came from your anus." Shane smacked his friend's ass for extra measure.

"Oh, real mature, Shane." Ray smiled when he said it though.

"I'm twelve. What do you expect?"

The men and women entered through a side door of the school and over the next half hour, a few dozen more had filtered inside. Eventually, the flow slowed, then stopped altogether and Garrett knew it was time.

They'd been watching from the cover given by a copse of pine trees. The moonlight filtered through the branches, casting a blue-green haze through which Garrett could see his friends.

"I think this is it," Garrett said. "I don't know why, it's just a feeling, but I do."

Shane nodded. "Yeah. I think so too."

"There's at least fifty in there that we saw. And who knows how many more got here before us." Garrett didn't know if he had a point, reciting these facts, other than stating the obvious.

"Do you think we can do it?" Jose asked.

Garrett wanted to believe they could, but he was a smart boy. Maybe too smart for his own good. He thought accomplishing such a feat was impossible. He almost said that, but Shane interrupted.

"So far as we know, we're the only ones who realize what's going on. If we wait even a few more days, they could infect everyone in the county." He looked to each of them, holding his gaze for a few seconds. "The way I see it, we don't have a choice."

"We have to kill the town to save it," Garrett said, then grinned.

Shane cackled. "I like the way you think, man."

They sat there a moment, working up the courage to venture into the school.

"Is anyone else scared?" Ray asked.

"On a scale of one to ten with ten being shit my pants, I'm an eleven." Shane said with a grin, but Garrett could tell by the look in his eyes that he wasn't joking.

"We all are, Ray," Garrett said. "And there's still time to back out if you want."

Ray looked from Garrett to the school, then back again. "And have you guys call me a pussy for the rest of my life? I don't think so." He worked up a weak, sick-looking smirk.

At least you'd be alive, Garrett thought. But instead of saying that, he rose from his crouching position and removed a box of salt from his backpack. He felt like he should say something inspirational because that's what heroes did just before the big battle, but his mouth had gone dry and besides, they weren't exactly heroes anyway.

He looked at each of them. Ray's permed hair glistened, the curls tumbling to his shoulders over which his shotgun rested. Shane's normally blushing cheeks looked almost scarlet, as they often did when he was nervous. And Jose's face was cleaved at the jaw by bits of metal and plastic that traveled up his cheeks and over his head.

When he saw it, Garrett couldn't hold back an exasperated sigh. "You put on your headgear?"

"It's after ten," Jose said, matter of fact.

"I think you could skip it for one night," Shane said and cackled.

Jose shook his head. "Mom would kill me if I forgot."

"I don't think it's your mom you need to worry about." Shane's smile became forced, then fled his face completely.

"Oh," Jose said. "Yeah."

Garrett patted him on the shoulder. *It's okay*, the gesture said and Jose flashed a sheepish grin. Then he stepped free of their cover and into the Byzantine blue moonlight and his friends followed. Together, makeshift weapons in hand, they went to the school.

CHAPTER FIFTY-FOUR

THE FOUR BOYS CREPT DOWN THE HALL, WHICH STRETCHED ahead of them like an empty cavern. Dim, vaguely green florescent lights cast a sickly glow onto the walls, lockers, and floors. The only sounds were their footfalls and Ray's heartbeat in his ears.

They checked each room as they passed by. So far, all had been empty. Vacant wombs awaiting the insertion of children. Shane and Garrett were on the right side of the hall, Ray and Jose on the left as they came to a T intersection.

"Man, of all places for these assholes to go, why'd they have to pick the school?" Ray hated school and hadn't wanted to set foot in the building until he was forced to in September.

"Want to go right or left," Garrett asked.

"How about both?" Shane grinned.

"Split up?"

Shane nodded.

"That's never a good idea. You know that."

"We've got two stories and probably eighty rooms to cover. We'll be here all night otherwise. Let's at least go two and two." He looked to Ray and Jose, who stood side by side, for their opinions.

"Fine with me," Ray said. "I want to get out of here as soon as possible."

Jose only shrugged.

"Good. Yell if you need help," Shane said.

He and Garrett headed right. Ray watched them for a few seconds, feeling like he should have said 'goodbye' just in case.

"What are you waiting for?"

Ray turned and saw Jose already two rooms down the hall. He hurried to catch up. "Coming."

They checked a dozen more rooms. All empty. Almost at the end of the hall and nearing the staircase to the second floor, Ray was starting to think they'd never find the aliens, that they'd already escaped into the night, when he came to room 128.

He gripped the lever to open the door and pushed down. It clicked and the door popped open. As he began to ease it inward, the door flew open so fast that Ray couldn't remove his hand and went along for the ride.

The door slammed into the wall, its halt so abrupt that the suddenness sent Ray sprawling to the floor. His shotgun clattered to the tile and skidded half way across the room.

Ray scrambled to his knees, looking to the doorway, but it was empty. He took one step toward that door, ready to run when—

RJ Petrillo's elephantine arm lassoed him around the waist. The tentacle constricted like a boa, squeezing the breath from him in a startled *oof*.

He could feel the arm pulsing around him, dragging him toward its source. Reeling him in.

Ray rolled onto his back, the tentacle squishing underneath him, and glanced toward RJ who looked almost nothing like the boy he'd been weeks earlier. His head now sat atop a neck that was a yard long. His legs had congealed and melted into one. His body writhed and thrashed on the floor as new tentacles birthed from him.

That was more than enough for Ray. He turned away, stretching for the shotgun, but it was out of reach. He couldn't even risk sticking his hands in his pockets to grab a pinch of salt because it would put the bare flesh of his forearms too close the tentacle.

It was only his ratty old shirt that was keeping him from being infected and Ray understood that if his skin touched the thing or it touched him, he'd be dead meat. All he could do was squirm and thrash, neither of which accomplished anything but exhausting him.

RJ's troll-like, huffing laughter grew louder. "Come on, Stinkpot. Let's play."

Even as an alien the kid was an asshole. "Fuck you, you ugly little freak!" Ray shouted the words, not caring if it angered the thing.

It drew him in closer and he heard another tentacle whipping through the air. It soared past his head and droplets of thick goo splattered the floor around him like hard rain. It had missed the mark that time but Ray knew it would have him soon enough.

He was going to die and he was surprised how easy it was to accept that cruel fact. He'd heard that you relived your life in your last moments, but it was different, at least for him. Ray's mind was overrun with things he'd never get to do. Experiences he'd never have. He'd never see his Papaw again. Never go hunting for mushrooms or ginseng or truffles. Never get to kiss a girl. Never drive a car. Never grow up.

If his end was near, he wanted to make it count. He was ready to reach into his pocket for some salt, damning the certain death it would bring, when—

A gunshot deafened him. He felt RJ's deformed arm loosen, then release him, then watched it fall to the floor. He scrambled over it, still careful not to touch it, and when he looked back he discovered twenty or more tiny, seeping holes in RJ Petrillo's face.

Ray turned and saw Jose standing in the classroom doorway, holding a shotgun, smoke wafting from the barrel. Jose said 'Thanks' or at least Ray thought he did but he didn't hear the word come out. Inside his head all he could hear was a steady, high-pitched ringing, like someone had tapped a triangle and its music never stopped.

The creature that had been RJ lay dying on the floor. Its face looked like that of a snowman on a day when the afternoon heats up unexpectantly and little of his physical featured remained. The flesh on his torso was expanding, bulging, and Ray had the good sense to climb to his feet and get out of range.

The explosion was muted. A burst of liquified innards shot a few feet into the air, then poured down, coating most of what was left of the body. Ray thought the bully deserved something worse, and turned back to Jose to say just that.

But when he looked to Jose, he found his friend enveloped in the arms of Nolan Haddix. The bully had one arm wrapped around Jose's forehead and the other around his neck. Even from ten or more feet away, Ray could see that the skin on Nolan's arms had attached itself to Jose's head.

Jose's eyes were wide with pain or terror or both. Tears streamed from them.

Ray opened his mouth and screamed, but heard nothing.

CHAPTER FIFTY-FIVE

GARRETT AND SHANE WERE CHECKING ROOM 146, MR. Fischer's science lab, when they heard a distant bang. Garrett felt his pulse quicken.

"Was that—"

"Could've been a door," Shane said.

"Or a gunshot."

"Yeah. That too."

"Damn it. I told you we shouldn't split up." Garrett lumbered toward the door.

"You always assume the worst."

"Considering what's happened the last month, I think that's to be expected." Shane had joined him. They exited the room and raced toward the T intersection where the quartet had splintered apart.

"Good point," Shane said.

CHAPTER FIFTY-SIX

JOSE FELT THE LARVA BURROWING INTO HIS HEAD. IF HE'D had to explain the sensation to someone, he'd have been unable to do so. It was unlike anything he'd ever felt. An alien feeling, he thought. A few minutes earlier that would have made him laugh. Not now.

The force that had been holding him hostage disappeared and the sudden change caused him to stumble forward. He looked back to see who or what had done this to him and saw Nolan Haddix. The bully's arms were gone, making him look oddly out of proportion and Jose realized that those missing arms were still attached to his own head. He tried to pull them loose, tear them off him, but they may as well have been sutured on for as strong as they were affixed.

The bully watched him with a wide, disfigured grin.

"Not getting away this time," Haddix said. "No way, Jose!" And he laughed and laughed.

Jose's temper, which was a rare and foreign beast even to him, came to life. He charged Haddix like a bull and his now deformed head slammed into the bully's chest. Jose felt the alien body give, absorbing the blow with its dense malleability, but his legs kept pushing forward and he drove them both out of the room and into the hallway, not stopping until they crashed into a row of lockers on the opposing wall.

The two hit the ground with Jose on top. And since he had two arms and Haddix none, he for once had the upper hand. He reigned blows on Nolan. His furious fists sunk into the bully's face, his chest, his abdomen. It was like hitting a punching bag full of snot and wasn't doing any damage, but it felt good.

All the while Jose could feel the things burrowing deeper into him. They squirmed through his face, down his throat. The pain became exquisite when they entered his chest. That's when he realized they weren't only invading him, they were devouring him.

A new force gripped Jose's waist, pulling him off Haddix. He flailed and fought against it before realizing it was Ray.

"Stop it!" Ray said, his voice incredibly loud, like he was trying to shout at someone on the opposite side of an auditorium during a rock concert.

Jose stopped struggling and Ray set him down. "They're in me, Ray." He was crying again, if he'd ever stopped.

"What?" Ray pointed at his ear. "I can't hear you?" Again with the shouting.

Jose didn't bother repeating himself. He watched as Ray picked up his shotgun and held the barrel tight against the center of Nolan's forehead and pulled the trigger. When he removed it, a small black hole, about the size of a nickel, was left behind.

From it drained a constant stream of diarrhea-colored discharge.

He wanted to see what came next. He thought he'd earned that much, but Ray grabbed him again and dragged him toward the janitor's closet.

"Stay in there!"

Ray opened the door and pushed him in. The room smelled of bleach and the fake floral scent of air freshener. Ray tried to close the door but Jose stuck his arm between it and the steel frame.

"No, Ray! I'm not hiding in there." From the dumb, clueless look on his face he could tell Ray still wasn't hearing him so he shook his head dramatically, then mouthed slowly. "I'm staying with my friends."

Ray seemed to understand that. Tears welled up and when he blinked, they ran down his cheeks.

Jose put his hand on Ray's shoulder and squeezed it. He mouthed, "Okay?"

Ray nodded.

The two of them retrieved their weapons and continued down the school hallway.

CHAPTER FIFTY-SEVEN

When Garrett saw Jose he wanted to throw up, but couldn't. He thought maybe the violent act of barfing would expel some of the guilt and sadness that had overcome him when he saw his friend looking like something out of one of the horror movies they'd spent so much time watching. Instead he was forced to deal with it.

Jose's head looked like it was ensnared in pink rubber hoses. One was around his forehead, the other his neck. Both had become part of the boy and it was hard to see his real features - the parts that made him Jose - through the macabre appendages.

"Nolan Haddix and RJ Petrillo are dead." Jose said, his voice bordering on prideful.

Jose gave the cliff notes of what went down and it confirmed Garrett's suspicion that he was right. They never should have split up. If they hadn't, Haddix wouldn't have been able to sneak up on Jose and infect him.

He was tempted to turn to Shane and scream at him. 'This is your fault!' and it was. But Ray had agreed to split up too and Jose didn't protest. And, in the end, Garrett had gone along with them. It was all of their faults. And it was far too late to go back and have a do over.

"Maybe, if we kill the source, the numero uno alien, everyone else will revert back to normal," Shane said. "That happens in movies sometimes. With vampires."

Jose shook his deformed, oversized head. "No way. I can feel them in me." He paused, wanting to say more but the words were hard to get out. "Eating me. I don't think it'll be long before there isn't much left."

Ray suddenly unleashed a hitching sob. The sound made Garrett want to bawl too but Jose wasn't crying and if he could manage to hold himself together, Garrett vowed to do the same. At least for now.

"It's okay," Jose said. "I mean, it's not. It's totally not, okay. But it is. Does that make sense."

It did. Garrett nodded.

Jose sat on the floor, leaning against a row of silver lockers. "I thought I'd be able to stick with you guys until the end, but I'm really hurting."

"It's all right" Garrett said. "You can stay here. We'll come back for you."

Jose tried to smile, but his face was a mask of pain. He held up his palms to show they were full of salt. "No, don't come back. This'll do the trick when it's time." He leaned back against the wall, catching his breath through jolts of internal pain. "I just need to know you guys will finish this, okay? Will you promise me that?"

Shane answered fast. Too fast, Garrett thought. "I promise. We'll end these fuckers."

"Promise," Ray said, wiping his wet, tear streaked cheeks.

Jose looked to Garrett. "Don't hold out on me, buddy."

Garrett swallowed hard. He knew Shane and Ray were lying. There was no way to be certain they could kill even a tenth of the aliens, let alone all of them. And now that he saw how fast and easy they'd infected Jose, even with guns and salt, he thought the odds teetered on impossible. But he lied, because that's what friends do. "I promise, Jose."

"Good. And watch out for Don for me, okay? You don't have to pal around with her or anything. That would be weird. But make sure she doesn't get picked on. And when she's older, don't let her date jerks. Stuff like that. Stuff a brother would do."

Garrett thought Jose looked like he was on the verge of tears now. He knew if Jose broke down, they'd all lose it and might not be able to recover. He couldn't let that happen. "I will." He looked to the others. "We all will."

"Good. Thanks, guys." Jose bent at the waist as a spasm of pain racked his abdomen. His mouth opened and a pint or more of blood and liquified tissue flowed out. He retched again and another glassful spilled free. When he looked at them, the noxious fluid trickled down his chin like he'd been drinking a strawberry milkshake.

"Go on now. I'll stay here and pray for you."

Garrett wasn't sure what he thought about prayers, but knew they could use all the help they could get.

With the still alive alien arms wrapped around Jose's head, they couldn't risk giving him a hug or even a handshake goodbye and Garrett thought that was almost the worst part. They could only nod and wave, then left their friend there to die alone.

CHAPTER FIFTY-EIGHT

THE THREE BOYS CREPT DOWN THE HALLS AT HALF THEIR previous pace. Seeing what happened to Jose had Shane on edge and he was sure Garrett and Ray felt the same. He was regretting not telling his parents. Even if they hadn't believed him, and he was sure they wouldn't, at least they'd have an inkling what their only son was up to.

Instead, they were home, believing Shane and his friends were camping out somewhere. His father was probably sitting on the couch watching Arsenio Hall who he called the funniest man on TV since Dick Cavett. His mom would be in bed reading something by Stephen King or Richard Laymon. He wished he was at home too, safe in his bed, sketching a superhero fighting some gross monster. Not doing the same thing in reality.

All of the classrooms had been empty with not a sign of the dozens of creatures they'd seen enter the building. They were approaching the far end of the school, where the gym, storage rooms, and weight room were located. Unless all of the aliens had suddenly teleported home Shane knew they must be in one of those three areas.

The weight room, which reeked of sweat and cheap deodorant, was vacant. Shane then took a quick peek into a supply area which housed cleaners, paint, tools, and various janitorial items but also an odd assortment of either confiscated or stolen student property. Shane spied a few skateboards, an archery bow, at least three BB guns, some knives, and a leather jacket with *Fuck the Man* stitched on the back. There was a pile of stuff and, amid it, he also spotted a tattered and clearly well-used edition of Penthouse. Like a proud father, he knew that was one of his as soon as he saw it and that made him grin.

His good cheer was interrupted by noise ahead and to their left. It was hard to pinpoint, but sounded hollow. He looked to the others to get their opinions.

"It's coming from the gym," Garrett said and Ray nodded in agreement.

Shane was certain they were correct. The noise was familiar now. The dull echo of movement over the hardwood floors of the basketball courts bouncing off the high metal ceilings.

They pushed through the steel double doors and stepped into the gym.

CHAPTER FIFTY-NINE

THE FLORESCENT LIGHTS IN THE GYM BLAZED OVERHEAD and Garrett had never been so wistful for the mysteries of the dark. What lay ahead of them was like every horrific, disgusting, grotesque sight they'd seen over the summer put together and multiplied by a factor of ten.

More than fifty men and women, their neighbors and teachers, familiar faces from the grocery store and bowling alley, stood naked in the gym. Garrett tried to take it all in and not really see it at the same time. He knew this scene would cause him night-mares for the rest of his life. If he survived the night.

The aliens were interconnected to one another. The tongue of Mindy the waitress from Luigi's had grown to four feet in length and it was embedded into the stomach of their Princi-pal. His penis had become a thick, rope-like tentacle that was affixed to the chest of a middle-aged woman with small, deflated breasts. That woman's left arm was long and thin like sinew and the hand was stuck up the ass of Matt Ross, one of Nolan Haddix's former cohorts. A trio of tentacles had birthed from Matt Ross's belly button, one of which was glued to the eye of an old man Garrett sometimes saw sneaking out of the Adult section of the video store. It went on and on and on.

All of their bodies were coated in thick, mucous-like slime that sloughed down their flesh and seeped onto the floor. It had formed random puddles, some several feet across and it bubbled and festered like it too was somehow alive.

"I fucking hate Steven Spielberg," Ray said. His voice drew Garrett out of his mesmerized daze and back to reality.

"What? Why?"

"Because *E.T.* didn't prepare me for this shit. Phone home my ass."

The boys had been standing behind the bleachers, peering out from the relative cover and even though the focus of the aliens seemed to be on one another, Garrett didn't want to take any risks.

"What do you think they're doing? Shane asked.

"Communicating. Maybe sharing knowledge. Reading each other's minds."

"Or having a fucked up alien orgy," Ray said.

"Or that." Garrett shrugged his shoulders. It was as good a guess as his.

Shane looked from his friends back to the creatures. "Either way, I'm guessing it's not good."

Garrett nodded. "Pretty safe assumption."

"We should probably..." He shook a box of salt. "Melt some of these bastards."

That sounded like a grand plan. Garrett opened one of his own boxes of salt. Ray shouldered his shotgun. Garrett held up one finger. Then two. They went on three.

Shane threw first, a high volley of salt that rained down over Matt Ross and the old perv from A&H Video. Both men reacted in a violent, dramatic manner. Their tentacles disconnected as their nude bodies spasmed and thrashed. Garrett thought they looked like they were doing one of those crazy new dance moves they showed on MTV.

The old man fell first. His torso ruptured and belched gallons of fetid goo. Ross wasn't far behind, but he fell face down onto the hardwood and his bloated belly burst like a water balloon, spewing even more of the muck.

The element of surprise was gone. Their cover was blown. And the dozens of aliens in the gym all turned in unison to the boys and moved toward them.

"Oh shit! Oh shit! Oh shit!" Ray chanted.

Garrett lobbed two fast handfuls of salt at the things and the granules took out five of the aliens. Shane threw again and the salt smacked into the face of Principal Ambrose, melting his skin on contact. Garrett heard Shane cackle at that and he didn't blame him. The guy was a dick.

"Oh shit! Oh shit!" Ray aimed the shotgun but didn't fire, like a hunter with buck fever.

"Stop saying *'oh shit'* and do something, Ray!" Shane shouted.

That did the trick and not even a second passed before Ray

pulled the trigger. A round of salt slammed into Mr. Whipkey who wouldn't be putting in any more hours at the hardware store. The round had opened a gaping, smoking hole in the center of his chest and his thick, gelatinous insides came pouring out.

The boys continued the barrage, throwing salt, shooting salt, watching with a mixture of glee and revulsion as men and women collapsed before them. A river of melting aliens and their liqui-fied remains spread across the floor like an oil slick and Garrett and the others had to keep backing away to stay out of the incoming tide.

"I'm out," Shane said. Garrett looked to his friend and saw him holding his box upside down as if to prove he was being honest.

"I have another in my book bag." Garrett motioned to his bag at the bleachers and Shane went for it. He also peered into his own box and saw he had two, maybe three small handfuls remaining. He checked the aliens and there were at least three dozen remaining.

Ray tried to shove shells into the shotgun but his hands were shaking and both tumbled from his grasp. They clattered to the floor, rolling toward the aliens.

"Damn it. Those are my last two shells." He went for them but his sneaker hit a puddle of slime and his foot shot out from under him. He skidded sideways, trying to regain his balance, but only made things worse. His right knee buckled under him and when he fell, the crack was so loud Garrett not only heard it, he felt it.

Ray screamed like a rabbit in a snare, his hands clutching his leg which was bent under him at an impossible, grotesque angle. Three aliens were within a few feet of him. One of them was Officer Hanes whose fingers were all so long they dragged on the floor.

Garrett moved as fast as his big body would allow, while being careful to avoid the slippery snot that had taken down Ray. He threw salt at the three things, hitting two but missing Hanes. The cop paid no heed as its brethren fell and melted beside it and kept going toward Ray. Hanes' long, slithering fingers whipped their way toward Ray.

Garrett knew he had no choice. He took a small fistful of his remaining salt and chucked it at the cop. It was a good throw and the tentacle fingers reeled back in toward the dying man's body as he spasmed and dissolved.

Ray sobbed on the floor, motionless until Garrett's hand fell on his shoulder. That made him jump and the movement elicited a pained yelp. He looked up at Garrett. "Do you think it's broke?"

Garrett knew it was broken when he heard it, but nevertheless he took a look. Ray's pantleg was soaked in blood and a shiny shard of white had poked through the denim. "Yeah. It is."

"Is it bad?"

You've got a bone sticking out of your jeans. I'd say, it's pretty damn bad. "No, not too bad."

"Oh, good," Ray said through tears. "I thought it was bad."

Shane had reached them, crouching down at their sides. He took one look at Ray's leg and the color drained from his face. He opened his mouth to speak but Garrett shot him a glare that put an end to that.

"We have to hurry," Garrett said, motioning to the remaining horde of aliens.

Shane nodded and together they threw handful after handful of salt, dropping two, three, sometimes four at a time. It took the remainder of their salt supply, but within a few minutes they killed all of the aliens in the gym. Their remains bubbled and gurgled on the floor, but there was no fight, no means of infection left in them.

Garrett stared at the carnage, almost unable to believe they'd actually done it. That they'd killed the aliens without somehow screwing it all up.

"Well, I have to say, that was easier than I expected," Shane said.

Garrett turned to him and found him grinning, but it was a tired, relieved expression void of any genuine good cheer. "Yeah. A little anticlimactic really," Garrett said.

Shane nodded. "Much ado about nothing if you ask me."

"Guys," Ray said, drawing their attention. They'd almost forgotten he was still there. "You might want to hold off on the celebrating."

"Why's that?" Shane asked.

Ray didn't speak. He only pointed at the rear doors where the gymnasium exited to the parking lot.

Garrett and Shane followed his finger and saw a pack of aliens moving into the building. And at the head of them were Larry and Harrison Roberts.

"Oh, shit." Garrett had managed to forget about the both of them and their presence killed his short-lived good mood. He had no need or desire to have a family reunion.

Larry Roberts' gray hair was alive, each strand a writhing undulating creature. He ripped off a handful and launched it toward the boys. It landed short but the worms slithered across the floor, through the muck and gore, coming for them. One of the creatures hit some spilled salt. It hissed and flailed, then went belly up.

"Help me with Ray," Garrett said and grabbed Ray's right arm. Shane took the left and together they pulled him out of the gym and he cried all the way. His leg flopped and wobbled and part of Garrett wondered if the only way it was staying attached was because of Ray's jeans.

Once into the hallway, they eased Ray onto the floor but it didn't stop his moaning. Garrett slammed shut the doors, but there was no way to lock them and they'd buy them a few seconds time, at best.

"What do we do?" Shane asked.

Garrett was startled to hear Shane asking him that question. Shane was the leader. He was the one with the plans. He was the hero of their group. Garrett didn't want that position, but he had an idea.

"Get him out of the school. Hide him somewhere. I'll lead them the other way."

Shane shook his head, his thin hair floating around his face. "No, we're not splitting up again."

"Do it, Shane."

"I'm not leaving you, Garrett."

Garrett realized he wasn't just saying the words because it was the noble thing to do, His best friend was on the verge of tears. That made him want to cry too and any leftover joy from winning the initial battle vanished. He didn't want to be apart from them either, but with Ray's broken leg it was the only way. The only chance. "You're not leaving me. You're getting Ray somewhere safe."

"And being a pussy."

"No. That's my thing, remember?"

"Where are you going?"

"The kitchen."

Some of the sadness left Shane's face as he realized what Garrett was planning.

Something banged off the steel doors of the gym and they both flinched. The time for talking was past, but Shane surprised Garrett by grabbing him and pulling him in for a short, but intense embrace. "I'll meet you there, I promise. So, don't go and die on me before that happens, okay?"

"I'll do my best."

Shane let go of him and turned his attention to Ray. Garrett watched as he grabbed Ray's arms and dragged him backwards across the floor, moving with surprising speed. They disappeared around a corner.

Garrett waited until the gym doors opened and his father stepped into the hall.

"Hello, Son." His voice was garbled and hollow. "Haven't seen you in a while. If I didn't know better, I'd think you were avoiding me."

"I'm here now."

Larry Roberts grinned and Garrett saw his tongue flailing behind his nicotine stained teeth. It whipped to and fro with so much frenzy that several of those choppers were knocked loose and tumbled to the floor. Brown pus seeped from his gums, dribbling down his chin like thick tobacco spit.

"Not for long," Larry said.

Garrett looked past his father and saw the rest of the aliens in human skin suits behind him. All of them moved toward him. There were dozens more. Fifty at least. Maybe one hundred. Garrett didn't bother with a headcount. Instead, he ran.

CHAPTER SIXTY

ALL TWO HUNDRED PLUS POUNDS OF GARRETT ROBERTS didn't stop running until he reached the cafeteria. His chest heaved and his lungs blazed but he refused to allow himself to succumb to the pain and exhaustion. He kicked down the stop to keep the steel door open, allowing easy access. The tables that typically filled the space were folded up and stacked in the back corner, creating a gaping, empty cavern. His plan was simple enough and as soon as he got to the cafeteria he went to the kitchen and found what he needed - a pallet stacked with fifty pound bags of salt. All that was left was putting it to use. When that was finished, he waited.

The aliens arrived less than two minutes later, funneling through the door and into the cafeteria. From his vantage point at the kitchen doors, Garrett saw they were all changing, transforming. Their features were less human now. They wore eyes that sat low on their faces, noses that were nothing but holes in the center of their heads, mouths that were impossibly wide and gaping and expectant. Their arms had become thrashing, oozing tentacles. Worms burrowed free from their pores, slithering along their bodies and onto the tile.

He didn't see his father or brother, but suspected they were somewhere in the pack. He did see other familiar faces. Skip the owner of A&H Video, Luigi from their favorite pizza spot of the same name, his homeroom teacher. There was a man that Jose would have recognized as Pastor Ted and several boys and girls from church camp.

"They're all here," Garrett thought. He couldn't know that for certain, but he understood it as the truth. They'd all come to the school for a purpose that was as alien to him as their origins. And he intended to end it.

When the aliens hit the center of the room, Garrett emerged from his hiding place. He clutched the remains of a bag of salt, twenty pounds or so, as he made his presence known.

"Are you in there, Dad?"

The aliens turned to him in unison.

"How about you, Harrison? Why don't you come out and show your ugly mugs?"

The group moved as one, their every motion in synch. They seemed to glide toward him on feet that were no longer feet, but tendrils of mucous-cloaked tissue.

Garrett skirted along the edges of the room, his back tight against the walls so nothing could surprise him from behind. There were five entrances to the cafeteria, counting the doors leading to the kitchen. Garrett had already taken care of four of them, dumping heaping piles of salt into the doorways. That left only the door they'd all come through and that was his intended finish line.

He was half-way there when Larry Roberts came to the forefront of the group. "There's too many of us, Garrett. And you're all alone," Larry said. "Your supposed pals are all either dead or they've turned their backs on you." Larry's grey, living hair fell in clumps to the floor. When they hit, dozens of worms wriggled and writhed. They raced toward Garrett.

His father was almost bald now. Along with his hair, much of his skin had sloughed off, leaving behind nothing but opaque, yellow jelly that held the vague shape of a human head. Garrett thought the stuff looked a lot like the pictures of human fat they displayed in text books as a warning sign not to overeat lest the stuff fill up your insides and coat your organs.

"I told you those boys were never your friends. You didn't believe me but now you can see it's the truth."

Skip, the man he'd so enjoyed talking to while renting movies, joined in. "I never liked you, Garrett. Every time you left the shop I laughed and laughed."

"I never saw a boy eat so much," Luigi said. You were one of my best customers but it made me sick to look at you, you pig."

Garrett's homeroom teacher opened her deformed mouth. "Even the teachers hated you. So sloven and lazy. That's why we never stopped the others from making fun of you. They only said what we were all thinking. That you were an ugly, worthless, piece of—"

More of them spoke. A Greek chorus of cruelty and hate.

"Fat."

"Disgusting."

"Pig."

"Ugly."

"Gross."

"Worthless."

"Loser."

Garrett felt as if his mind was going to break. These people, these things, were saying every negative thing he'd ever believed about himself. Repeating the loathing that he felt when he was excluded from activities or picked last for class projects even though he was almost a straight A student. Picked last because they'd rather team up with someone like RJ Petrillo who was stupid but normal, rather than get a good grade with Garrett's help because Garrett was fat and gross. Because Garrett was a pig.

The aliens started squealing.

Reeeeeee! Reeeeeee! Reeeeeee!

He'd been frozen in place and the things were close now. Five feet away, well within the reach of their tentacles. And as their words and sounds pummeled him into submission, he was tempted to accept their perverse form of death with relief because it would put an end to the hate he'd felt so often in life. The hate he could never understand because he was a kind person. Why was that never enough?

"You're such a goddamn pussy, Garrett," his father said. "I wish you'd never been born."

It was his father's voice rising over the drone of the others, that brought him back. His father's face which, even though it was disfigured, transformed into a grotesque Halloween mask, that woke him up.

"You were a shitty dad!" Garrett shouted. He resumed his side-stepping movements along the wall. The aliens followed him. "I loved you, you asshole and all I ever wanted was for you to like me. But now..." Garrett made it to the main entrance. He took one small step backward, his body filling the open space and looked to his father. To all of them. "Now I'm done caring about what any of you think about me."

Garrett dumped the salt onto the floor, creating an ivory Maginot line across which the aliens could not cross without dying.

His father screamed. The sound started off as human but rapidly descended into something decidedly not. It rose to an almost deafening level, a sound like yelling through a throat clogged with broken glass and phlegm and insane rage.

Larry's tongue shot out of his mouth like a streamer from a New Year's Eve party horn but there was no accompanying sound effect. It was ten feet long but Garrett was twelve away. The tongue dropped to the floor with a wet splat. It disconnected from Larry's mouth, allowing it to slither closer.

The tongue hit the salt, sending up yellow puffs of smoke. Its outer layer of skin popped and putrid, festering snot splashed out.

The aliens abandoned their taunts. They scrabbled through the large cafeteria, seeking a weak spot where they might escape. Their tentacles whipped against the safety glass of the windows. They attempted to climb the walls. But they were trapped and Garrett knew it was of his doing.

They couldn't hurt him any more. He smiled, then began to

laugh. The stress of the night - of the summer - became less oppressive with each chuckle. He felt like he hadn't beaten only the aliens but the entire town of Sallow Creek.

And just as he began to feel worthwhile for maybe the first time in his life, a vise tightened around his waist. The force was crushing and sent him to his knees, then to the floor.

He rolled onto his back and saw the tentacle ensnaring him. It pulsed and constricted sending shockwaves of pain through his torso.

"What's the matter you little fag?" It was Harrison's voice and Garrett looked past the tentacle and saw the thing that had been his brother leering at him. His eyes had turned the color of spoiled milk. His ears had slid off his skull, his nose off his face. His toothless mouth was a gaping black hole from which came a steady stream of pus-filled drool. "Not such a tough guy now."

The tentacle squeezed again. Garrett felt like his insides were on the verge of bursting, of being turned into the same pulverized goo that spilled from the aliens when they died, but he didn't want his brother to see his pain.

The Harrison-thing's humanoid body was turning less recognizable by the second. Its head had become part of its shoulders, the neck gone. "I'll give you a choice, little brother. Do you want to be one of us, or should I just kill you? Not gonna lie, I'd prefer the latter but it's up to you."

Garrett opened his mouth to answer, the tell Harrison to go ahead and kill him, when he heard a shotgun rack.

Harrison turned around, toward the source of the noise. When he moved Garrett got a good look too.

Shane held a shotgun at waist level. "How about I kill you instead?" He wasted no time waiting for an answer and pulled the trigger.

A spray of salt rocketed from the barrel and hit Harrison in the chest. Garrett watched his brother flail, stumbling in a wide, clumsy circle. He crashed into a row of lockers, then bounced off. Garrett felt the tentacle holding him let go and it flopped to the floor, seeping its diarrhea-colors snot.

Free, he pushed himself to his feet and joined Shane in watching Harrison fall, melt, then burst.

"No offense, man, but your brother was such an asshole."

Garrett nodded. "None taken."

He saw a wheeled cart and hose beside Shane. Then he realized there was a new, pungent odor in the air. "What's all that? And what stinks?"

Shane grabbed the hose and proudly showed that it was connected to some sort of spray gun.

"I don't get it," Garrett said.

Shane motioned to the tank. "I found it in the supply room. It's a paint sprayer. I filled the tank with paint thinner. And this," Shane held the sprayer to Garrett. "This is what you've been asking for."

"Remind me again, what was I asking for?"

"A flame thrower!"

Without further explanation, Shane grabbed the cord to the air compressor and gave it a yank. It sputtered and died. He tried again and on the second try it rumbled to life. Then he reached behind himself and pulled a flare from his back pocket. He struck it and the tube blazed red, filling the hall with its crimson glow.

"Well?" Shane asked. "What are you waiting for?"

"Are you sure this will work and we won't, like, blow ourselves up?"

"Totally sure." Shane nodded. "Eighty percent sure."

"Eighty?"

"Seventy percent. Sixty, at worst."

"Good enough odds for me."

Garrett raised the paint sprayer and turned toward the cafeteria. The aliens inside the room had congealed into one gigantic, flailing mound of flesh. It was fifteen feet high and, Garrett realized, reaching for the ceiling where a row of skylights allowed moonlight into the room. They were less than two feet from the thin panes of glass.

"Ready?" Garrett asked as he aimed the nozzle of the sprayer at the mountain of aliens.

"Oh yeah."

Garrett squeezed the trigger. Clear, noxious fluid jutted from the nozzle. Shane leaned in and held the flare in the spray. Garrett half, or at least forty percent, expected them to get blown to bits, but instead the paint thinner burst into flames. Flames that arced through the air and rained down on the aliens like Hell itself.

Even over the roar of the air compressor, Garrett could hear the creatures screaming as they burned and burst and died. He heard their flesh sizzling. Their fluids boiling. In seconds the entire cafeteria was aflame.

Garrett released the trigger. What had happened in that room was gloriously horrific, but he wasn't done yet.

"Is there any more of that paint thinner?"

Shane nodded. "A shitload."

"Good." Garrett put his free hand on Shane's shoulder. "Let's burn this fucker to the ground."

They did just that.

EPILOGUE

By the time the volunteer fire department arrived, the Sallow Creek Middle School was fully engulfed and beyond saving. At sunrise, all that remained was concrete and metal. There was no trace of the aliens nor the hundred or so men, women, and children who disappeared. It was presumed they had died in the fire, but no one could explain what they were doing in the school, at night, in the middle of July. Garrett, Shane, and Ray didn't attempt to educate them.

They went along with the prevailing theory, and they mourned Lynn and Jose at a candlelight vigil a week later. They kept their secret and life moved on without further ado.

For a little while.

September 23, 1989

THE START OF THE SCHOOL YEAR, AND SEVENTH GRADE FOR the boys, had been pushed back over a month while the town scrambled to make room for the displaced middle school students who were without a schoolhouse of their own.

Garrett added an armload of dry sticks and twigs to a small pile of embers that Shane had set ablaze. The kindling quickly caught fire and flames reached into the air like grasping fingers. Garrett flinched and bounced backward two steps even though the fire was in its infancy and harmless.

Shane emerged from a large tent, which had become their temporary clubhouse. It wasn't comfortable and didn't have a TV or VCR, but they could move it from place to place, always in search of a new adventure. On this night, they were camped out on Whitehorse Mountain.

"That's a good start," Shane said, tilting his head toward the fire. "Need some meatier stuff though."

"Ray found a tree limb this big around." Garrett held his hands about six inches apart. "He's dragging it back. I would've helped but my hands were full."

"Convenient."

Garrett grinned.

Dusk was rapidly transitioning to night and the illumination from the fire dominated, throwing its orange glow haphazardly into the campsite. The color made Garrett think about Halloween and he wondered if Shane's parents would go along with them trick or treating one more year.

His mother was still MIA in Cincinnati and he'd been living with the Vinyan's since July. It was occasionally awkward, like when

Sara took them shopping for school clothes and insisted a large sweatshirt would fit and told him to try it on. He did, and ended up looking like the Michelin Muffler Man. Sometimes he still felt like an interloper in their home, but that feeling faded a little with each passing day.

"Thanks for all the help, Garrett."

Both of the boys looked toward his voice and found Ray pushing through the brush and into the clearing. He huffed and puffed and glowered as he awkwardly pulled the heavy branch across the forest floor.

Garrett shrugged his shoulders. "We needed tinder."

Ray placed the branch over a fallen tree that they used for a bench.

"I'm practically handicapped here." He pointed to his leg, which was still encased in a cast, then flopped onto the tree.

"Your recovery has been so impressive, I almost forgot." Garrett said. "Here. I'll do the hard part." He stomped on the branch, snapping it in half, then added both halves to the fire. He dropped them hard, sending up puffs of smoke and sparks.

"I know what'll improve your mood, Ray," Shane said, reaching into his backpack.

"What's that?"

Shane pulled out a pack of hotdogs. "All beef. Footlongs even!"

Ray only shook his head. "Anyone ever tell you you're an asshole, Shane?"

"Everyone."

"Well they're right."

Shane skewered a wiener on a stick then handed the pack to Garrett. He stabbed two and hoisted them over the fire, then glanced at Ray. "Grab my bag."

Ray did.

"I've got s'mores stuff in there. Help yourself."

Ray's scowl faded and he rummaged through Garrett's pack, pulling out a jumbo marshmallow.

The boys toasted and roasted their food in peaceful silence but Garrett missed Lynn's constantly yapping mouth. He thought about Lynn and Jose every day and wondered if they'd ever fade from his memory. He supposed it was inevitable that they would, but he hoped that didn't happen for a long time. Even though thinking of them made him sad, he didn't ever want to forget about them and their friendship.

"Remember Jose with the marshmallows?" Ray asked out of the blue. Apparently Garrett wasn't the only one thinking of their friends.

They knew what Ray was talking about. Earlier in the spring, right after Jose got his braces, they'd toasted marshmallows and he shoved three at once into his mouth. They became so gummed up in the metal wires that were supposed to remove the gap from his front teeth that it took him almost an hour to get it all out.

"Yeah, and Lynn told him that if he'd drink a coke the acid in it would dissolve the marshmallow goo. So, he tried and it fizzed up in his mouth and he choked and it came spurting out his nose." Shane laughed, remembering. "Good times."

They had been. But these are good times too, Garrett thought.

As night grew darker and the serenading birds traded places with the buzzing insects, the boys discussed the important things in life. Like whether *Thundercats* or *He-Man and the Masters of the Universe* was the better cartoon. If Rowdy Roddy Piper could beat Macho Man Randy Savage (Garrett was convinced he could, the others disagreed). About which of the girls would show up for the school year having grown boobs over the summer.

Ray wanted to know if Steve Vinyan would take them all to see the *Halloween 5* in October, but Garrett was more excited about *Shocker*, the new Wes Craven movie that was supposed to be even scarier than *A Nightmare on Elm Street*. They talked until they had to struggle to keep their eyes open.

It was Ray who caved in first. He was debating, mostly with himself, who was prettier between Elle MacPherson and Kathy Ireland when his words slowed, then stopped mid sentence. The others looked to him and his eyes were closed.

"Did he just fall asleep sitting up?" Garrett asked?

Shane poked Ray in the stomach with his hot dog roasting stick. Ray didn't react. "I'd say that's an affirmative."

Garrett giggled. "Help me get him in the tent."

They rose and each grabbed an arm. As they got Ray to his feet his eyelids fluttered and half-opened. "Elle's got a better body but Kathy's face, it's just so sweet. Like the girl next..." His words ceased again and they shuffled him toward the tent.

As they walked, their own sounds of crunching footsteps were accompanied by similar sounds in the woods. Only those sounds were much louder.

"Do you hear that?" Garrett asked.

"It's kind of hard to miss."

They pivoted, still holding Ray, in the direction of the noise. It was still coming. Faster. Louder.

Shane gave Ray a shake. He slowly came back to reality. "What?"

"Listen," Shane said.

Ray's tired eyes cleared as the noise came closer.

It bordered on thunderous now. Garrett half-expected to see trees falling in its wake but as they waited to see what was coming from within the woods, they saw nothing but black forest.

"If that's a fucking alien, I'm gonna be so goddamn pissed." Ray shrugged off their arms, ready to fend for himself. To fight.

That gave Garrett an idea. He dove for his pack, hands tearing through it, throwing aside Twinkies and Ho Hos and jerky. Fistfuls of candy bars hit the ground and then, at last, he found what he wanted.

Packets of salt and pepper, little bigger than postage stamps.

He ripped three of them open at once and handed one to each of his friends.

"Here!"

Shane accepted it, his expression fearful and bemused. "This doesn't instill a lot of confidence, buddy."

"It's better than nothing."

Shane nodded. "You got me there."

The noise was on the verge of the clearing. It would be on them in any second.

Garrett looked to his friends. "This might sound lame, but I love you guys. I just wanted to say that in case, you know."

Shane nodded. "Love you too, Gar. And you, Ray."

"That's kind of gay," Ray said. His fearful face stared unwavering at the approaching force.

"You're kind of gay." Shane's trademark grin made an appearance. "And let me tell you something else, friend-o. If we have to run for our lives, you're screwed."

Ray stole a glance at his cast. "Shit."

"Yeah." Shane said. Then all of them stared into the black abyss before them.

It was seconds away. And then it arrived.

Apollo exploded through the thicket, his mouth filled with a dead squirrel.

"You damn, dumb mutt!" Ray said. He was breathing hard.

Apollo dropped the squirrel and barked at Ray as if insulted.

"Don't you disparage my dog." Shane laughed, but his face was void of color. "He brought us breakfast."

Garrett thought Shane looked more scared than ever before and he wondered how long they'd go on like this. Flinching at every loud noise. Cowering at the unknown. Afraid for their lives. He suspected it would last a good long while, but that was okay because they were alive. And they had each other.

———

A QUARTER MILE FROM THEIR CAMPSITE, THE STYGIAN

waters of a pond gurgled. From deep in the muck a bubble arose, rising lazily through the murky depths until it reached the surface.

When it collided with the cool, night air, the bubble popped and a worm remained in its wake. The creature floated motionless for a long moment, then swam for shore.

THE END

IF YOU ENJOYED "WITHIN THE WOODS" PLEASE VISIT MY website and sign up for my mailing list so I can tell you about my new books and stories. You'll also get 3 free short horror stories just for signing up. That's better than a mouthful of worm/tentacles, right?

AFTERWORD

First, let me thank you for reading my tale of monsters run amok in the woods of Pennsylvania. I've had this idea brewing for almost two years but had to finish up my zombie series, LIFE OF THE DEAD, first.

When it finally came time to bring this story to life, I immediately fell in love with the characters who each carried parts of my real life friends and me. I was twelve in the summer of 1989 and while I didn't have any adventures involving aliens, great portions of the rest of the story are true-ish.

We had an awesome clubhouse(courtesy of my pap and my mother). We rented horror movies at A&H. We collected cans for spending money. We played Heads Up, Seven Up. We were a bunch of weirdos and outcasts, but I would never dream of changing a thing.

I've been writing stories since I was in elementary school. I read those missives on the school bus and occasionally in English class, but never dreamed my writing would reach an audience beyond that. Now, two years into my writing career, and I've made the #1 horror best-seller list on Amazon (briefly) and have readers around the world.

To say it's a dream come true is trite, because its more than that. It makes me feel whole. And for that, I thank you, dear reader. I hope you'll stick around and see what I come up with next.

Much love,

Tony Urban

ABOUT THE AUTHOR

A professional writer and photographer, amateur cryptozoologist, and fan of general weirdness (both real and imagined), Tony has traveled tens of thousands of miles seeking out everything from haunted places, UFO crash sites, and monsters like Bigfoot and the Mothman. In a previous life, he worked in the independent movie industry but he finds his current career much more exciting.

Tony's first writing memory involves penning a short story about taking a road trip with his best friend and his dog (two different creatures) to watch KoKo B Ware in a professional wrestling event in Pittsburgh. He wrote that epic saga while in the 3rd grade and it was all downhill from there.

His favorite time of the year is Halloween and he would pretty much live inside a pumpkin if such a thing were possible. Since it's not, he'd take a cabin a log cabin in Maine. Or a log cabin just about anywhere. He's not picky.

His first books were a series of offbeat travelogues but recently his zombie apocalypse series, "Life of the Dead" has been a bestseller online and grossed out readers all over the world.

His ultimate goal in life is to be killed by a monster thought by most to be imaginary. Sasquatch, werewolves, chupacabras, he's not picky.

If that fails, he'd enjoy making a living as a full time writer. Which of those two scenarios is more likely is up to the readers to decide.

For more information:
tonyurbanauthor.com
tony@tonyurbanauthor.com

ALSO BY TONY URBAN

72811352R00224

Made in the USA
Columbia, SC
01 September 2019